HONEYBECK'S TREASURE

Iris Button

Pen Press

First published in Great Britain by Pen Press

All paper used in the printing of this book has been made from
wood grown in managed, sustainable forests.

ISBN 978-1-78003-795-0

Printed and bound in the UK
Pen Press is an imprint of
Indepenpress Publishing Limited
25 Eastern Place
Brighton
BN2 1GJ

A catalogue record of this book is available from
the British Library

Cover design by Jacqueline Abromeit

PROLOGUE

The small Caribbean island of Barbados has long been a tropical paradise; it attracts tourists every day to sail and swim in the warm aquamarine sea and to sunbathe on its golden sandy sundrenched shores. But the beaches have not always been so popular, years ago the beaches were found to be too hot and too dirty. Archaeological evidence showed that inland was cooler and there had been settlements of Arawak Indians on the island for up to a thousand years, some scholar basing his findings on the year 2000 BC. That is, until the hostile Caribs settled in and drove the Arawak out. There were still Carib settlements here in the first quarter of the sixteenth century but no one knows why they left. The occasional ship called here for fresh water, it seems that Barbados has its own fresh water springs. It is said that the pirate Captain Kidd hid a treasure here. But lying east of the main chain of the Leeward and Windward Islands, ships were infrequent in these waters as the tides and the trade winds blew them further north.

It was in 1625 after trading in Brazil that an English ship called the *Olive Blossom* was caught in a bad tropical storm and was blown way off course by gale force winds and a driving rain; she would have been sailing north-west along the southern island chain towards the Carolinas, then to finish the triangular crossing to London, but being lost and possibly badly damaged they anchored off the west coast of Barbados to take on fresh water. She was captained by Henry Powell. He found the island to be 21 miles long and 14 miles wide and completely uninhabited at that time, except for wild pigs that were left there in 1537, so it is written, by a passing Portuguese ship captained by Pedro Compos to provide food for shipwrecked mariners. It was also written that it was the Portuguese who first named the island Los Barbados meaning 'the bearded ones' after the bearded fig trees that grew along the beach. Henry Powell took possession of the island in the name of King James the 1st of England by having members of his crew carve out on a fustic tree: THIS ISLAND IS TAKEN IN NAME OF KING JAMES 1ST OF ENGLAND THIS YEAR 1625.

Then on arriving back in England some months later, he reported the information of his taking of the island to his employer William Courteen.

It took Courteen four weeks to find investors, suppliers and stores, then an expedition of 40 to 80 people sailed from England captained by Henry Powell in the ship called *William and John*, and landed on the west coast of the island in February 1627. It was later written that this was a mistake, and that they landed on the 17th February 1626 and not 1627 as previously documented. It was also written that the Portuguese deportment of the pigs happened some ninety years before. The English arrived and the settlers made their homes a few hundred yards from the beach where there was a huge hole, a great swamp that water from the hills drained into; it was a flat swamp stretching for 400 yards across. At first the small settlement was christened Jamestown after the king. Shortly afterwards more ships arrived, more settlers moved in, and more small wooden houses known as chattel houses were built, and a town emerged – it was quite often referred to as the Hole, and became eventually what is known to this very day, as Holetown.

When Powell landed with the settlers in 1626 he did not stay long, but sailed to Guyana to obtain a variety of food crops and brought back with him a few Arawak Indians to teach the settlers how to plant. Tobacco was the main crop, but the climate was found to be too hot making the leaves dry. Some cotton is still grown here, but when sugar cane was introduced to the island by a Dutchman of unknown name some planters became very wealthy and large plantation houses were built further inland and on higher ground to catch the cool sea breezes. Then slaves from West Africa were brought in to tend the land, more and more slaves were brought in, and soon the white population was in the minority.

The island, once covered by dense forest, is today the most advanced and the most populated island in the Caribbean.

Julie Read, having a successful hair and beauty salon in London, was about to marry Gavin Anderson eldest son of Lady Elizabeth and Sir Gabriel Anderson, a very successful property developer. They had been together for four years and the planning and the organizing for the wedding had taken a whole year, and the last few weeks had been really hectic. They had planned their honeymoon in Barbados where they had enjoyed several holidays, sometimes twice a year; they loved the island and always stayed at the famous Sandy Lane Hotel and this had been booked now for nine months. But then suddenly a month before the wedding Gavin was notified by the bank in London where he had worked for eight years that his application for transfer to Barbados had come through and he was to take on the position of CEO at the bank in Holetown. This was a dream come true, and Julie was so excited as it had coincided with their wedding plans. There was also accommodation to be provided, and they were to live on this paradise island. And so the plans for the hotel were cancelled.

On Saturday the sun had shone on a hot June day in Surrey, England, and Julie had never looked more beautiful in white silk and lace and masses of veiling. Her brown eyes shone with love and excitement, and today her long dark hair had been swept up with diamante pins, by Miranda her top stylist. The sun was a blessing after a week of pouring rain when the marquee was put up in her parents' garden, and the 150 guests had wined and dined and then danced to an eight-piece group from London, until the early hours of the morning. Julie and Gavin had left the party before midnight, with kisses and hugs from family, and then excited friends shouting well wishes as the car moved off into the darkness with a rattling of old tin cans and shoes dragging behind. The driver was to take them to London Gatwick, where they spent the night in a hotel and left early the next morning for Barbados.

CHAPTER ONE

The eight-hour flight had been smooth and they were now looking down on the blue Caribbean Sea with strips of golden beaches and lush green vegetation. Gavin squeezed Julie's hand and excitement ran though them both as the 747 touched down in Bridgetown, Barbados, where they were about to start a whole new life.

The terminal was crowded as usual for the passport control that was slow and then there was another long wait for the luggage, but it was eventually collected and they were in no hurry as they followed the porter out of the terminal where Gavin spotted his name, ANDERSON, on a board held by a tall and handsome well-built black man who introduced himself as Rick Holland, the house manager. He led them and the porter to a silver Mercedes which he said also went with the house and would be available to them at any time, or if they wanted he would be there to drive them. Gavin and Julie in the back seat clasped hands and exchanged silent excited glances; they had not expected a car, least of all a Mercedes.

Rick made easy conversation. He had an American accent and was well educated going to university in New York; he said that his parents had moved there when he was five years old, and he had moved back to Barbados six years ago having met a Barbadian girl at university, and they now lived together on the island. They drove past green grassy fields and waving sugar cane. Rick asked if they had been to the island before and they both said "yes" together. Gavin asked if the house they were going to in Speightstown was near the beach.

"No," Rick slightly shook his head, "it's up in the hills, it's much cooler up there with a nice view of the sea but it will only take you about five minutes to get down to the beach, and ten to fifteen minutes to get to Holetown."

"We don't know much about the cottage," said Julie, "only that it's called Silver Lady."

"It's a nice property," Rick slowed down as the car in front turned left, "it's 300 years old and it hasn't been lived in for ten years, but the roof has just been repaired, and the guys have done a good paint job on the window frames and fencing – it looks quite tidy now."

As they drove through Holetown, Rick pointed out the bank and then another ten minutes they were going through Speightstown. The car turned off the main road to the right and began to climb the hill; they drove through small villages, and eventually came to a large black wooden gateway, with SILVER LADY COTTAGE painted in large white letters. They drove on through an avenue of tall trees and thick jungle-like greenery for about half a mile until they came to a rounded sandy and gravel stone clearing. The car stopped in front of a thick hedge, they got out of the car and followed Rick through a small and open black wooden gate that was almost hidden between the wild untamed shrubs. A thin and very narrow uneven coral stone path snaked its way in to a few steps up under an old and blackened coral stone arch then they went on to an age-old wide coral stone patio. To their right the patio was shaded by tall mahogany trees and the scarlet flowers of the huge Flamboyant trees, the petals now scattered at their feet. To their left, the house that had five coral stone arches in a row, and through them they could see a long dining table and high-backed chairs. They entered the house through the middle arch; the black painted gothic front door was wide open and a man stood there with a tray of champagne. Rick introduced them to Charles Bray, the butler – a well-built black man aged about fifty, his tight curly hair greying at the temples – who welcomed them with a bow of his head and a warm smile and offered them the tray. They thanked him, taking a glass, and followed Rick through into a wide circular hallway with a dark polished wooden floor that creaked under their tread. A large round mahogany table stood in the centre and held a tall vase of fresh exotic pink ginger lilies, above which was a large chandelier suspended on four long chains, "Oh that's lovely," said Julie.

"Yes at one time it would have been lit by candlelight," said Gavin.

"Gosh a bit dangerous," Julie glanced at him.

"Yes," Rick smiled, "but now it's converted to electric candle-like bulbs. At that time there were no bees on the island, the candles were brought in from Africa; they found that English candles burned out in the tropical heat – in fact I think there have been a few minor fires here, there is a burn mark on this table," he pointed it out, "I should think that was done by a candle probably falling from there." Beyond the table a polished mahogany staircase went up to a landing with a dark wooden balustrade. The newel post at the bottom was exquisitely carved with the head of a sea serpent with big staring eyes and gnashing teeth; the snake-like body continued up the handrail in delicately small hand-carved scales finishing at the top with a large curling fish tail, giving the impression that the serpent had slithered down the stairs to ward off unwelcome visitors. The wall on the right of the staircase was hung with several paintings of ladies with white pompadour wigs and low-cut silken gowns, two wore large hats adorned with flowers and feathers. In a recess near the serpent's head a grandfather clock stood strong as if in command and ticked away steadily. There were more paintings of Victorian ladies, and coral stone alcoves which held fine china ornaments and jardinières. Rick opened a door off to the right of the circular hallway and they followed him, finding themselves in a long and wide mahogany-panelled hallway with a Persian blue carpet and doors on either side. The vaulted ceiling was of dark wooden beams and narrow skylight windows. They entered a door to their right. "This is the main drawing room," Rick swept his arm around the whole room, "there are four reception rooms in all, but this is the most popular – I think it has been well used."

"But I thought that we were going to stay in a cottage?" said Julie.

"This *is* the Silver Lady Cottage," Rick smiled, knowing the reaction he would get as they glanced around the spacious room and then at each other in amazed surprise.

"But it's huge," Julie almost squealed, "it can hardly be called a cottage, how many bedrooms has it got?"

"Nine." It took her breath away, and Rick smiled, "It hasn't been lived in for ten years, but the roof has just been retiled, and of course the electricity was put in some years ago and that's only just been rewired. The furniture has been under dust sheets for years, it's all original antique, as you can see, and I think the house is sixteenth-century. There's always been staff here, and the bank has kept it in good condition."

Gavin and Julie stood in awe of the grandeur of the spacious and well-furnished room. A darkish red and midnight blue Persian carpet covered most of the floor; it was well worn and surrounded by at least two feet of highly polished dark wooden floorboards. Two long arched windows, and between them arched French louvered doors that were painted white, looked out across the patio on to manicured lawns and a round gazebo with eight tiled pillars. Rick pointed to the outside white-painted louvered storm shutters, "We do get some bad storms on occasions, but these are rarely used, but of course they are there, if you want them, the staff usually leave the doors wide open all day, it of course lets the air in."

"Staff?" Julie queried, "How many?"

"Eight in the house," Rick turned to her, "but only four live in – the butler and the chef have separate apartments downstairs and two maids live in the attic."

Julie gave Gavin a bewildered glance.

The heavy dark red velvet drapes that were half closed against the strong afternoon sunlight gave the room a shadowed look. It was very warm; Rick flipped a switch on the wall and two ceiling fans soon brought down the temperature. In front of the windows stood two antique armchairs; they were wide, low and covered with rich thick deep purple velvet cushions, a low mahogany carved coffee table stood between them, in the centre of which was a large well-used silver ashtray with burn marks on the side lips. In another corner there were more heavy armchairs with beautifully carved arms and deep ruby cushions, and there was a high-backed wooden rocking chair facing the window. There were smaller chairs and small tables dotted about the spacious room and, to the left of the door, a large carved sideboard with a black flecked marbled top which took up most of the mahogany panelled wall that faced the wide open French doors, leading out onto the arched patio where they had first entered the house. Placed upon the sideboard were silver ashtrays and a silver candelabrum with new tall white candles and a large exquisitely carved ivory elephant's tusk, and a telephone that looked completely out of place in this grandeur. Around the wood panelled walls were alcoves with ornaments of fine porcelain and exquisite glass, hand-painted pots and dishes. A tall jade figurine of a beautiful oriental woman stood on a small table in the far corner to their right, and there were lamps with pink silken shades and fringing, and golden menorahs were attached to the walls with new white candles. There were French bracket clocks, one French clock with a musical chime. Paintings in gilt frames of ships adorned the walls, with full-blown sails and seas so rough you could almost feel the salt in the air. Two enormous gilt-framed mirrors faced each other at either end of the long room, and two large chandeliers hung from black heavy beams, the glass droplets glittering as they were caught by the late afternoon sunshine coming in through the half-closed drapes and reflected in the mirrors.

Although modern furnishings were more to their taste, they couldn't help but catch their breath at the old-world charm and the richness of it all. "It's beautiful," said Julie shaking her head.

Rick showed them the rest of the house – all the rooms had dark mahogany beams and polished floorboards. The music room held a large grand piano, and apart from the dark green walls the whole room was furnished in old gold, with comfortable armchairs, and two silk sofas with old-gold coloured satin cushions that matched drapes at the two long windows, a gold and green patterned Persian carpet covering most of the floor. The three other reception rooms were furnished in a similar style, one in a deep rose pink, no doubt used by a lady, with its fine and feminine furnishings of pink satin chairs and lace chairbacks, and delicate ornaments and gilt mirrors. "This is the library," Rick just opened the door and they had a quick glance, it was a big room.

In the very spacious kitchen they met Oliver Mason, the chef, and his assistant Robbie, a tall dark-skinned lad wearing white who was busy chopping vegetables on a long marble-topped table. Oliver was a heftily built Barbadian man with a lighter brown skin, and dressed in whites with a tall chef's hat, he had a wide shy grin. He was pleased to show them his kitchen, saying that the two gas cookers that were now fitted into the enormous old-world style brick fireplace were new just three weeks ago and he would be pleased to give them a good try out. He also said that he had planned on chicken for dinner tonight but if they wanted to change it, it was no problem.

On leaving the kitchen they followed Rick from the main circular hall and up the wide wooden stairs, their feet clopping loudly with every step. Julie held on to the handrail and admired the delicately hand-carved scales of the serpent. Rick led them across the blue Persian carpeted landing to the first door, "This is the master bedroom, and this is how it originally was, it's of course cleaned but nothing has been touched." It was a vast room; facing them was an extra large four-poster bed, with a white canopy, the headboard and the posts carved with birds and vines, the counterpane was of multi-coloured patchwork, the dominant colour being red that was now faded. Either side of the bed were two large windows, the long drapes from ceiling to floor were once bright red, but now after years in the blazing sunlight were faded to an orange-pink and looked as if touched they would fall to pieces. To their left was an enormous dressing table with three mirrors, the drawers carved with leaves and vines and was highly polished, and on the top were stuffed exotic birds – one had a red head, now faded, the feathers dusty, and a black feathered body and a long tail; one bird had a yellow head, green body, and one had once been bright blue but was now faded to a pale blue almost grey. To the right of the room a wash stand, with a large willow-patterned bowl, and on a pedestal stood a large seagull, its wings spread wide as if in flight, its beak open as if screeching. The floor was highly polished and there was a thin faded and well-worn red Persian carpet.

"And it has been like this for years?" said Gavin in surprise, "Why?"

"I don't really know," Rick shook his head, "it's probably the room where Captain Desmond Honeybeck died. I know a little history of the house but no one has mentioned this, it's only my opinion."

"It looks as if it's been untouched for a hundred years," Gavin smiled with disbelief.

"It most probably has," Rick smiled as they came back into the hall again. He opened the next door along the hallway which was also a large room, neat and clean with a four-poster bed and mostly white. "These four bedrooms are the largest," he said, "the five on the other side of the staircase are a bit smaller." He opened a door at the end of the hall, "This room has just been refurbished especially for you," he smiled at them both, arching his eyes at Gavin, "being that you are just married," he inclined his head shyly as if it was a secret.

"How did you know that?" Gavin grinned, his eyes wide, "does it show?"

"You *are* on your honeymoon, *aren't you,* Sir?' Rick inclined his head again with a smile and a nod, there was a twinkle in his eye, but he didn't disclose his source of information.

The bedroom was beautiful, spacious with enormous cream-coloured antique wardrobes and gilt-framed mirrors and an equally enormous cream-coloured dressing table and a pale blue velvet stool. Two pale blue velvet armchairs stood either side, and a very new sky-blue patterned silk carpet covered the whole floor. There was an enormous antique four-poster bed, the mahogany headboard carved with two mermaids with flowing wavy hair holding a large shell

11

between them, the four posts carved with vines and shells. The counterpane was cream to match the new long drapes at the two windows, and louvered doors opened out on to a long balcony that was enclosed with a newly painted white iron balustrade The house was built on a ridge, and from here there was a beautiful view of the sea that was beyond the trees. Rick said there was a swimming pool down the steps just before the trees, also with a view of the sea, there was the patio where they had first come in and well-kept lawns and flowering shrubs, mahogany trees and sweet-smelling white frangipani, and tall waving palms that shaded parts of the garden.

"The statue you can see down there on the lawn is the Silver Lady," said Rick, "she's the figurehead of a galleon, that's where the house takes its name; she's painted silver and white, and she shines in the dark, I don't know why, I guess it's some sort of phosphorous paint. I thought I'd better tell you this, as you might get a bit worried if you look out here in the dark and see her glowing, it gave me a bit of a start the first time I saw it, she looks like a ghostly figure. This house was built by a pirate – he was an Englishman called Desmond Honeybeck, I guess the master bedroom down the hall was his, maybe that's why it's still in its original state. He had been pirating in the Caribbean waters for years around the sixteen hundreds. Apparently there was a battle with a ship called the *Sea Gull* – whether it was a pirate ship or not, I don't think anyone knows, but there was cannon fire and gunpowder exploded and both ships were sunk. Honeybeck and one of his crew were the only two to survive, it's said that they were fighting for their lives in a stormy sea and then amongst the debris suddenly the figurehead of his ship *The Silver Lady* bobbed up out of the water, they both clung on to it, and after hours in rough water they managed to get ashore. When Honeybeck built this house, he was convinced that she had saved his life, and he put her there in the garden where she had stood for three hundred years; whether she has always glowed like that I don't know."

"That's interesting," Gavin nodded, "I suppose he eventually died at sea, and the house was left unattended."

'No," Rick arched his eyebrows and shook his head, "he died here at the house ten years later, he was wounded in a sword fight, attacked by the crewman that was saved from the shipwreck with him. It seems that Honeybeck had accumulated a great fortune over the years from his pirating days, so they say, and it's hidden here somewhere but it seems that nothing has ever been found. I would imagine that all of these antiques have been stolen too, this may even be the treasure." He smiled.

"How old was he?" Gavin asked.

"I think he was about fifty when he died, somewhere around sixteen hundred and something – that was a good age, most pirates died around thirty; if they were extremely skilled with the sword they may have made it to forty. I suppose the house was empty for some years after he died, and then people named Turner, a wealthy family from England, lived here for generations – it was a sugar plantation and it was handed down from father to son and it grew and grew to many acres. Up until just a few years ago, when Ben Carding, bought the land, it was still a sugar plantation. The Cardings live a mile or so down the road, they're your next door neighbours," he grinned, "I don't know much more about it than that. Only that the bank have looked after everything for years, putting their top people in here for some months at a time, so there has always been staff. There are two guards that come on duty after dark, both Bajan guys – Dan Calder and Bill Elliot. Dan has a dog, a German Shepherd, so if you see someone wandering around with a dog after dark you'll know it's him. They are both ex-policemen and very reliable but the old place has been empty now for some years, apart from the live-in house staff of course, but they are all fairly new now within the last six months and they have been chosen very carefully by the bank, because of the antiques. One of the three gardeners has been here forever; the others have only been here in the last three months, but the renovations have been going on for nearly a year."

Their luggage was brought up by an old man who suddenly bundled noisily through the door, huffing and puffing and dumping the heavy bags in the middle of the room. Rick introduced them, "This is Mr Gibbons, he's the head gardener, been here almost as long as the house," Rick grinned.

The man nodded and grinned, he was a Barbadian man, aged well into his seventies, very dark skinned, his head balding with a white curly fluff around his neck and ears, he had a wide and friendly grin through a white beard showing a set of yellowing teeth with one gold one in the front. He left the room, bidding them good night.

"Goodnight?" Gavin frowned with a grin, looking at his watch, it was mid-afternoon. They grinned at each other knowing from previous holidays that early evening was quite often referred to as night.

Rick was about to leave and said that a maid would unpack for them, but Julie said that she preferred to do it herself, and Rick bid them good evening, saying that he would be in the office until 6.30 if they needed anything. He gave Gavin his mobile number, and left the room.

Julie stood at the French windows looking out to sea, "It's all so beautiful I really can't believe the house, I expected a small cottage."

"Yes so did I," Gavin walked out onto the balcony with her, "It's so warm and the sun is still out." He put an arm around her. "We're going to be so happy here, aren't we darling?"

She nodded, her brown eyes shining, taking a deep and contented breath, "Yes it's wonderful." He kissed her, and they stood in each other's arms gazing out to sea. "It's like a film set," said Julie dreamily, "I'm not dreaming am I?"

'Nooo." He grinned.

Arrangements had been made with the chef, Oliver Mason, and they were to have dinner in the gazebo at 7.30. It was dark by seven o'clock. They had showered and changed and were now sitting in the comfortable armchairs in the gazebo, with a glass of champagne. The dark night sky was starry and very warm. Charles switched on the ceiling fan that cooled the humidity and the fan flickered the candles on the table before them that was laid with sparking cut glass and polished silver. The bowl of fresh flowers in the centre of the table was picked from the garden by Charles, the butler, and he had arranged them himself.

Charles came to replenish their glasses; he felt a tug at his heart, seeing them gazing at each other and holding hands, and asked politely if they would like the music turned on. Gavin thanked him, the lights got brighter and then Charles dimmed them and soft music played.

Shortly afterwards they were enjoying a superbly cooked meal, and then sat at the table finishing the wine. It was about 9.30 and Julie felt magic in the air – the night sky was like black velvet dotted with a million stars, and the night air was warm and alive with the tropical sounds of tiny whistling frogs that were never seen in the daytime. Flashing small green lights appeared as fireflies came out to play, darting amongst the leaves of the sweet smelling blossoms of the frangipani and around the low security lights, and the loud buzz of crickets and unseen insects filled the tropical warm night scented air. It was the first real night of their honeymoon, and it was all so romantic, so magical, Julie hoped that nights like this would last forever. Gavin kissed her tenderly, vowing his love, and their soft whisperings were unheard by the glowing Silver Lady that stood with her back to them just a few yards away, staring with her sightless blue painted eyes out onto the dark and distant sea.

The morning light was streaming through a gap in the cream drapes when Julie awoke in the king-size bed and stretched. She turned, still a little sleepy, reaching out for Gavin but he was not there, she blinked against the light. The French doors were open and a warm breeze moved the palest ice-blue sheers. She got out of bed and put on a pink satin dressing gown and stepped out onto the veranda, Gavin was there, as she came close he put an arm around her and kissed her forehead, "Oh it's so wonderful here, smell that sea air. Sleep well, darling?" She nodded still a little sleepy, looking up at the early morning sky, a clear blue grey and apricot tint, it was going to be a lovely day.

After a light breakfast of orange juice, fresh fruit, toast and coffee, they settled themselves on deck beds beside the large swimming pool. Rick had not showed them the pool, it was reached via rough coral stone steps with a sea view. The pool surprised them and was so beautiful, a brilliant blue now reflecting the cloudless sky, surrounded by rugged rocks and framed by waving coconut palms and sweet-smelling frangipani, and pure white orchids clung in huge clusters to the gnarled branches of an old and wizened yam – it gave the appearance of natural tropical lagoon and through a clearing in the trees a view of the sea. You could almost imagine Tarzan swinging through the trees, but instead it was Charles who had come with ice cold drinks, and to open the tall green and white umbrellas to shade them from the hot rays of the sun.

"Oh what a lovely way to spend Monday," Julie sighed, closing the book she was trying to read, then leaning back closing her eyes behind dark glasses, "this is heaven, I bet it's raining in England."

"Hmm," Gavin mumbled behind the newspaper, "but you've seen all this before."

"NOT!" she sat up very quickly, "as Mrs Gavin Anderson I haven't! It all feels so different now, there seems more warmth in the sun seeping though my skin."

"Naaah, it's not the sun, it's you, you're hot stuff," he grinned, peeping around the paper and then dodged back again quickly with a grin as she lashed out and hit the paper with a giggle. He chuckled, then glanced over the paper again at the beautiful slim figure in the pink bikini.

"Want me to turn the heat down a bit then?" She grinned, bracing her shoulders and pushing her small rounded breasts forward."

"OH! Nooo!" He frowned, shaking his head, "I can stand the heat, some like it HOT!" He inclined his head and grinned with his eyes rolling comically, "I've always liked a bit of hot stuff." He smiled sexily, his eyes still rolling.

"But you're a MARRIED MAN!" her voice rose in absolute amazement and then gave him a disgusted look.

"And you're a MARRIED WOMAN!" the eyes still rolling and the eyebrows flashing up and down, "*and*," he stressed with emphasis, you shouldn't be giving me the come-on!" He was still half hidden behind the paper.

"Well, why don't *you* come *on!*" She sat up, breathing in to display her full young rounded breasts again, preening like Marilyn Munroe, and throwing her head back glamorously and lifting her long dark ponytail, fluttering her sparking brown eyes and smiling at him like a model in a glossy magazine. Then reaching out her arm sexily she was about to strike the paper again when he caught her wrist, giving her a playful yank over on top of him and she giggled as he held her tight and kissed her, and they chuckled happily together. "I'm glad that you don't look any different for being Mrs Anderson, I want you to look like Miss Read for the rest of our lives."

She giggled, "I'll try even when I'm old and grey, but I do feel different." He kissed her.

On hearing a squeal, Charles looked down from the top of the steps through the trees but seeing only the tops of the umbrellas, and hearing giggles he rolled his eyes and smiled to himself, *honeymooners,* and made his way back to the kitchen with an empty tray and a grin showing even white teeth in his back face.

The musical signal of Gavin's mobile phone interrupted the romantic moment and their lips parted as he jumped away from her quickly to answer it. "Hello."

His father's voice was loud in his ear, "Settled in have you?"

"Yes thanks, the house is great," said Gavin.

"Good," Sir Gabriel Anderson smiled, "I thought you'd like it."

Gavin looked surprised at his father's tone. "Why? Have you seen it then?"

"No, but I've seen a video. Staff OK? There's eight isn't there? Did Rick pick you up OK?"

"Yes," Gavin frowned a bit bewildered, "how did *you* know?"

"I bought the house for you, it's a wedding present."

"You WHAT!" At Gavin's loud gasp, Julie sat right up, on the end of his deck bed.

"What is it?" she said, sitting up straight-backed with a look of alarm. "What's happened?"

Gavin shook his head and waved his hand at her as his father's voice went on, "Well I know you love Barbados, and the bank were going to give you a small pokey little place to live in – I didn't think it was good enough, so I bought the Silver Lady." He went on explaining how he had found it and eventually clicked the phone off. Gavin sat for a few minutes, dazed.

Julie was anxious, "What's happened?"

"That was Dad, this house is ours! He BOUGHT IT! It's a wedding present!" She caught her breath. She was aghast. "Apparently he met Sir Robin Law, they were talking about my application for transfer out here, and Sir Robin said the accommodation was not very good, and so Dad pulled a few strings, phoned Robert Prescott – he has a holiday home here – and *he* got hold of Rick Holland. Dad's never met him, but Rick has organized everything, and sent him videos of the place."

"But it must have cost your father millions with all those antiques," said Julie. "Does he know it's not a cottage?"

"Yeah!" Gavin was still a bit bemused, "I suppose so, he's seen a video."

The phone rang again, Gavin answered it. "Oh hello, Robert!" It was Robert Prescott, chairman of the bank, and a friend of his father's. They had not met but had spoken on the phone several times before. Robert said, "I've just had a call from Sir Gabriel, he said you were here, and he gave me your phone number, I hoped you're settling in – nice house isn't it?" He went on to say that they had been here for two weeks and had a small holiday home on the beach. "I wondered if you might like to come to dinner this evening, sorry it's such short notice but my wife and I are flying to Florida the day after tomorrow – our son is getting engaged and they are having a party. And I'd also like you to meet Alan Stone, the new C.F.O. Stone was in charge of finance in Surrey, he also has just been transferred from the UK. He's been here a week now, I met him a couple of nights ago at the bank a meeting – he starts in a couple of weeks' time, I thought you two might like to get together."

That evening Rick drove them to 'White Waves'. The house was on the beach, a butler opened the door and Robert Prescott came forward, hand outstretched, with a beaming smile. He was a small man in his sixties, of medium height, bald-headed with a trim of grey. He then introduced his wife Mary. She was small and delicate, about the same age as her husband, she had a sweet smile, dark brown eyes and dark hair greying rolled up into a pleat. She shook hands warmly, "So pleased that you could come, I'm sorry it's such short notice," she indicated chairs, but just as they were about to sit, Alan Stone and his wife Suzie were coming through the front door. Rob again welcomed them, with a warm handshake, and then was introducing his wife and also Gavin and Julie.

The butler, Tompkins, offered them wine and the evening went very well, ending with the men sitting together talking business, and the ladies sitting in the garden under the stars, Mary apologising for the short notice that evening. "I know you have only just arrived," and saying that their son Michael suddenly sprung it on them two days ago that he was getting engaged to this girl named Mellissa. "It was such a surprise, we didn't even know he had a girl," Mary chuckled, splaying her thin hands and looking wide-eyed at them both, "and we do hope he is doing the right thing."

"So you are going over to check her out are you?" Suzie Stone smiled.

Mary sniffed, "Well yes, I guess that's what you'd call it, but what can we do, they have to live their own lives." They went on to talk girls' talk, of make-up and clothes, and then Mary was saying that Rob was semi-retired and now they could spend two to three months a year here on the island, but only had two weeks left to go now, and that they were going to spend them in Florida. And then Suzie and Julie were both asking Mary questions about living here on the island. Suzie said that they had been here twice on holiday, but she never thought that she would actually live here.

"Oh neither did I," said Julie, "we've been here several times over the last four years, staying at Sandy Lane, and we were thrilled when Gavin got news of the transfer and that we were to live here."

"We're at Sandy Lane now," said Suzie, with a shy smile, "we've been sitting on the beach most days, but I have to be careful being so fair-skinned." She was very petite with a pale skin and natural medium-length wavy blonde hair. "We arrived at the house last week and a water pipe had broken and everything was wet, so they put us in Sandy Lane, it's lovely, but I am so looking forward to getting my own home."

The men stood up and were saying goodnight, then Robert and Mary walked with them to the door. As they were going to get into their cars, it started to rain quite heavily, "Oh I hope it won't rain tomorrow," said Suzie, "we're going out on a catamaran."

"Oh I think you'll enjoy it," said Mary looking up at the dark sky, "it's only a shower."

"You should go with them," Robert suggested to Gavin, thinking that the boys could get even better acquainted.

"Why don't we all go?" said Mary, "we haven't been on a catamaran for years." And she had enjoyed their young company.

"We can't," said Robert, "we're flying out early the next morning."

"But we'll be back in the middle of the afternoon – I'm half packed anyway." Mary looked at him in surprise, "Come on, let's go."

"Oh, OK then," Robert agreed a bit reluctantly, seeing that she was anxious to go, and they arranged to meet at the wharf.

CHAPTER TWO

Rick was driving and they picked Suzie and Alan up at Sandy Lane on the way. They arrived at the wharf around ten o'clock in the morning, where people were already boarding the catamaran, *Sunny Days*. "Let's sit up the front," Suzie was excited, "we did this last year."

"Forward," Alan corrected comically, "It's forward, there's no back and front on a boat, it's forward and aft."

"Oh listen to him," mused Suzie, raising her eyes, "he's been sailing about twice in his life."

They made their way, *forward*. And they all sat in a line on their own towels, their legs dangling over the front of the wide white deck. There was a safety net between the two floats, Julie sat over the right float she mused in her mind, *starboard*. Suzie sat next to her, and then Mary, then Alan and Gavin, and Robert; there were more people in the line but the majority of the sixty passengers were spread over the broad white deck in an array of swimwear or shorts and tee shirts. Four young teenagers sort of plonked themselves down on the safety net giggling and pushing each other, they were to get very wet when the cat started to sail. The trip was to take about four hours, including lunch and swimming, and it wasn't the most comfortable of rides sitting on a towel on the deck, "A bit hard on the backside," Gavin remarked.

Julie and Gavin had never been on a catamaran before, although they had been sailing several times in the Caribbean. Gavin's father, Sir Gabriel, had chartered a luxury yacht and they had been for ten days in the British Virgin Islands and the Grenadines with the family – that included Gavin's younger brother James and their older sister Celia, with a crew of eight. Celia had been most discontented from the first moment she got on board, the wind blew her hair and the shower was too cramped, her husband Tom had been most patient, but how he put up with her no one knew.

As the catamaran moved away from the dockside the sun was blazing down, most had now discarded shorts and tee shirts, and the pungent smell of many different suntan creams arose with the heat. The cat soon picked up speed and a cool breeze blew, and a group of five young guys let out WHOOPS and WHISTLES of excitement as loud disco music was switched on and the throbbing of the engine was faded out and they were proceeding along the west coast of the island.

The water was a little choppy, and the floats dipped in the swells, much to the delight of the four teenagers on the net enjoying every wave. A steward made his way cautiously among closely knit sun-seeking bodies, offering a tray of mixed drinks – most took rum punch. The catamaran dipped and bobbed as they sailed steadily under sail now, the captain giving a running commentary on the houses and hotels and places of interest along the shoreline, and by now with the third rum punch everyone was in a party mode, chatting and laughing with everyone else. Then after two hours they slowed to a stop a few yards out from the shore, the anchor was dropped and the sails were being lowered and music turned down. The wind no longer rushed in their faces and their ears, and the intense heat from the sun blazed down and had most of the women lashing on more suntan cream.

The announcement came over the loud speaker that a buffet lunch was now being served at the stern, and the passengers moved to port or to starboard, queuing in an orderly line along the deck to the well of the cat where chicken, fish, rice and salad was displayed and of course no limit to the drink. Everyone took their plates back to their places on the deck where there was no shade. After a good lunch, those that wanted to could swim – a lot of the passengers went in, Gavin and Alan among them while the others watched from the deck. There were turtles close by and the crew threw bread to attract them and people were diving off the deck to swim with them; those watching could see more from above and many cameras flashed as the turtles surfaced and dived. After a while the horn was sounded calling those that were still swimming to get back on board. At one o'clock sharp the anchor was raised and the engine shuddered into life and they were on the move back to Bridgetown to shouts of excitement from the group of young guys who, by this time, had had plenty of rum punch. They motored out some distance from the shore and the sails were hoisted and they turned into the wind, and the breeze although warm was welcomed, the music now turned off and they sailed peacefully with just the dipping and swishing of the sea. A dark cloud came over and there was a short light rain shower that lasted just a few minutes, and then hot sunshine again.

Then the captain gave an announcement over the speaker, saying that whales had been sighted, and they were heading out to sea to see them. This caused a lot of clapping and excited chatter and the passengers, some now standing and straining their necks and their eyes, were all hoping to be the first to spot one. The captain also said that whales were sighted on rare occasions here in Barbados, and at one time the small island of Bequia (pronounced Bek-way), in the Grenadines, used to be a whaling station.

As they moved further out into deeper water it was more choppy and now the engine was switched on. The cat dipped up and down and from side to side. "Anyone want another drink before it gets too choppy?" Gavin asked, looking along the line. They all nodded yes, so he and Alan got up and made their way carefully across the moving deck that was now wet and slippery from the swimmers towards the galley on the port side.

The forward floats dipped deep; the teenagers on the safety net were getting very wet with the white foam splashing continuously.

"There's a whale!" somebody shouted and everyone looked but it seemed to be a hoax, and it went very quiet although all eyes were looking to the horizon, the swells getting deeper as they went further out. Then the starboard float where Julie was sitting lifted under a big swell that jolted the whole catamaran, and the teenagers screamed with delight as one of them was thrown a few feet into the air. Julie grabbed the rail beside her for support, a man nearby laughed and said that they'd got a puncture, and everyone was giggling and jeering.

Gavin and Alan were leaving the galley, each carrying three rum punches, when the starboard float suddenly lifted again right out of the water, and the head of a huge whale came up. Only those in the front knew what happened. Everyone screamed as some started to slide down the deck to the port side. Julie gripped the handrail tighter, as the float lifted even higher and the huge grey back of the whale humped the whole starboard side of the catamaran up out of the water. The four teenagers were flung high into the air, and tossed over the side as the starboard float was rising even higher as the whale humped its back again. Suzie screamed and slipped, Julie quickly grabbed her hand, seeing both Robert Prescott and Mary sliding away helplessly with looks of terrified surprise, following the other passengers, screaming and shouting. Julie, with one hand on the rail, hung on to Suzie with her left hand both her arms now stretched wide and to the limit in either direction. Suzie was now flat out on her stomach and dangling loosely away from the deck and struggling to get a grip with her feet but it was slippery, and the deck was now almost vertical, and Julie was a scary thirty feet in the air and now lifted from the deck herself and dangling, hanging by one arm and holding Suzie with the other. Their fingers were slipping and Suzie screamed, "Don't let me go!" But then their hands slipped apart and Suzie was hurtling down to the port side with a blood curdling scream. Julie watched as she plunged feet first into the sea and disappeared and the hungry black swells just swallowed her up. Julie, still hanging on to the rail, was swinging in mid-air trying to get a grip with her feet and her left hand but now the float was high and at its peak and beginning to turn. There was another shudder as the whale humped its back again, and her hand was slipping on the rail; she could hang on no longer and was flung helplessly forward with a mighty thrust with all the others that were on the starboard rail hurtling high through the air out and down into the sea as the starboard float was on the apex of the turn. She plunged feet first, hitting the water like a brick wall, plunging down into the deep black swells and seeing bubbles float up before her eyes. She was a good swimmer and managed to kick her way to the surface and came up gasping for air and floundering around as if drowning, and then seeing the huge tail of the whale flapping just a few feet from her and disappearing under the catamaran as the starboard float was plunging forward. Then the forty-foot mast seemed to fall as if in slow motion and the mighty canvas crashed into the sea sweeping all and sundry under it, the huge float crashed and dipped deep into the water and the black swells rose to four to six feet above her head and she was dipped deep below the water again and felt the current sweeping her and lifting her out away from the cat. As she rose again the spray rained down taking her under again, and for a split second all was deadly quiet, and then as she surfaced yet again, gasping and taking in deep breaths, her ears cleared and she heard screams and shouts. She saw heads bobbing and disappearing between the deep swells, then the huge float suddenly popped up like a cork out of the deep sending more deep waves before coming to rest on the surface. There were shocked and terrified screams of help, gulping and coughing, names being called; a woman nearby was calling between gulps and splutters "JOHN! JOHN!" Everyone was splashing and struggling. Julie was calling "Gavin!" her voice like everyone else's choked and lost in the swish of the waves. Although struggling and gasping breathlessly she managed to do a few strokes reaching up way above her head to hold on to the bouncing capsized float that was slippery, black and green with sea grass, sea grime and sea slime.

Debris now floated all around items of clothing, towels and food paper plates, and a man's trainer floated amongst plastic glasses, silver foil and bags; suntan bottles bobbed up from the depths hats and sandals but there was not a sign of a life jacket. She clung on desperately calling Gavin's name, but found that it was useless and better to save her breath. They would find each other later, Gavin was a good swimmer. She looked for Suzie, she supposed that she was now amongst the bobbing heads. A child was screaming, and splashing helplessly a few feet from her, and she was about to go to her, but the mother was suddenly there. The child desperately grabbed at her and they both went under, but reappeared again between the swells and the woman grabbed the float, the girl about eight years old clinging around the woman's neck. Julie watched as heads were appearing and disappearing as the waves rose and fell, the desperate screams and shouts had now subsided a little as everyone was catching their breath, a lot now hanging on to the float for support as she was.

They were a long way from the shore so there was no chance of swimming in, but two men had started to swim away – they probably might not make it, but there was a slim chance that someone would pick them up. She changed arms, her hand slipping on the green slime, and she still was desperately trying to see Gavin among the bobbing heads; she wondered about the whale – was it still lurking below, and would it surface again and take the cat from them? She wondered how deep the fathoms were, and were there sharks nearby?

Then a ski boat roared up at great speed, churning the water in a huge white swirling circle and two young black men jumped into the sea. The first man swam a few strokes and grabbed the child who screamed desperately clinging on to her mother and wouldn't let go, but the mother pushed her away saying "GO" as the man grabbed her, taking her to the boat where the driver lifted her in, and the man came back for the mother – he was struggling, trying to get her into the boat helped again by the driver who was also struggling to keep the boat steady as the water splashed heavily over the side. Two men were trying desperately to clamber over the side and others came and the boat dipped dangerously taking on water to shouts from the driver. Another ski boat came roaring up, again churning the water and making those still trying to keep afloat scream for help. Three jet bikes arrived all at once with a great roar of engine power and people scrambled on to two of them, each taking two people, and they roared away; one capsized, the driver now struggling in the sea as people were scrambling and fighting to mount the bike, but they managed to right it again and the driver took off with two extra passengers. One of the young men from the ski boat came to Julie, he asked "are you alright," she nodded, "can you swim," she nodded, he grabbed her under her arms and turned her on her back and dragged her in a life-saving hold to the ski boat, pushing her up over the side. She fell into the seat at the back gasping for breath as an inward smile crossed her lips hearing Alan's remark, *it was aft*, and she felt relief with the solid wood under her back, but exhausted and breathing heavily she struggled into the seat. The woman opposite her clung desperately to the child who was shaking and crying, "Where's Daddy?"

It was chaos with shouting and screaming as people tried to clamber on board the ski boat, the driver shouting as the boat dipped and bounced dangerously from side to side in the deep swells as people were scrambling and fighting each other to get aboard and the water lashed over the side. There were about fourteen of them now in the boat, the driver, shouting "NO MORE, NO MORE," they were already overcrowded and had shipped enough water, and before the driver revved up the engine the man that had helped Julie aboard was pushing people away from the motor at the back. The engine roared into life and the driver shouted that he would be back and the boat turned and roared away, slower than normal with the extra weight, passing another ski boat just arriving which had a rubber banana float on the back which could seat six people. The banana, wet and slippery, bobbed and bounced as people scrambled to get on and then they all fell off again – it happened every day and caused many laughs but not today under such tragic circumstances, and the driver and his co-driver were shouting at them to go steady as they were trying to clamber on the boat and it was dipping precariously low enough to sink on the port side.

The beach was crowded with onlookers and police, and there were many helping hands. Julie was helped over the side by a boatman who was in the water up to his chest, he took her off her feet in a strong arm as he waded ashore and then on the beach another very tall and athletic black man scooped her up in his arms and almost ran up the beach with her to where an ambulance was waiting and a blanket was wrapped around her. The woman and the little girl were already there, then a man and a woman were helped in, they were all shivering, with exhausted sounds of relief, there were about eight of them in all crowded in and then the doors were closed and they were on the move.

Arriving at the Holetown Clinic that was just five minutes away, about three miles or so down the road, it was chaos – wet and bedraggled passengers now all shivering in the air conditioning, tearful, snivelling, scared and nervous, and most crying with relief, one woman was vomiting in the corner and a nurse was trying to make her way to her, everyone in despair and looking for their loved ones and friends. Nurses, trying to help with blankets and taking names and addresses, most were tourists and were staying in hotels, private cars and police cars were arriving with four or more passengers, and another ambulance. One woman being carried on a stretcher, a man with a towel around his head his face covered in blood. There was no sign of Gavin. There was a short wait and Julie was taken into see a doctor; he examined her, and found all was well but like everyone else she was badly shaken. She asked him if he had seen her husband, he said that he had not seen all the passengers yet, but to ask one of the nurses who were taking names.

Julie felt sick with anxiety, she was tearful and shaking with nervous agitation – where was Gavin? Everyone else was here, where was he? The waiting room was packed, he could be there somewhere and still more were arriving. A woman appeared to have a broken leg and was being carried by one of the black men rescuers. There was a lot of crying, sniffling, sad and anxious mumbling, a child screaming for its mother who it possibly would never see again. But no one seemed really seriously hurt, all of course were very shocked, and scared. Julie managed to find a seat, wrapping the blanket closer around her and anxiously watched every head that came into the waiting room until Gavin made an appearance. For nearly an hour people streamed in and out. Suddenly she saw Alan Stone, he beamed on seeing her; he came anxiously over to her, he looked fine, his tee shirt and shorts had dried, he said he had been waiting down on the beach, but he had not seen anything of Suzie yet, and then he asked about Gavin.

Julie shook her head sadly, shedding a few more tears and pulling the blanket closer around her, "I'm getting very worried."

"Oh there's still a few more to come yet," said Alan, although, in himself he didn't feel very confident, but he tried to sound reassuring, "the coastguard is out there now and divers. Do you know exactly what happened?"

Julie nodded a bit surprised, "Yes, it was a whale humped up under the catamaran, right under the right float where I was sitting."

"Good God, *really?* Is that what happened? I thought we'd hit part of the reef. Gavin and I were just coming back from the galley with the drinks and the next thing I knew, I was in the sea. Good God! It's unbelievable, a *whale?*"

"Did you see Gavin?"

"No." He shook his head wildly with a pained frown, there was a sick and empty feeling in his stomach. "But the ski boats are still going out." He hoped that would comfort her, but in his own mind he knew that it was now hopeless, if Suzie and Gavin were not here now there was little hope. A man sitting next to her was called into the doctor, and Alan took his place and sat down.

Julie was tearful, "I tried to hold on to Suzie, but our hands slipped and she went down into the water, I just couldn't hold her," she shook her head and cried, "I just couldn't hold her." Alan put an arm around her, and she cried bitterly into his shoulder. "I'm sorry, Alan," she shook her head, "I, just couldn't hold her, I just couldn't hold her," the tears ran down her cheeks, "I'm so sorry," she wailed bitterly, as he tightened his arm around her.

A tall uniformed Bajan policeman came into the waiting room, they heard him tell the receptionist quietly that this was the last; there were no more to come, as yet.

Julie took a deep breath and sighed, wiping her eyes on the blanket. Alan felt his heart sink, Suzie must be here somewhere, but he held a choking feeling back in his throat. He put a hand out and covered both of Julie's hands as she was twisting them tightly in her lap. There were no words to say.

Through her tears she mumbled, "Gavin has to be somewhere, he's a strong swimmer." Alan squeezed her tightly to him, trying to comfort her, over her head tears ran down his cheeks feeling every bit as distraught although he tried not to let go fully, telling himself that this was not happening, Suzie would turn up any minute, and he had to be strong now to comfort Julie.

The policeman turned their way and Alan asked, sniffing, if all the passengers had come here to the clinic.

"No, Sir, some were taken to the hospital in Bridgetown," he nodded with a slight sympathetic smile, "don't worry maaan, there *is* still hope." He put a comforting hand on Alan's shoulder. He took both their names and jotted them in a book, and suggested that they go back home or to their hotel so that they could be contacted. He also mentioned that some passengers had refused to see a doctor and had already gone back to their place of residence and may be awaiting news. And said that the police would be in touch.

Alan phoned Sandy Lane and asked to be put through to his room but there was no answer. He then phoned the Silver Lady Cottage, asking if Mr Anderson was there, Rick answered saying that he hadn't seen him and that he was out for the day. He was surprised when Alan asked him to come down to the clinic to collect Mrs Anderson. Rick jumped back in his chair, "WHY! Have they had an accident?"

"Yes!" Alan said, "Can you come quickly?" He didn't go into detail.

The waiting room was clearing now, just a few passengers remained. One or two people drifted in to see the doctor, one or two came into the pharmacy for a prescription. Alan still had his arm around Julie when Rick suddenly pushed open the door. He was shocked when Alan started to explain about the catamaran disaster.

They dropped Alan off at Sandy Lane Hotel, and Rick drove Julie home, she explaining through tears what had happened. She went straight to her room she stood feeling a bit disorientated, her heart was racing and hot tears still welled and ran down her cheeks. She shook her head and covered her face with her hands and sat down in the blue velvet chair and sobbed bitterly. Lucy, the maid, tapped on the door and came in – Rick had done some explaining and had sent her up – she asked gently if she could do anything. Julie shook her head. Lucy stood by the door watching her mistress, and feeling her pain, she bit her lip not knowing what to do, and then she left quietly closing the door and went back downstairs to where Rick and the rest of the staff were in the staff room, all in shock. She herself had done nothing, she shook her head feeling so helpless.

Julie shook her head, her hands still covering her face, *she was never going to get over this. Oh God, where was Gavin, where WAS HE? He couldn't be dead, HE JUST COULDN'T BE! Not her darling Gavin.* She sniffed, wringing her hands so tight together that she winced with the pain, and looked around the room through blurry eyes in utter despair, then took a deep and faltering breath. *But if it was true, what would she do?* It was true, it *was true*, she knew it in her heart he was dead, but she refused to believe it. But now, *what would she do without him? She was telling herself that she would just have to try to get over it. But NO! NO! He would come through. He would. He would... There was some simple explanation, there had to be. He WOULD COME... She pressed her fingers hard over her lips. He HAD to come, he wouldn't just leave her!*

She dried her eyes blew her nose and sniffed, she had to stop this silly crying, he would phone and everything would be alright. She stood up weakly and made her way to the bathroom where she bathed her puffy eyes with cold water, telling herself *crying wasn't going to help, she must be strong.* She must think positive. Her breath faltering, she picked up his shaving brush from where he had left it that morning on the shelf, feeling the softness of the hair in her fingers – it was still wet – she touched it to her lips then burst out crying again. *Gavin just had to be there somewhere,* there had to be an explanation, she sniffed back the tears again, *maybe in the hubbub they had missed each other, maybe he had been waiting on the beach like Alan. Maybe he was still there waiting anxiously for her. Maybe he was at the clinic now, or* perhaps at the hospital and not able to contact her, yes that was it – he's lost his phone, or it was too wet and not usable. Maybe, he had hit his head! Her heart panged! Maybe lost his memory, *maybe they were operating on him...* She was looking in the mirror, she looked a mess, hot tears streamed down her cheeks again. *Maybe she was doing all this crying for nothing, HE WOULD come back, soon. He would contact her, HE HAD TO, he wouldn't go and leave her alone...* He wouldn't! He wouldn't! She shook her head and sniffed again and tightened her lips. *She must stop crying...* She must get ready, she didn't want him to see her in such a mess when he came back. She discarded her still damp bikini.

After a hot shower, she felt a lot better. She did her make-up and lashed a bit of mascara on the still puffy eyes – it was a little improvement and made her feel a bit better. She put on a light white cotton dress, the one he had liked, and then wandered about the room from the French doors to the dressing table, then out again looking out to sea and maybe the air would clear her head and her eyes. She stood for a few minutes and she came back in again and looked into the mirror, and then walked out on to the veranda again, knowing that it wasn't doing any good, but she just couldn't settle, feeling worried, nervous, and in despair, twitching her face and wringing her hands, and her inside still shaky after the ordeal in the water. Then, clenching her fists very tight and taking a deep breath, she pulled her shoulders back, and taking another deep breath, before opening the bedroom door, she lifted her lips in a tight straight line. She made her way downstairs, a tissue to her nose, hoping that she wouldn't see any of the staff, but Lucy was there at the bottom of the stairs.

"Good evening, Mrs Anderson." She sounded a little wary, maybe she should have said nothing, but she *was* concerned, her tiny voice wavered nervously, "Can I do anything?" She put her head on one side, and clenched her hands up underneath her chin, pityingly.

Julie had a pained smile behind the tissues, dipped her head and shook it gently in tearful acknowledgment appreciating the girl's concern but unable to answer. Lucy watched her go.

By now, it was almost dinner time, she was not a bit hungry but nevertheless made her way to the gazebo and stood looking out on to the distant horizon and the flaming sunset. *Was Gavin out there?* The thought welled tears again. *There had been no news or Rick would have told her.* She was rubbing her hands so tightly that it hurt, she heard a footstep behind her, and she spun around hopefully, but it was Charles with a glass of red wine, "Thank you, Charles," it was a whisper, "I really need this." He smiled gently with a nod, not daring to ask how she was, but the unsaid words showed on his face, he bowed his head and left. She sat in one of the easy chairs, her head still in a whirl and on the brink of tears again and trying hard to hold them back but it was impossible. She sipped the wine, it perked her up a little. *She must think positive, Gavin would come! HE WOULD! And there WOULD be a perfectly normal explanation – his phone was wet, he got tied up in the hospital with no access to the phone, a nurse should have phoned but had lost the number... And all these tears would be for nothing and they would be laughing about it... BUT THEN... If he didn't? What WAS she going to do...?*

Rick was coming across the garden, Charles had phoned to tell him that Mrs Anderson was in the gazebo; she stood up, anxiously hoping Rick had some news. He came up the gazebo steps, a sympathetic look on his face as he asked if he could do anything. She shook her head with disappointment, he had no news. Her lips quivered, she tightened them not able to trust herself to speak, she put a tissue to her nose and pinched it hard and turned away from him. And then turned back, "I'm sorry, Rick."

"It's alright, I understand."

She sniffed hard, "Rick, I know it's really your time to go, but please don't leave the house yet! Please stay. I, I just want to sit here alone, but then, I don't want to be in the house on my own," it was a scary heartfelt cry, "I know that Charles and Oliver and the maids are still here, but… Rick…" She took a breath, the tears were coming again and she turned away from him, "I'm sorry," it was a whisper behind the tissues, she put her hand to her forehead and shook her head, "I really don't know what I want, but please stay for a while, I just want to know that you are here."

"It's alright, I understand." He stood for a few minutes, just looking at her, feeling her sorrow, feeling her grief, wanting to put an arm around her, not knowing if he should, or not, it wasn't really his place, he wanted to comfort her but… Then nodding his head sadly, "I'll be in the staff room if you want me, Mrs Anderson, and I'll stay all night if you want me to in the small blue guest room and you can phone me at any hour of the night."

She looked up over the tissue that she was holding to her nose, "Thank you, Rick. But I'll be alright, just stay for a while please," she could hardly get the words out.

He nodded and left the gazebo and walked back across the garden, feeling a little awkward, but hearing her sobbing he hesitated, half turned – should he go back, then thought against it, hoping that there would be some good news during the night. Back in the house he had phoned his girlfriend, Chrystal, saying he would not be home tonight, he'd made his mind up to stay.

Julie was sitting down again feeling quite deflated, the phone rang and she picked it up quickly. Charles' voice said it was Alan Stone, there had been no news but he'd just phoned to asked if she was alright, and they had not much to say to each other. Then Charles came to serve her dinner; she took a seat at the table, thanking him. She sat with her elbows over the plate, she wasn't hungry, and then played around with the food, she had another glass of wine, and then told Charles when he came back to collect the dishes, to apologize to Oliver for not eating.

She had sent Charles off duty after he had poured a glass from the second bottle of red wine, and she sat there until well after midnight, her ears alert to the slightest sound, hoping to hear a car in the driveway and hearing Gavin's voice coming out of the darkness, but the night was quiet but for a slight breeze that rustled the trees and she felt the dark cloud of loneliness gripping her, and with a feeling of disappointment, she finished the second bottle of red wine, and decided to go to bed. She got up a little unsteadily and walked very carefully across the garden to the house, that seemed to be moving before her eyes, the lights were still full on but the house was unusually quiet. Entering through the side door she walked slowly from side to side along the hallway to the main circular hall, watched secretly by Charles and Oliver from the top of the servants' stairs waiting in case they were needed.

Hesitating she screwed up her eyes, measuring the wide spacious distance between her and the stairs – could she make it? *Could she?* Yes, she decided, then taking one cautious step, and then another, she made it, about to mount the stairs one hand on the serpent's head, she balanced wavering back and forth, the stairs rippling like waves before her blurred vision, when Rick came into the hall. "Can I help you, Mrs Anderson?" She turned as if in slow motion, her head wobbling and her eyes narrowed, she viewed the figure of a man through blurred vision, and waved a hand, "No." He watched her as she mounted the stairs, holding on to the scaly serpent banister rail for support... and he heard the bedroom door close with a bang. He exchanged glances with Charles and Oliver.

Once in the bedroom she clung on to the door, she had to make the space between the door and the bed – it was a long way but she made it unsteadily, glad to sit on the bed and picked up the phone, the numbers dancing before her eyes.

She managed to call Rick in the staff room telling him he could go, and apologizing for keeping him there so late. On hearing the slurring words he asked if she needed anything and was she alright and could he do anything, and she replied, "Nooo! I'm fine, but I've had too much to drink." He heard her giggle and he smiled, saying that he would stay in the small blue guest room and she could call him at anytime in the night. She nodded but didn't answer, her arm flopped down as if she had lost all use of it, and the receiver went down with a bang. Rick on the other end jumped back with a grin, thinking he wouldn't have any trouble tonight.

Julie flopped down on the bed, and fell into a deep sleep.

Rick went up to the small blue room, undressed and got into bed, but although it was late and he was tired, the thought of the master, Mr Anderson, never coming back, was sadly worrying and kept him awake. He lay with his hands under his head, his elbows spread wide, thinking that he must try the police again in the morning and the hospital, hoping for some solace. The night was alive with the whistling frogs and the nightly buzzing of insects as always; being most used to them he rarely heard them, but maybe being here in the house the sounds were different – it was the first time that he had ever stayed the night in this house. He was alerted by a noise; he listened, someone was on the stairs – Mrs Anderson! He sat up and swung his legs over the bed, and sat for a moment, then thought he should go and see, but on opening the door he found that there was no one there – he must have been mistaken; he waited a minute, listened, but all was quiet... He went back to bed. About fifteen minutes later, he heard footsteps on the stairs again, maybe it was Mrs Anderson coming back up. He jumped out of bed again and went to the door, there was no one there and the footsteps had stopped. He waited a minute, and listened as before, but the house was quiet; he frowned, puzzled, and went back to his room and walked to the window, thinking that it may have been something outside, but the garden was bathed in moonlight and the lady glowed, but all was still. He went to bed and eventually fell asleep.

Alan Stone had done much the same thing as Julie – he had sat at the beach bar at Sandy Lane until after midnight. Everyone seemed to be talking about the catamaran disaster. He'd got talking to some guests who had sympathized with him, and they told him of another young couple staying in the hotel who had not yet returned, they had also been on honeymoon. People were asking him if they could do anything, but of course he thanked them and said no, it was just a case of waiting and hoping for some good news. But then, in his own mind, he knew there would be no good news not now, but there was always a possibility that Suzie could be in the hospital maybe unconscious and they didn't know who to contact, no one would have had any identification on them. And although he was sitting at the bar, he was on edge, his mind was not really on the conversation and it was not on the drink he was consuming. Everybody had their own opinion of what had caused the disaster, even he didn't know for sure – Julie said it was a whale, he thought perhaps they could have hit the reef. He asked the barman for a bottle of whisky, and then slipped away to his suite taking the bottle with him. Whisky was a thing that he never drank, but he sat down heavily on the bed, glass in one hand bottle in the other, tears in his eyes. The next morning he had a terrible hangover.

Julie had slept all night and awoke early, surprised to find herself still dressed, and then the realization came back to her again; she blinked her sore and puffy eyes, and got up with an exhausted feeling. After showering she felt better, she left the bedroom hoping there was no one about, but Lucy was at the bottom of the stairs again, cleaning, she said, "Good morning, Madam." Julie answered keeping her head low and went out making her way to the gazebo. The morning was bright with sunshine that hurt her eyes and she quickly put on her sunglasses. Charles said, "Good morning, Madam," and poured her black coffee; she needed it badly, but luckily she hadn't got a hangover which surprised her, although she couldn't remember much about last night. She felt tired and lifeless but the coffee did help. The morning was clear and warm, the birds were singing, but there was an emptiness in the air, she felt numb.

Rick came up the gazebo steps, "Good morning, Mrs Anderson Mam," his voice sounded grim, "how are you this morning, Mam?"

"Oh, not too bad, thank you, Rick," she sounded pensive, he knew she didn't mean it, "I'm sorry to have kept you so late last night, I just couldn't stop drinking," she had a slight smile then took a breath, "I suppose there's no news?"

He shook his head, "No. Mam. But I'll try phoning the hospital again," he stood for a moment watching her as she just blankly stared into space, there was nothing more to say and he turned and walked back across the lawn.

She turned her head slowly watching him go, her elbows on the table rubbing her hands hard together and then turned back to stare down the garden. *Anticipating Gavin coming up behind her and putting his arms around her as he had done so many times, she thought that he might come, but in her heart she really knew he wouldn't. She had always felt so safe in his arms, but now she felt such emptiness as if she was exposed to the whole wide world, and alone.* Those words kept running around her head, *she was ALONE.* But then another thought, *she was alone, and in a strange country, what was she to do?* She frowned, still tearful, shaking her head gently, she *couldn't believe that she would never see him again... Only two days ago they had been so happy.* But she had to keep believing that he was out there somewhere and *HE WOULD come back.*

She put her elbows on the table again, her hands either side of her face, *loneliness was a feeling of nothingness, an empty word, but it was so painful.* She screwed her eyes up tight, trying to rid herself of the pain that she knew would never go away. Having flashbacks of his smile, hearing his voice, his laughter, the touch of his hand, she smiled, her mind going back to the time *when they had first met at Jan and William's wedding, they had sat next to each other at the table, she a bridesmaid, he the best man, but although Jan and William were their best friends, the two of them had never met before the wedding. Will and Gavin had known each other in their teens and later had worked together in the bank. She had met Jan, when she had been one of her regular clients at the salon for hair and beauty treatments. His face appeared before her again, brown eyes shining with that special look of love that he had for her alone... There was that word again, ALONE...* She covered her face with her hands, and cried, *she really was ALONE,* she knew no one here in Barbados. *She knew the staff were feeling her sorrow, but they were strangers.*

She took a deep breath and wiped her eyes. Her mind going back again *to Jan's wedding. They had enjoyed the day, drinking and dancing...* She caught her breath *feeling his arms around her now, as they were then; it had been love at first sight. A few days later he had phoned the salon and made an appointment to have his hair trimmed, which of course didn't need trimming, and he had asked her out to dinner that evening.* She took a breath, blinked and sighed with a slight smile, *their romance had lasted longer than Jan and Will's marriage that had been such a lavish affair – Jan's father had spared no expense, but it had only lasted barely a year, and Jan had come crying to her, that Will had found someone else. And she had not heard from Jan now for some long months she hadn't even answered her wedding invitation, and she didn't know where to contact her, even other friends knew nothing of Jan's whereabouts. I suppose to be left like that, is like dying. Jan had loved him so much and she had been so devastated, and the divorce had been so traumatic, that Jan had taken to drinking and had gone in to rehab and she hadn't heard from her since.*

She said quietly to herself, "And now Jan will never see Will again." For the last four and a half years William had made his life, so he had told Gavin, in Australia with the other woman... *It had all happened so fast. LIKE DYING! Here one minute and gone the next... NO!* She shook her head, *No, no! It wasn't at all like dying. Dying was all so final. So very final... William could come back, but Gavin...* She shook her head gently, *Gavin, NEVER would!* The tears flowed again, *she must pull herself together,* she squeezed her hands and her toes tight, *she had to stop, she couldn't cry for ever.* She sniffed hard and turned as Rick came up the gazebo again. He was very concerned, and said that there were two policemen here to see her, or should he send them away until later? She agreed to see them.

They came across the patio and the lawn to the gazebo, "Good morning Mrs. Anderson," they were both black Barbadians and they did not look a bit like policemen, both wearing light grey trousers and white open-necked short-sleeved shirts, they looked more like tourists.

"Thank you for seeing us, I'm Detective Inspector Murray, and this is Detective Sergeant Collins." She indicated the easy chairs and they sat. She offered them coffee but they refused. "We're taking statements from all those that were on board the catamaran." She saw Murray wince at her tearful look, she guessed *it was a hard thing to say it sounded so casual,* "it is the worst disaster that has ever happened here on the island, and I wonder if you could you tell us in your own opinion what you think really did happened?"

"Yes! It was a whale!"

Both policemen straitened their backs and looked at each other in surprise, "A *whale!* Are you *sure?*" Both showed the whites of their eyes, they had heard about a freak wave, the water was rough, and they hit the reef. But no one had mentioned a whale!

"Yes, definitely a whale," she nodded, "apparently whales had been sighted and everyone was anxious to see them. I was sitting at the front right over the right float, and the head of the whale came right up out of the water lifting the catamaran high, and everyone was just slipping away down the deck. I hung on to the rail but the float went up vertical as the whale humped its back and dived. I was up thirty feet in the air and thrown away from the cat, and I suppose I was one of the lucky ones... The mast fell and the huge canvas came down and just swallowed everyone and everything in its path, taking them under the water... I lost my husband..."

"Yes, I'm very sorry, Mrs Anderson, your house manager just told us," Inspector Murray sympathetically dipped his head in sorrow. She shed a few tears, then sniffed hard, trying to dismiss the thought of it all that was so vividly planted in her mind and telling herself that she must not break down in front these men.

Sergeant Jeff Collins who was jotting down notes looked up. "There is still hope, Mrs Anderson, don't give up." She nodded at him gratefully, a tissue to her nose, "Thank you," it was a comforting thought.

"Yes," Inspector Murray added, "We are sorry for your loss, Mrs Anderson, but there *is* still hope, we have found several people," he didn't say dead or alive, "they were scattered – some were taken to the clinic in Holetown, and some went to the hospital in Bridgetown, some of course just went home or back to their hotels, we haven't located them all yet. A man has lost his memory after receiving a blow to the head, he was found by a diver under the catamaran in an air pocket."

"What's this man like?" Julie asked anxiously.

Inspector Murray described the man, with grey hair and a beard. Julie felt disappointed and shook her head saying that was not her husband.

Inspector Murray thanked her for her time and the information she had given, saying that she had been most helpful and said again not to give up hope, they were still looking into the disaster and that they would be in touch. They left.

No more than a few minutes after the police had left, Charles came to say that there was a Mr Stone here to see her, "Oh, show him up here to the gazebo please, Charles."

"Alan!" she said anxiously, as he came across the lawn, "have you had any news?" He shook his head sadly pulling a face. "The police have only just left."

"Yes I passed them on the way in. They're interviewing everyone – they came to Sandy Lane early this morning."

"They were most intrigued when I told them about the whale." Charles brought them coffee and they sat in the easy chairs in the gazebo.

He asked about the whale again, he had seen nothing. He said he had come from the galley with the drinks, Gavin was behind him, and the next thing suddenly he was thrown into the sea, and feeling the pull of the undercurrent he swam away from the float, and then he had seen other people splashing in to the water but he had not seen anything of Gavin. He had seen the mast fall and the canvas taking people under – he had been at the stern then. There was a long pause while they sat with their own thoughts. Julie was glad that he was there, and yet she had mixed feelings thinking she would rather be alone with her grief. In fact, she didn't know what she wanted she rubbed her hands together nervously, "There *is* no hope is there?" She looked at him tearfully.

"You mustn't think that way," said Alan. "The police are still looking into the disaster…" he paused. "They might find something…" there was another long pause. "A man lost his memory, maybe there are others."

She sniffed, "Yes the police told me." She took a deep faltering breath, "It was going to be so wonderful here… We were on our honeymoon," she sniffed again, "we only got married last Saturday."

Alan had a grin and nodded sadly, "So were we, we got married the week before," they looked at each other in surprise. He squeezed her hand gently, it was a friendly gesture, "It'll be alright, we'll get by."

She nodded at him, tight-lipped, the tears beginning to well in her eyes again and feeling that she had a friend that really understood.

"How long have you and Gavin been together?"

At the sound of his name, she tightened her lips, and dabbed at her eyes, "Four years. We had a wonderful wedding," her voice wavered she sighed and sniffed tearfully, "We have only been married just four days. How long had you been together?"

"Two years, but we never lived together. Suzie lived with her parents and I live with a couple of other guys, we had a small flat in Surrey.

'Oh we came from Surrey too," said Julie.

"Suzie was so looking forward to us having our own home. But the house here is not ready yet, there was a tropical storm a week before we came out and a water pipe had broken and everything was wet, so they put us in Sandy Lane. I haven't actually seen the house yet. We were thinking later of buying something – that was our plan," he choked a bit, and coughed to stop himself from breaking down, God knows he had cried enough through the night and now he felt he must be strong in front of Julie. There was a long pause.

"What will you do now, will you stay here?" She looked at him tearfully.

"I have to for a while," he spoke quietly, "I have to start this new job, I can't let them down, I've just got to stay for at least three months, I'll just see how it goes. Will you stay here?"

"Well I don't know yet what to do, Gavin's parents are arriving this afternoon. My parents want to come out but I told them not to come yet. And I suppose without Gavin and the bank I will only be able to stay here for a few months, I don't really know what the rules are. But *now* I have *this house*. Gavin's parents bought it for us for a wedding present."

"WOW!" Alan flicked his eyebrows, "some wedding present." He nodded, "Suzie's father is coming tomorrow, her mother is ill and can't come, I think it's the shock. My parents are both dead I have no family."

She nodded sympathetically. "Do you want some more coffee?" She checked her watch, eleven thirty, "Perhaps it's time for a glass of wine," she phoned Charles.

Alan left before lunch. He hadn't been gone ten minutes, when Charles phoned to say that the police were on the phone.

"Hello Mrs Anderson, this is Sergeant John Simms, I don't want to get your hopes up, but we have retrieved bodies..." There was a short pause, "...from the catamaran disaster – they are in the morgue here at the Queen Elizabeth Hospital in Bridgetown and I wonder if you would be kind enough to come down and maybe make some positive identification."

Julie's heart jumped at the thought that they might have found Gavin, but hesitated. It was a whisper, "Yes, sergeant. Yes alright. Yes. I'll come."

She put the phone down slowly, her hand shaking, a deep sickly sour feeling in the pit of her stomach. She shivered, she felt stunned, numb, anxious, she felt she wanted to run and scream, it was kind of excitement and sadness all rolled into one, but, *at least she would know for sure... it was the not knowing that was eating her away, but the thought of going alone scared her. She didn't really want to go at all. She wasn't really ready for this, she didn't feel strong enough. Could she really face seeing Gavin... DEAD!* She was shaking inside, she felt sick, her mind in a whirl, *she couldn't go alone. No! No! She just couldn't go anyway. That was it, she just couldn't go at all... But on second thoughts, Rick would drive* her and he *would have to come in with her...* Just then the phone rang, it made her jump and her heart pang, she caught her breath and picked the phone up slowly with a shaky hand, hoping it had all been a mistake, and for a moment she hesitated...

"Hello?" It was Rick, "Mr Stone is calling you, Mam."

"Hello, Alan?" It was a kind of question, her voice was weak and strained.

"Are you all right?"

"Yes," she was nodding while she spoke, "But the police just phoned they want me to go to the morgue." It was a breathless whisper. He could hear the terror in her voice.

He hesitated, "Yes, I know. They have just phoned me too, I expect they are phoning everyone, there's nothing to worry about, it won't be very nice but it's the only way they have to identify people."

"I feel afraid. I don't know what to do, but I said I'd go, but I don't really want to, and yet, I really want to know. But *I am afraid*, Alan, I really am."

"So am I," he nodded, "It won't be pleasant, but I have to know for certain. We'll go together. I'll pick you up, in about an hour... Alright...? An hour?"

"Yes," it was a whisper, she broke down and sobbed, "I'll be ready." She put the phone down very slowly, and went to her room. Her clothes were all light colours. Gavin's clothes hanging there in the closet moved as she took out the darkest green dress that she had. She gathered all his shirts in her arms and rubbed her face against them lovingly, holding her breath as tears welled in her eyes again.

"Oh my darling," it was a weak whisper, she hugged the shirts tightly to her face for some long minutes, and then turned tearfully to go to the bathroom – his shorts were still there where he had left them hanging over the bath to dry when he had come out of the pool. She looked in the mirror about to brush her long dark hair, and his shaving brush was still on the shelf – she picked it up, again feeling the softness of the hair – it was still damp as before, she touched it again to her lips, feeling the softness, and the familiar smell of his shaving soap and the tears welled again. She sniffed hard telling herself that she really must stop this crying it was making her feel awful and it wasn't going to bring him back. She knew it, but just didn't want to believe it. She brushed her hair back into a ponytail, then put on some lipstick, putting a mascara brush to her eyes, thank heavens it was waterproof but with all the tears it really wasn't working that well. Blinking back the tears once again, sniffing and taking a deep breath, she put on her green dress and went down to the drawing room to wait for Alan Stone.

A uniformed policeman showed them through white painted swing doors into the morgue; it was a large white tiled room with a high arched ceiling and sunlight streamed in from high windows. The air conditioning was full on, it was cold as she had expected and she shivered, and an unbearable deadly silence hung heavily on her ears. There was no smell of anything which surprised her, she had expected strong disinfectant; she rubbed the goosebumps that ran up her arms, and she could feel her inside shaking. She was very conscious as Alan's hand tightened on her arm, she suspected that he was also feeling anxious as they followed the male nurse across the white tiled floor, his soft white shoes unheard, their shoes tapping loudly in the empty hollowness. He stopped at a table, a white sheet covered a body; he hesitated before turning back the white sheet and looking at them both to see if they were ready, it seemed to take ages, and she felt so uptight she wanted to screams *for God's sake hurry up!* She took in a deep breath holding it, anticipating what to expect and wishing that she hadn't come but Alan's hand on her arm was reassuring. She reeled back, with a soft gasp – it was like a blow to the head and she was glad that Alan was there, she turned to him, her hand tightly covered his on her arm. She held her breath as tears welled in her eyes and she put a tissue to her nose and pinched it tight, her eyes blurred and hot tears ran down her cheeks. She had a stifling feeling as she slightly shook her head and turned away from the pale and sleeping figure, not sure if she was relieved that it was *not* Gavin. The nurse, realizing the shock that everyone goes through in these awful circumstances, said gently and quietly, "I'm sorry, Mrs Anderson, but there is another one I would be pleased if you could possibly identify…" She nodded tearfully, holding her breath as he removed another white sheet and she glanced at Alan sadly. It was one of the young teenagers; she turned her head away shaking it slowly, not able to put a name to either man. The nurse thanked her, then looked at Alan, "We have three women, Sir."

The tall uniformed policeman standing close by took Julie by the arm and led her outside, she was glad of his support as her legs felt weak. He sat on the white bench seat beside her, "Thank you for coming, Mrs Anderson, I know it must be a traumatic ordeal for you, but it has to be done." She nodded, her breath stifling her, she couldn't answer, she was wringing her hands tightly and shaking, she noticed the heavy gold wedding ring that he wore as his large black hand covered hers in a comforting gesture.

Alan proceeded to follow the male nurse, the second body broke his heart. He nodded, "It's my wife," his knees felt weak and he gripped the table. Suzie looked so pale so serene, so peaceful, the nurse seeing the same reaction so many times before, put his hand under Alan's elbow to steady him, and sat him down, keeping a comforting hand on his shoulder, while Alan put his hands to his face and wept.

CHAPTER THREE

The days went on, Alan knowing for sure now that his wife of only two weeks was confirmed dead, and although it was an awful shock it did make him feel a little better, at least he knew, it was the *not knowing* that was so painful and it had worried him, although he knew in his heart that she had not survived, but a relief to think that she had been found. He knew now that it would be very hard to come to terms with, but that he must put this episode of his life behind him, and get on with living, but the pain would never go away.

For Julie, not knowing about Gavin, would have to live with the uncertainty – did he die instantly or did he suffer, did he manage to survive, was he out there now not knowing who or where he was? Although she was resigned now to thinking he was dead, without a body the uncertainty would always be there.

It was during the week that Michael Prescott phoned Julie. She had not met him, but he said that he was here staying in his parents' house; he had been there for a few days, but he had only just found his father's diary, and realized that they had all had dinner together the night before the accident and had all been on the catamaran together. He wondered if he could come and see her and perhaps she could give him some information as to what did actually happen. He said the police had informed him of the disaster and they had been very helpful, but the details were sketchy.

She said that she was sorry that she couldn't have let him know; all she knew was that his parents were going off to Florida but she didn't know where to contact him. However, she would be pleased to see him and fill him in on the details.

"Well you can come for lunch today if you like, I'm not doing anything. It's all very casual."

"Thank you, Mrs Anderson, I'd like that very much, we're going back in a day or two – oh, I'm here with my fiancée – is that alright?"

"Yes of course, come about twelve o'clock, I'm sure you would like a drink first." She came off the phone and arranged with Oliver to cancel the salad for one, and there would be four of them for a full Sunday lunch of roast chicken. She then phoned Alan who she knew would be pleased to have the invitation.

Alan arrived at 11.45, Charles brought them a glass of champagne, and right on midday Michael Prescott was introducing himself and his fiancée Mellissa. They were both tall and painfully thin – Michael very thin-faced with a mop of brown curly hair, and not at all like his father who had been short, bald and wiry. Mellissa was attractive, Julie saw Alan's eyebrows go up and they stayed there, as she waltzed in, swinging a large white beach bag and wearing a tight white skimpy tank top over voluptuous breasts, the very shortest shorts and so tight they could have been sprayed on, and the longest legs finished in scarlet four-inch stilettos. The make-up was for a command performance, with the brightest lips, silver blue eye shadow and sweeping false black eyelashes. The long, loose, white-blonde hair reached to her waist. She was a model – well you didn't have to be told that – she modelled swimwear, so Michael said. Julie thought that she could have been a model for a Barbie doll.

Charles brought them champagne, and of course they chatted about the terrible disaster, both Julie and Alan still feeling the sadness as Alan filled them in on the details that they did not know from the police. They were both shocked at the news of the whale.

"Well, it sounds most catastrophic," Michael sounded sincere, and it wasn't that he didn't care, but it seemed that the tragedy of losing both his parents had not really hit him yet. "But I'm glad that you both came out of it alright, Mr Anderson."

"Oh no!" Both Julie and Alan said quickly together, "No, I'm Alan Stone…"

"Alan lost his wife, and I lost my husband, we only met at your parents' house the night before…"

It went a little quiet, Michael held his breath. "I'm sorry. I thought…" he hesitated, a bit lost for words.

"They found my wife…"

"Alan is to have a funeral…" said Julie. "My husband was not found."

"Oh! I'm sorry," Michael swallowed hard, "I'm sorry." He shook his head gently. What else could he say?

"Yes I'm sorry too, how sad!" Mellissa bowed her head, she had to say something but there was no warmth in her words, it all sounded so false. There was a long pause, and an awkward moment.

"But, we have to get over these things," Alan said brightly, filling the uncomfortable silence, "life has to go on," he had the slightest smile.

"Yes, of course…" Michael nodded sadly, it went quiet again and the atmosphere was now strained. Mellissa blinked her long black lashes and turned her head slightly as if tired of the conversation, but then she didn't feel the pain and sadness like the other three and she had not met Michael's parents.

"Julie just asked me for lunch," Alan went on filling in the awkward moment. "We are still both in a state of shock," he turned to Julie, seeing her wipe away a tear, he touched her hand with a sad smile as a comfort, "but as I said, life has to go on, and we are both new here. We don't know anyone yet."

Julie smiled, "Yes, neither of us has any friends here at the moment, Gavin and I just moved in here. And Alan is still at Sandy Lane, his house isn't ready yet. Gavin and Alan were both ready to start a new job with the bank, that's why your father asked us to dinner, so they could meet."

Charles replenished their glasses and said that the lunch was to be served and they took their places at the table in the gazebo. The conversation was light, mostly about the island. Julie could see why Michael had fallen for Mellissa, she *was* quite beautiful – well, with the professional make-up. And not at all the housewife type. She recalled Mary's words, *we haven't met her yet*. But Mary surely wouldn't have approved, she probably would have had the shock of her life. Mellissa was the sort of girl that every man dreamed of, and was every mother's nightmare.

Michael said that he was a photographer for a fashion magazine, and that was how they had met, only three months ago, Mellissa had been modelling swimwear. *No!* Julie thought, *your mother would definitely not have approved.*

"What are you going to do, Mrs Anderson?" Michael asked, "Are you going to stay here in Barbados or are you going back to the UK?"

"Oh! Julie, please, Mrs Anderson is so formal. Well I don't really know yet, I love being here, we have been here many times on holiday and I will stay for a while hoping that the police will find my husband, it would be good to know – they say there is still hope."

"I doubt it now," Alan grimaced sadly, "it's been too long."

Tears welled in Julie's eyes again, knowing that he was right, they all saw it and looked away, so as not to embarrass her. She tried to hold the tears back, "I have to keep hoping, Alan."

He nodded and touched her hand again. She got up and went to the edge of the gazebo, turning her back on them and looking out onto the back of the silver lady, trying desperately to hold back the tears and the sobs.

"What about you, Mr Stone, will you stay here?"

"I have to, I've just started a new job, I can't let them down so soon. It's Alan by the way. What about you?"

"I'm staying here for as long as it takes," said Michael, "I have to sort out Dad's affairs, here and in London, but I like it here in Barbados, I might even move out here now I've got the house."

"It's very humid!" said Mellissa sourly, "I couldn't live here in this climate, it's far too hot, I shall be going back in a day or two," she shrugged her shoulders. Michael glanced at her in surprise, "Oh really?"

Julie turned and came to sit down again, thinking to herself, *well that was a good start to a romantic engagement, something that important and they didn't agree!*

Michael and Mellissa left mid-afternoon, and after seeing them off at the front gate, Julie and Alan walked back towards the patio. Alan looked up at the trees, "This is a lovely garden isn't it?" He smiled but there was a sadness in his tone, and as they began to slowly walk around they came to the silver lady. "Not a great beauty is she?" He looked at the bright staring blue eyes and the bright red painted mouth, the silver face was quite hideous.

"No, but apparently she was responsible for Desmond Honeybeck's survival."

"Who was he?" Alan asked.

"He was a pirate, he built this house, *he* and one of his crew by the name of Thurgold were saved by the figurehead of his ship the *Silver Lady*. There was a battle and the ship sank, and apparently she floated up out of the sea after the ship exploded."

"*Thurgold?*" Alan was surprised, "the new guy that's coming from the UK, to take over as CEO, is called Henry Thurgold."

"Really? I wonder if he could be a relation."

"What, from way back, no." Alan wrinkled his nose.

Julie flipped her eyebrows, "Could be, Thurgold was English. Rick told us."

Alan, laughed, "That's all we need, a pirate running a bank?" They laughed together, it was the first time that they had really laughed easily. They looked at each other, it was the first time that either of them had really relaxed. He put an arm around her shoulders and gave her a friendly hug.

It was too hot to walk around, and Julie suggested that they sit in the gazebo in the shade, she put the fan on and called Charles for some cold drinks, "Oliver makes super fresh lemonade," she smiled at him, "not unless you would prefer another glass of wine?" He shook his head.

Charles brought tall glasses of ice-cold lemonade, and left quietly.

51

They sat chatting, more relaxed now, and finding out about each other. He said that he and Suzie used to play tennis; Julie said that she had never played, she wasn't sporty, but Gavin had planned to join the golf club here in Barbados, he had been a member of the golf club in the UK. She had gone to the club house on occasions, and she had found it very social, and they used to go to polo at Windsor. "We also went to Ascot horse racing every year for the whole week, Gavin's father had a box."

"Oh, the high life. Sport of kings," Alan smiled.

"Gavin's family are very wealthy, I told you his father bought this house for us. Gavin really loved the house, we were making such plans, but of course he had not had enough time to enjoy it. I like it too, but it won't be the same without him, I haven't had much interest in anything yet, I haven't actually been all round the house, it's about the first time that I've really walked around, out here – it's a lovely garden but I haven't explored it all yet."

"Come on then, let's explore," Alan got up, full of eagerness, putting his drink on the table, knowing that to do something would take both their minds off the sadness and they strolled across the lawns.

"How many acres here?" asked Alan.

"Fourteen, I think a lot of it is wooded and rough, so Rick said, and part of it used to be a sugar plantation, but some of the land has been sold, so I don't know how many acres there were originally."

"Wow, I wonder why they call it a cottage. What's over there?"

They walked across the lawn to a far corner where there was a sort of a ragged overgrown and half dead arch of entangled vines and flowering weed, and into a shaded wooded part of the garden that obviously hadn't been touched for years. There was a mound of dried and brown entangled grass and overgrown shrubbery. Julie frowned, "Do you think there is a grave here?"

Alan grimaced, "Dunno, might be old Honeybeck."

"Oh, I hope not, Alan! Do you believe in ghosts?"

"No!" he said automatically, then frowned, then grimaced, "Well! I don't really know. Why?"

She took a deep breath and thought for a moment or two, "Well! For two or three nights, I've heard footsteps coming up the stairs and then a door closes. I've not seen anyone. I've asked the staff if anyone has been up there at night and I'm told no one comes up there, they are not allowed, only the maids of course to clean in the daytime."

"Sounds spooky."

"Yes it is a bit. The other night I opened my bedroom door very quickly hoping to catch whoever it was, and I'm sure I saw another bedroom door just closing. I plucked up courage and went and stood outside for a moment or two listening, and then opened it quickly hoping to catch someone but the room was all in darkness there was no one there. It's an old room, Rick said it had once been the master bedroom." She shook her head, "I don't think it has ever been touched."

"Oooh, even more spooky. Do the staff live in? Have you mentioned it to Rick?"

"No I haven't actually. Charles and Oliver share a large apartment in the basement, and two of the maids live up in the attic, the rest come in daily. It was Charles who said that they were not allowed upstairs."

"Rick doesn't live in then?"

"No, he lives in one of the cottages on the estate, it's over there somewhere, not far," she nodded across the garden, "he lives with his girlfriend Chrystal. I haven't met her. Oliver has a girlfriend that stays sometimes. Charles – I don't know – I think he has a girlfriend. He has a son about twelve years old."

"It's not *him* is it, running about the house at night?" He looked at the mound again, and thought *it could be a grave*, but he didn't air his thoughts, better to say nothing. "Come on," he took her by the arm. They wandered the lawns and flower beds that were neatly kept and looked into the faces of several stone statues – all had demure expressions and you could feel the solitude and the loneliness that radiated from them. "They give me the chills," said Julie, "I've never felt like this looking at a statue before." He just looked on with the slightest shake of his head knowing what she meant, it *was* a weird feeling, he glanced behind him thinking there was someone in the garden.

The garden was shaded by tall mahogany trees and at this time of the year by flaming red flamboyant and sweet-smelling ever-flowering white frangipani. A ball of fire had now set the sky aflame as the sun sank slowly out on the horizon; they saw a sail boat caught in the orange mass and for a moment it looked as if it was made of pure gold. The sun sank fast and disappeared in a flash as if switched off, leaving the sky streaked in flaming orange and grey shadows. And now as the evening dusk came on, bats flitted from tree to tree silhouetted against the gray and dusky evening sky, and once again the garden seemed engulfed with a certain silence as birds began to sleep, and the shadows crept across the garden as they had done for hundreds of years.

Although there was nothing outside but the rustle of the trees in the light breeze, it seemed so much quieter as they entered the drawing room. "Would you like a cocktail?"

Alan grimaced, "We had a lot to drink lunchtime."

"Oh that was lunchtime."

He smiled, nodding his head sideways, "Well, yeah. Go on then, you talked me into it." He smiled, "I must say I've done more drinking in the last few weeks, than I have ever done."

"Me too," Julie smiled, 'but I guess we have good reason." She phoned Charles who came within a few minutes and they were sitting in the purple easy chairs, the French doors still open wide to the now orange fading dusk.

"Would you like me to turn the lights on, Madam?"

"Yes please, Charles, just the table lamps." He flipped a switch on the wall near the door, the pink silk-fringed shades filled the room with a soft pink glow, leaving part of the room in shadow.

They clinked glasses, "You look a lot more relaxed now," Alan smiled.

"Yes I feel a lot better now. I have to get used to living without Gavin, but I keep expecting him to come walking through the garden. He will forever be on my mind, I'll never get over this."

"Yes I know what you mean." There was a long pause while they both sat staring into space, lost in their own reverie. Out of the corner of his eye Alan, seeing the rocking chair moving, turned sharply and stood up, "It's suddenly getting a bit chilly here isn't it. Can you smell cigar smoke?"

She looked at the rocking chair, "Yes, I think it's a ghost."

Alan frowned looking somewhat surprised, *"Honeybeck?"* His mouth stayed open.

"Yes, it could be," Julie stood up, twisting her lips nervously. They stared at the chair as the momentum was increasing, Julie took a deep breath and slowly backed to the door.

Alan grimaced, "No it's the draught from the window," he went to close the French doors.

'Look!" Julie whispered, "the rocking chair has stopped!"

"It was the draught," said Alan. But the atmosphere grew even colder – it was eerie. There was no doubt that something was there in the room with them. Alan could see that she was nervous, he felt uneasy himself, and he crossed the room to her. They were now near the door, he turned quickly and flinched.

"You alright?" She looked at him quickly.

Alan scratched back of his neck, looking around, "I thought something touched me." Then they both gasped in alarm, seeing the purple chair that Alan had just left, sag on the seat and the back with a small hushed sound as the air was puffed out of the cushions as if someone or something unseen sat down in it. They stood motionless holding their breath, both hearing a silent pang of anxiety in their heads, Julie had her hand clamped across her mouth staring at the chair in awe.

"Did you hear a sigh? Let's go," he whispered, tapping her arm and nodding sideways to the door and they both backed out as he opened it, not daring to take their eyes off the purple armchair. The house was quiet as they stood in the long wood panelled hallway, their hearts beating fast. Alan listened at the door; hearing nothing he shook his head, about to open the door again.

"NO! Don't! Come on," Julie sounded nervous, "there's another room we can go to." He followed her along the wide hallway, and she opened a door – it was dim with just the faint dusk light coming through the windows. She felt on the wall for the light switch and the library lit up with small blue shaded table lamps around the spacious room. "Oh I'm sorry, I thought this was another drawing room, there are four in all so Rick said, it must be the next door along." She started to close the door again, but Alan pushed it open, "This is OK, it looks comfortable in here. Big room."

They sat in rose-patterned tapestry winged-back easy chairs, a coffee table between them, both still feeling short of breath. "Whatever *was that?*" Alan frowned.

Julie shook her head fearfully, "I think we need another drink." She chuckled and raised her shoulders with a sort of cringe. "You don't think it happened because we've had too much, do you?" She smiled with some relief then phoned Charles to bring fresh glasses of wine, saying that they were in the library.

"This is a nice room," said Alan, "should be some interesting books in here." He looked around the specious room, cooled now from the afternoon sun by the ceiling fan that she had put on with the lights; the pale blue shades on the table lamps and the dusky blue grey carpet also added to the coolness. Hundreds of books lined the walls from floor to ceiling. "Wow, this is fabulous – look at this," Alan pointed out one here and one there, hoping that it would take her mind off the spooky incident.

"Yes, I should think there are," Julie came to look, "it's the first time that I've been in here. We just had a quick glance in that's all, when Rick showed us round; in fact I haven't really explored the house at all yet. I wonder if there is anything here about old Honeybeck. Do you think that's a painting of him there on the wall?" She walked over to stand in front of the oil painting of a middle-aged man with deep suntanned skin, the features lean, strong and handsome in a rugged sort of way. He had a diamond stud in both ears, his long black hair tied back in a ponytail, although that could not really be seen, under the tricorn black hat trimmed with gold and a red ostrich feather. He wore a white stock at his throat pinned by a large sapphire broach and the dark red velvet frock coat had wide turned-back cuffs to show wide wristbands of French lace, beneath which he wore a crimson damask waistcoat with intricate carved gold buttons that went down over a broad chest. There was a wide gold silken sling that went over his right shoulder and across his chest, also a wide leather strap with a silver buckle to hold the scabbard and a sword at his left hip, a strong bejewelled hand with heavy gold rings of rubies, emeralds and sapphires, rested on the hilt of the sword and a thick brown leather belt was around his waist with a large silver buckle which held two leather sheaths – one with a flintlock pistol and another with a wooden-handled knife. His fine red breeches of crimson patterned damask were tied with a bow beneath the knee, over white silken hose, and his feet were shod in polished brown leather with shiny silver buckles – it was the dress of a gentleman.

"Handsome brute wasn't he?" Julie was studying the portrait, "Fancy dresser too. I bet that was him in the drawing room wasn't it?"

"Yeah!" Alan flicked his eyes, "I didn't think I believed in ghosts, but I've never experienced anything like *that! Have you?*"

Julie shook her head, "No it's a bit scary, isn't it. I wonder if the staff have seen anything."

Alan tightened his lips, twisting them sideways, "Don't mention it! They'd be scared and leave! They'll tell everyone, and you'll never get any staff here again." Alan pulled out a book, "Here's something about pirates! *Hey*, look at this – there's a safe here."

"Is there, where?" Julie looked around and came over to look. "Wonder what's in it, there must be a key somewhere, probably in the desk." She started to open and close drawers.

Alan, dumped the heavy volume on to the desk, and it fell open at a page that said, HONEYBECK! "Here, come and look at *this*!" Hearing the excitement in his voice she came quickly across the room. "It just fell open at this page," he swivelled the book around and sat down in the high-backed black leather chair.

She stood over him, "What does it say?" But just then, Charles came in with the drinks. She thanked him, and then just as he was at the door, "Oh, Charles, tell Oliver that Mr Stone is staying for dinner." She looked at Alan, with a nod, "You will stay won't you?"

Alan arched his eyebrows with an eager grin, and Charles, said, "Yes Mam," and left the room.

"Thanks," he smiled at her.

"Well, you're only going back to the hotel, and I need a bit of support if this Honeybeck has moved in here, I really don't want to spend too much time alone, *with him!*"

Alan grinned. "Yeah, I know what you mean, but I don't know what I can do…"

"Just be here," she grinned, "Anything in the book?" She looked down over his shoulder.

"Hmm! Not much." He ran his finger down the page then read out loud, "He was a pirate! His ship was the *Silver Lady*! We know that already!" Julie smiled. "She was sunk on the west coast of Barbados, in October 1628, fired on by a Spanish pirate ship *La Gaviota* in brackets it means (*The Seagull*). Her crew boarded *The Silver Lady*, and took possession, a fight broke out and Juan Callietto the captain was killed in a sword fight with Desmond Honeybeck, and then gunpowder exploded and both ships were sunk and all hands were lost."

"Rick said he died here in the garden," said Julie.

"Yeah!" He looked up at her a bit surprised. "Wait a minute, there's a bit more here. Honeybeck escaped with a crew member." Alan read on, "Captain Desmond Honeybeck, and James Thurgold, a member of his crew, survived after hours in a raging stormy sea clinging on to the figurehead of the ship the *Silver Lady* which had suddenly risen up from the deep among the debris; they managed to hold on to the figurehead to keep them afloat and eventually got to the beach. Many tales have been told that Honeybeck and

Thurgold came ashore near Jamestown, and they terrorized the few English inhabitants that had settled on the island just two years before, robbing them of their few meagre possessions. Honeybeck and Thurgold then lived rough on the beach for some weeks, until they stole a rowing boat and set off for the harbour at Carlyle Bay on the south coast which over a few years had become a busy anchorage. It took them a whole day to row. They then lived rough on the beach again and stealing food where they could, while they watched and waited for months to seize a sloop – a speedy vessel was essential. Single-masted sloops were the most popular vessels with pirates, they were often built in the West Indies and were between 9 and 18 metres long and could be easily hidden in shallow waters for repairs or careening, and also while lying in wait for a rich merchantman, or a Spanish vessel with a cargo of riches such as gold and silver. Then one mid-afternoon such a ship appeared on the horizon; she was a merchantman, she proceeded slowly taking her time, and the waiting seemed endless but eventually *The Golden Shark* made her way serenely into the bay late afternoon, and anchored among a hundred or more peacefully swaying masts. Honeybeck and Thurgold still watched and waited their time. Then while the crew of the *Golden Shark* were busy with the rigging and the anchorage, they rowed out under a flaming orange sunset and managed to climb aboard unseen, terrorizing the captain and two officers at pistol point then commandeering the ship. Over the months she had called at many ports and so, they found her to be loaded with a cargo of half a million silver coins, 20 tons of gold dust, jewels, silks and precious spices used for preserving food, barrels of wine and casks of Jamaican rum. Also, chained below deck there were seventy West African slaves. Honeybeck selected the strongest slaves, who were not sailors, and forced them and the ship's crew to get the ship underway again. Thurgold, a rough cut-throat, had this all in hand – those that refused to obey Honeybeck's command instantly, were slain with one thrust of the sword and thrown overboard, three went very quickly the rest obeyed. The lesser slaves Honeybeck took to the beach and sold at top prices to the waiting plantation owners who needed them for working the land. He then returned to the ship and killed the captain, John Cooper, and most of the officers, and they sailed out of the bay watched from the beach by the plantation owners.

"For some months Honeybeck and Thurgold had caused havoc on the west coast of the island, and the settlers lived in fear, and were glad to hear that they had sailed away. But it was after a year that they came back with a new ship. *The Green Dragon* sailed into Carlyle Bay with a cargo of slaves from Africa which Honeybeck sold once again on the beach to the waiting plantation owners. Once again he'd kept the best and the strongest for himself as he intended to stay on the island of Barbados, and they were taken to the west coast and forced to build him a house..."

"This house I suppose," said Julie.

Alan read on, "...then after the house was built, he again kept the best of the slaves for his household staff and gardeners, the rest he sold. He then raided villages and took all he could, including young girls for servants and it is suspected for pleasure. Thurgold who, when sailing, was the first officer and held an important position had now became a servant in the house which Honeybeck ruled like a king. Roaring through the house demanding instant attention, Thurgold didn't like this, but knowing there to be a big hoard of gold and jewels which of course he had helped to steal over the years while pirating, he was prepared to wait his time, quietly and secretly watching Honeybeck, on several occasions going to what he supposed was his hiding place, although he was not sure. But one day Thurgold challenged him with a sword demanding a half share, but quicker than the eye could see, Honeybeck had manned his sword and they fought fearfully, Honeybeck driving him back and Thurgold turned and fled to the garden where the battle continued now watched by the terrified servants who had been alerted by the sound of steel clashing. Honeybeck was the stronger of the two but they were both excellent swordsmen, both had drawn blood on their arms and then Honeybeck lashed out badly wounding Thurgold who was a tall thin man, the sword going right through his body and he fell flat on his back onto the patio the sword still in his hand. Honeybeck stood with the blood dripping from his now raised sword, his face a mask of surprise, and somewhat relief that the fight was over, and then of sorrow – they had fought many a battle together and won over the years, and now Thurgold his long-term friend was dead! Honeybeck knelt sadly beside him. It was then that Thurgold mustered his last ounce of breath, lifting a weak arm and surprising Honeybeck by stabbing him close to the heart and both men lay dying together. The watching servants in their hiding places were afraid and kept their distance. It was then that one came forward and they found that Honeybeck was still alive; he lingered for three days in a state of delirium. It is supposed that they buried both men somewhere in the grounds. There is no mention of a grave, and still to this day, Honeybeck's treasure, as far as I know, has never been found…

"So!" Alan leaned back and looked up at her, slapping his hand on the page, "all we've got to do now is find the treasure." He grinned.

"You've got to be *joking!*" Julie smiled.

"Well, you've got nothing else to do with your time. I'll buy you a spade tomorrow," he laughed.

She grinned, "You don't think I'm digging up the garden do you?"

"Well that's usually where you'd find a body and possibly buried treasure. That's of course if the servants didn't find it and become rich." He flipped his hands out palms up and shrugged his shoulders.

She clipped him playfully across the head, he got up and they chuckled together – it relieved some of their tension. "What about the key for this safe?" She opened every drawer in the desk, but found nothing.

"It'll be a hidden drawer I would think…" Alan looked around, "…you wouldn't leave a key to the safe just lying about would you, and this is an old desk – there's bound to be a hidden drawer somewhere." They searched…

CHAPTER FOUR

Alan had now moved into his small house in Holetown, he was glad to get out of the hotel. He had taken Julie down to see the house and it was comfortable; it was on the opposite side of the road from the beach but had a close view of the sea. He had employed Cleo to do his cleaning washing and ironing and sometimes cooking if he needed it. Cleopatra O'Hanovon was young, barely thirty and pretty, very fat, very black and very jolly, with a beautiful white smile. She was the granddaughter of an Irish sailor who came into port on a merchant ship called the *Pennypacker*, and stayed for two days only, then sailed away never to be seen again. Cleo worked happily around the small house, keeping it spotless, polishing and cleaning, and singing along to the radio all day, and when Alan came home about six o'clock in the evening she would quite often still be there, and surprise him by having a hot meal ready. He gave her extra cash, and they got along together very well.

Alan and Julie didn't see much of each other, perhaps only at weekends as he was busy working, but he phoned her nearly every day just to keep her spirits up. Sometimes he took her to a restaurant in the evening and she would invite him most weekends for Sunday lunch at the Silver Lady, which they both enjoyed and they would relax and spend the whole day together by the pool, and some evenings when the sun went down they would go into the library, still intent on finding the key to the safe and sorting out Honeybeck's treasure – if of course it did exist. But Alan also thought that by keeping things going it kept Julie's mind busy, and it saved her moping about, it gave her something do every day. During the week she kept herself busy with emails, and moving around the garden planting seeds in pots and with the hot sunshine and the rain they grew quickly, and while poking around in the garden she kept her eyes open in case there should be any signs of treasure, she supposed it would be a grave. She eyed the silver lady every day, sure that one day she would reveal her secret.

Some weeks she and Zena would go shopping although it wasn't a regular outing and there was nothing much to buy, but then they would have a girlie lunch and it would fill in her day. She had met Zena and her husband Perry at Gatwick Airport while waiting for the flight out to Barbados – Perry Frazer, Zena's husband had started talking to Gavin, and then on the plane they had seats across the aisle and the conversation had carried on. They were both black Barbadians, and Perry was a lawyer; they had been on holiday in London and were on their way home.

It was a few weeks after the catamaran disaster that Zena had phoned asking them for dinner. Of course she was shocked to hear the sad news of Gavin, and she and Perry had come to the Silver Lady Cottage post haste to give some comfort to Julie, and now every few weeks she phoned and they went out on a shopping spree and lunch, and Julie was glad of her company. She also kept herself busy emailing her mother and Gavin's parents, and Miranda whom she had left to run the hair and beauty salon for her – Miranda had said that all was well and they were busy. She also kept in touch with other friends in England, and had found out that Jan was now remarried to a Theo Shawden, and now lived in Spain where they ran a restaurant. Now, having the email address, she had contacted Jan, and they had also spoken on the phone. She was still sitting at the computer in the study when the phone rang on the desk beside her, she picked up the receiver – it was Michael Prescott, "Hi Julie, I'm back on the island, I was wondering, would you like to go out for dinner tonight?"

"Oh, hello Michael!" She smiled, holding the receiver away as his loud voice full of excitement blared in her ear. "When did you arrive?"

"Last night! Came in on the late flight. Bit warmer here. Damned cold in New York."

"New York! I thought you were in Florida. Have you moved?"

"No, I've been working there for a month. What about dinner?"

"Yes alright. Thank you."

"Pick you up at seven, OK? Can't stop now,"

The line went dead. Putting down the receiver, with a smile at his vibrant enthusiasm, he had sounded in a hurry.

When he picked her up she was surprised to find that he was alone, she had expected Mellissa. The restaurant was busy, and they sat now, just the two of them under the stars, the sea just fifteen feet below them thundered heavily against the rocks. Julie tried to concentrate on his lively conversation, but being so close to the sea her mind was on Gavin – he was still out there somewhere, she knew it was ridiculous but she still had thoughts that he might come back. Even here in a busy restaurant with Michael, who was a nice guy and pleasant company, she had that lonely feeling, and with every rolling wave that hit the rock she winced – Gavin was out there in the dark. Michael was asking how she was coping alone, it brought her back to reality. "I'm coping," she nodded quickly with a slight smile, "I have to," she nodded, "it's hard, but I have to."

"Do you see much of Alan?"

"Yes, we go out occasionally, and we keep in touch on the phone, and spend nearly every weekend together; we go to a restaurant, and he comes to my place for Sunday lunch – it gives him a break from living in a hotel, and it gives my chef more to do," she smiled, "as a matter of fact he has just moved into his own home. Guess he's a bit lonely now, we both are, but we are company for each other." Michael nodded with understanding as they sat quietly after dinner sipping the last of the red wine. She asked him about Mellissa.

"We got engaged two months ago, we had a big party! Glamorous! As you can imagine with all the models." He grinned, but not with happiness. "It was more like a fashion show." He sighed, putting his elbows on the table and rubbing his hands together, "but since then, well! We've rarely been together, the modelling took her away for the next two weeks, and then another two weeks in Paris, and now she's down in Mexico for a month! I wanted her to come here, I'd made plans, but she wasn't keen." He pulled a face, "and I expect she'll be modelling in South Africa, she doesn't have to go..." He sounded disappointed, and there was a pause... "But while I'm here I'm going to make arrangements to do the house up, it's in pretty good shape, Dad kept it going although it was only a holiday home, but they spent quite a lot of time here. They loved it. And I wish I'd come more often, since working in America I didn't really see enough of my parents..." There was another pause... "When I'm here in the house with all their things about, I feel I'm intruding... It's the same with their house in London, but my sister is sorting that out... And I really haven't had the time to mourn yet with so much going on... We had a memorial service, my sister organized that." There was another pause... He was still rubbing his hands together thoughtfully, "I feel I've missed out..." The earlier vitality just seemed to have ebbed away at the thought of his parents and there was sadness in his tone.

"So you're not so busy now, with the photography then?" Julie raised her eyebrows, changing the subject.

"Oh yes, I've been photographing the winter collections, it's been all go in the last few weeks, but I didn't get the Mexico job!" He flicked his eyebrows and looked a little disappointed. "But we are still busy, we're photographing antiques for the next few weeks for an antiques' fair, it's a big thing, we do it every year, it also includes models and this year the clothing theme is 1920. But I needed a break..." Julie thought he looked pained and that the thought of his parents' death had only just hit him. He went on, "...and Mellissa is away. And I still have some of Dad's affairs to sort out, so I've left it to Brian Forbes, he's my assistant, he's just a young guy, but very talented."

"My house is full of antiques," Julie smiled trying to brighten him.

"Have you photographed them?" Michael looked at her keenly.

"No! Why?" She looked surprised.

"Well it's good to keep a record, say you had a break-in, at least you could show the police a photo."

"Oh, I never thought of that! I'll take a few snaps."

"I'll come and do it for you if you like?" He smiled, and she agreed, he would obviously take better photos than her snaps. He said he could come around in the morning if it was OK.

Michael arrived about ten o'clock, and she went around the house with him. He had brought a large camera, a tripod and arc lights, angling things to get the best light, all very professional. In the drawing room, he took photos of the tall green jade lady, the hand-painted china, the French chiming clocks and the chandeliers. He went into each room; he was fascinated with the polished staircase and the serpent handrail – he thought that would make a good front cover. And then she walked with him in the garden and he photographed the silver lady, from all angles. It took him the whole morning, and they then sat in the gazebo and had coffee, and he left before lunchtime.

Julie had lunch alone. It had been an interesting morning, and she told Alan about it when he phoned. It was after lunch that Zena called, asking if she would like to go shopping and have lunch tomorrow as Perry was playing golf. They arranged to meet in Holetown. "There's a thing on at the golf club tonight, if you want to come?" Zena smiled, "Perry's playing in a tournament, and there are drinks and canapés afterwards, it's very casual just from five until eight." Julie agreed to meet her there.

It was the first time that she had been to the golf club; the club house was very large with a high ceiling, a bar at one end, and several tables and easy chairs around, and the view across the greens was spectacular. They sat at a table with a drink. The golfers came in, in dribs and drabs, hot and grubby but all saying what a wonderful day it had been, and they were served with drinks and canapés.

Zena and Perry introduced her to some nice people, and then there was prize giving – Kathy Forland and Jenny Smythe took the first prize of beautiful vases, each having the highest score of the day, both were white Bajan ladies and were avid golfers playing every day. Zena suggested that Julie should take up golf, it would keep her busy, but Julie shook her head – she was not sporty. She also met Tom Powers, who had lost his wife in the catamaran accident, she recognized him as the man that had come into the clinic with a towel around his head and blood running down his face; he now had a scar on his forehead. They had a long chat about the terrible disaster, commiserating together. His wife, Lily, he had kept afloat because she couldn't swim, and she was brought to the clinic, alive but died half an hour later, "I think she just died of fright, and I flew her body home, it was terrible," he grimaced sadly, then said that he'd just come out again now for a week's golfing holiday, with his sister and her husband. He said he hadn't wanted to come but they had insisted now that he was living alone, but now, looking out to sea made him feel very sad. And he hadn't been near the beach. "And you do have to try and get over these things," and she agreed, he grimaced again, "But it's hard when you've been married thirty years." He grimaced again. "How long were you married?"

"Just four days," she smiled sadly. He caught his breath, "I'm sorry." His eyes sparkled, and she was glad when his brother-in-law caught his arm, and he turned away, wiping a tear from his eye.

Julie drove home, thinking, *thirty-eight years of marriage, she had only had four days…* But she was feeling good after a few drinks and it had been a pleasant evening meeting people, and it was too early to go to bed yet. She went into the drawing room, turning on the lights and the ceiling fan, then she turned on the TV. Finding a film, she relaxed back in one of the purple armchairs, and she was just settling down, the ceiling fan was on, but the atmosphere seemed very *chilly*.

Suddenly the thought came to her of just last week when she and Alan had seen the purple chair move – goosebumps ran down her arms, just as the rocking chair caught her eye it was beginning to rock. She sat bolt upright staring at it for a long moment feeling the panic rising in her chest, then relaxed – it was *just the draught from the ceiling fan.* She inclined her head, and thought she heard a sigh. She stood up quickly, her eyes widened as she scanned the room – the rocking chair was gaining momentum, *it wasn't the fan,* and there was a strong smell of cigar smoke. She rubbed her arms and began backing slowly away to the door her heart racing, staring hard at the rocking chair, she ventured a timid whisper, "Who's there?" Of course there was no answer. Then again, "Is that you, Captain Honeybeck?"

"Umm!" A muffled grunt, *or was it?* She caught her breath he eyes wide, "Captain Honeybeck?" She ventured again, still staring hard at the rocking chair.

"Yessss," a whispered hiss and a low sinister chuckle made her hold her breath, it had come from every corner of the room.

Her eyes widened and her whole body tensed and tightened. Not daring to breathe she reached the door, her hand fumbling behind her for the door handle, afraid to take her eyes off the rocking chair. She ventured again, a very timid whisper, "*Captain Honeybeck...?*" The rocking chair jumped as if someone suddenly got up out of it, and there was a very quiet muffled chuckle, but it was clear enough, she didn't imagine it, she flinched with fright feeling a cold breath on her ear. She turned quickly with a little squeal and rushed out of the door slamming it shut! And spun round fast bumping full pelt into the arms of Rick who was about to knock on the door. She squealed and he grabbed her by the upper arms to steady her, he was as surprised as she was at the sudden impact. "Are you alright, Mrs Anderson? What's the matter?" He looked at her anxiously.

She caught her breath pulling away from him, and shook her head, her breath coming in short pants, "Um, NO! NO!

There's something in there!" He could see the fright in her face and hear the alarm in her voice.

"Why! What's in there?" She stepped aside and he clicked the door opened cautiously, not knowing what to expect, and then he flung it wide open with a quick intake of breath. They both stood in the doorway, all was still. Julie put her hand to her mouth, her heart was racing and thumping loudly in her ears, but there was nothing, the rocking chair was still. All was still. Rick glanced at her, she glanced at him, they both turned back to the room.

"He chuckled!" she said nervously.

"*Who* did?"

"She looked at him a bit sheepishly, "Captain Honeybeck." And although she'd said it, she found it hard to believe.

Rick turned to look at her quickly and leaned back blinking, in a sort of amusement, *"Honeybeck?"* he repeated with a frown and feeling a bit bewildered and wondering if he had heard her correctly, then his eyebrows rose with a sort of amusement and there was a slight twitch at the corners of his mouth, but he held back the laughter that was ready to burst. He turned back to look at the room, biting the inside of his mouth. All was still. "I think it's alright now, Mam," he said gently bending his head a little as if talking to a child that had awoken from a bad dream, "you can go back in now."

"I'm not going BACK IN THERE!" said Julie, very firmly, and started to walk off down the hall. He watched her go, covering the grin with his hand. She reached the library and turned the door knob, looking back up the hall before entering. She saw him watching her. She put her hand around the door and found the switch, all the pale blue table lamps came on, she closed the door and stood dead still scanning the deadly silent room.

Rick was still standing at the drawing room door, he grinned and rubbed his chin, taking a deep breath, then crossed the room and turned off the TV. Turning to check the room while in there, and scanning it again before turning off the lights and coming back out, he closed the door. Then stood for a moment listening, and looking down the long wood panelled hallway, thinking that Mrs Anderson had been under a lot of stress just lately. It was probably the TV that she'd heard. Then he suddenly remembered why he was there – he went down the hall and tapped on the library door. He listened but heard nothing; he tapped again, and then opened it and poked his head inside, she was deep in one of the winged-back armchairs. He went in, "Excuse me, Mrs Anderson, Mam, but what I came to say was that Mr Stone rang while you were out, and he would like you to ring him back."

She glanced up, "Thank you, Rick. Is he still there?"

"No Mam, Mr Stone wants you to ring him."

"I mean Honeybeck."

Rick swallowed hard, not knowing what to say, "No Mam, I don't think so." Julie nodded an unsaid thank you.

Rick wasn't sure whether to stay or go, he was hovering, watching her sitting there wringing her hands. He made his way quietly to the door, waited, and turned around, then left, closing the door quietly, then stood in the quiet hall for a minute or two… He grimaced, wondering should he go back in. But then thought better not, and walked away down the hall, stopping outside the drawing room door again. He listened, there was not a sound; he opened the door cautiously and looked in, the light from the hall lit up the darkness but all was still, though he did notice the slightest movement of the rocking chair, thinking it was the draught as he had opened the door. He closed the door quietly again and then made his way out to the car and went home.

In the quiet darkness of the drawing room, the rocking chair was gaining momentum.

Julie looked around the books, still rubbing her hands, and feeling the nervous thumping of her heart. The table lamps caused shadows around the large room and it was eerily quiet. She glanced cautiously into every corner before getting up and walking around looking at the books. Her every movement, her breathing, the rustle of her skirt, the tiniest crunch from the sandals and the soft pat as the underside of her heels flapped on the leather sole, every sound disturbed the stillness of the air. It was eerie, she wished Gavin was here. She looked behind her scanning the room and looking into every dark corner. She sniffed, *there was no cigar smoke… It was creepy, Honeybeck could be in any room.* She took a deep breath, *ghosts can't hurt you, can they? They're not real… No! But they could scare you to death…* She tried to clear her mind. Wandering around the books, she wondered *if there was any more about Honeybeck, perhaps if she knew more about him she could make him go.* She pulled out the large and heavy volume, knowing now that the safe was behind it, and it fell from her hands with a loud slap on to the desk, the sound echoed eerily around the room and she stopped! Listening, eyes wide and holding her breath, every little movement seemed eerie, waiting any minute for something to happen…

The switch for the ceiling fan was on the wall near the door, she crossed the spacious room warily almost on tip toe, then switched on the fan. The sudden soft whirring seemed to quell the dense silence, she felt easier – and stupid, *what was she expecting to happen? This was her house now, why should she feel afraid? Honeybeck was not going to walk in the door – or, was he?* She glanced at the door expecting it to open, then shook her head, saying to herself, "stop thinking like that, it might cause it to happen!"

She turned her attention back to the safe, and crossed the room, she and Alan had already days before looked everywhere around the desk for the safe key, and so now she pushed at the safe door and pressed around the bookshelf, moved other books, stamped on the floor, *there must be a trigger to open it somewhere, although they didn't have modern mechanical hydraulic methods in those days, did they? So there must be a key. There was a large keyhole, and so… there must be a large key… mustn't there?* "But where? Not, in a small hidden drawer that's for sure?" she muttered aloud. *The key hole was large, but then that could be false couldn't it?* She was convinced that there was a trigger somewhere. *I wonder what's in there, could be the treasure, a map perhaps for finding the treasure, but then why have a map, Honeybeck, already knows where he hid it, and he wouldn't leave a map for someone else to find, would he? OR, was the treasure in there? No... No...* She shook her head. *Pirates didn't hide treasure in safes. Because a safe can be opened! Well some of them can... If one had a key. And it was not the thought of what the treasure might be, it was just the excitement of finding it. But no it wouldn't be in the safe, it was buried or hoarded somewhere else, wasn't it,* "But where?" *Some... where... Like... Like...* "Mmm," she drummed her fingers thoughtfully on the desk, "somewhere like... The Silver Lady, *of course! The Silver Lady, yyyesss!" Why else would he put her there in the garden? She'd seen in it in films, a chest being opened and jewels pearls and golden goblets brimming out over the open lid, and wasn't it then, that men came in with guns...* This made her feel a bit creepy.

She turned quickly, feeling something behind her... There was nothing, she was jumpy, her thoughts were making her jumpy, but *it was all imagination.* But still she looked over her shoulder cautiously, wide-eyed. *It could be Honeybeck, he could be in this room now. He could be anywhere in the house,* she shivered, *he could follow her everywhere. Was he watching her now, somewhere in the shadowed corners of the room? She looked into them all again. No, it was all imagination. But... what would he do if she found the treasure? What could he do? WOULD HE grab her! COULD HE grab her?"* She *was alone! In a haunted house...* Well almost. The staff would never hear her if she screamed. She rubbed her arms against the goosebumps. "YES," she muttered, and took a deep breath, *the treasure is in the silver lady, that's where it was... In the silver lady! It had to be. Why put her there...? Stuck in the middle of the garden for all to see, she wasn't just an ornament surely she was there for the purpose of guarding the treasure. She would look in the morning. No! Why not look now? If Honeybeck could be in the house, he could also be in the garden, so what was the difference? He was a ghost he could be anywhere.*

She remembered seeing the torch in the drawer when Alan was here; she took it, switched it on checking that the battery was OK and then opened the louvered doors. It was a lovely moonlit night, stars twinkled in a light grey sky, there was no need for the torch, the whole garden looked as if it was bathed in a soft grey velvet. The very dim security lights were enough to see as she nipped quickly and quietly across the lawn, walking around the gazebo and down to the lady. The night seemed to enclose her in unseen arms and she felt a nervous shiver go through her whole body as she approached the silver lady. She looked warily around her, there was a buzz of insects in the warm still night air and the frogs whistled loudly. She came cautiously around to face the lady – the moonlight enhanced the silver face and the wide blue eyes, and the glowing hideousness in the night light was quite alarming – the eyes appeared to blink, the red lips seemed to move, *but of course, it was just the trick of the moonlight. WASN'T IT?*

She clenched her lips tight together, then taking a breath and bringing the air down her nose with a slight shush, she straightened her shoulders feeling a little braver – it was amazing what a few drinks at the golf club could do. She stood for a minute or two, just looking. In this light, the silver face was quite frightening. Thinking that *she must be mad to be out here in the night.* But nevertheless, she *was* here, and she stepped nearer, *wondering what Honeybeck would choose as a trigger for opening up his treasure,* then looking at the silver voluptuous breast and the impression of the nipples showing through the silver and white painted swathes of the dress, she decided, *yes, that's the most likely place a man would pick.* She reached out her hand, pointing a finger to the right nipple then hesitated, *what if alarm bells rang alerting the whole house? No,* she pulled a face, *Honeybeck, wouldn't have an alarm system not in the 16th century, would he? Well would it matter if alarm bells rang, it was her house now anyway.* She wondered if Honeybeck was there in the garden. She glanced around feeling a little uneasy and switched on the torch, *not that that made any difference to a ghost,* it just made eerier shadows in the trees, and beyond the beam all was dark and deadly still and quiet, *a bit too quiet, even the frogs were not whistling now and there was no rustling of leaves on the trees, no breeze, no air, nothing, everything was dead still.* Then thinking again, *just what was she doing out here? Just wandering around the garden at this time of the night! Was the warm night air making her more intoxicated, well WAS IT?* She shrugged her shoulders.

She turned back to the lady, hesitating again, her finger just an inch from the right nipple, then she quickly pushed it hard, standing back quickly and holding her breath as if it had burned her finger. Nothing happened, *well, what was she expecting – bells and coins to come pouring out like getting the jackpot on a one armed bandit? She didn't know. Maybe it was both breasts.* She put the torch down in the grass, the lady looked more menacing in the shadowed light. Julie cringed, looking around her and feeling a cold shiver go down her spine, expecting to see or hear Honeybeck. But she wasn't going to give up now. She stood facing the ugliness of the red lips and the bright blue eyes, staring now into the shadowed light they appeared to blink. She stared back waiting any minute for something to happen, ready to run. She reached out both arms at full length, fingers pointing to the nipples, she was half an inch from them when suddenly there was music! Her heart leaped, she squealed in fright, stepping back and catching her foot and losing her balance as she kicked out, and the torch went flying in the air. She lay there, her own breast heaving, her heart beating fast, the music still coming from her phone ringing in her pocket. She jumped up quickly, breathlessly fumbling with nervous fingers to get the loud musical tone out of her pocket, pressed the button and put it to her ear – it was a breathless fearful "Hello" – it was Alan.

"Hello, you didn't ring me back, What's the matter?" Hearing her nervous breathing, he became anxious, "Julie! What's the MATTER! JULIE! JULIE!"

"Oh! It's nothing, the phone just gave me a fright that's all."

"Why? Did it wake you, sorry if you're in bed, were you asleep? What's going on, what's the matter with you?" He frowned into the receiver, "What are you doing?"

She finally got her breath back, "I'm alright. And I'm not in bed, I'm in the garden."

"The *garden!* What at this time of the night?" What the *hell* are you doing in the *garden?*"

"Looking for Honeybeck's treasure."

"WHAAAAT!"

She explained, about the rocking chair again, and the voice in the drawing room.

"I'm coming over."

"OH! NO!" she said, but he clicked the phone off. "YOU!" she said, pointing to the lady, "are causing a lot of problems." She came close and quickly pressed both breasts hard at the same time. Nothing happened. She felt a little disappointed, then she poked at both the eyes, and then pressed her finger on the nose, and the mouth – still nothing happened. A sound close by made her turn sharply, and pick up the torch shining it into the trees, a slight panic rising in her breast, and goosebumps running down her arms again. The slightest breeze rustled the leaves, she swished the torch beam across the garden, eyes glinted through the trees, then came a low harsh growl.

She was about to run but the dog burst through the trees and stood there baring its teeth, just as a voice said, "SIT" the dog sat on command as the two security men came out of the trees. The dog gave one sharp bark, the man Dan Calder corrected him and apologized, then asked, "Are you alright, Mrs Anderson Mam?' We heard music and a shout, but we were right over the other side of the garden."

Although breathless she smiled, her heart racing, "Yessss! Thank you. I was just getting some fresh air – it was so quiet out here, and the phone rang, it made me jump and I stumbled, but I'm alright thank you."

"I'm sorry if Buddy startled you, Mam, he's got ears like an elephant, I usually keep him on a lead, but he just took off through the trees."

She nodded. "Yes he did startle me, but it's alright thanks." They were smiling as they bid her goodnight, about to walk away, "Oh, er… Excuse me, Mr Stone will be here in a few minutes."

"Oh, thank you for telling us, Mam, we'll look out for him," said Dan, and they disappeared back into the trees again.

She made her way back to the library – the door was still open, her heart was racing and she leaned on the desk for support, her breath coming in short pants. The dog had given her a fright, its bright eyes had glistened in the torchlight through the trees before it had actually appeared. *She must have been mad to be out there anyway.* She spun around quickly, her eyes wide as the curtains swished back, she thought her heart had stopped beating. "ALAN! Oh my God!" Her hand went to her throat, "How did you get here so quick, you gave me such a fright?"

"Sorry," he smiled, "I was going straight down the garden, I thought you were there but your security man said that you had come back in. You should lock this door you know," he turned and shut the louvered doors, turning the key in the lock, and pulled the curtains over. Then, seeing the look on her face as he turned back, he came to her quickly taking her upper arms and turning her to him. "Say, are you alright? What on *earth* were, you *doing* out there?"

She looked at him with such relief, and leaned on him. He put his arms around her and held her tight. "Oh Alan, I'm so glad you are here." She told him in a quick gabble about what had happened in the drawing room, "It's HONEYBECK! I'm sure. And then in the garden the dog made me jump – it came bursting through the trees."

"Well, fancy wandering around the garden at this time of the night!" he scolded, "perhaps it was your security men you heard chuckling. Have you been drinking?"

"Yes, I've been to the golf club with Zena and Perry, but I haven't had that much. And, oh no, I wasn't in the garden when I heard the chuckling – it was Honeybeck in the drawing room I'm sure. But I didn't tell the security about that. I was really convinced that I would find the treasure out there in the silver lady – why else would he put a thing like that in the garden? I came out of the drawing room in a bit of a rush and bumped into Rick, I told him about the chuckle and there was the smell of cigar smoke, but he didn't see or hear anything. I don't think he believed me, I think he thought that I was mad..." She took a breath. "You know, Alan, I'm beginning to worry about this house, it's scary... Well, I'm not, really *that* scared, I mean I'm not terrified, but I do find it eerie and now I think I'm being watched, I have this feeling all the time, I think Honeybeck is here and I think he's guarding his treasure."

Alan thought to himself, *he wasn't too happy about seeing the rocking chair and the purple armchair moving the other evening, it certainly had been eerie.* He tried to put her at ease, saying, "Oh, it's a bit scary, but ghosts can't hurt you." *He didn't really think that they could, and why would they want to anyway? He didn't really think that he even believed in ghosts, but now he'd seen it for himself and there was no doubting that there was something in the drawing room, it had made his skin creep.*

Alan stayed the night in the guest room, not wanting to leave her alone in the house, well she wasn't really alone but the staff being in the basement would never hear her if she called out, but luckily the night had been uneventful. They had breakfast together and asked her out to dinner that evening. She wrinkled her nose, "Can I think about it? I sometimes don't feel like going out."

He knew how she felt, they were both still grieving, and sometimes it was an effort to go out, but he thought that going out did ease the pain and the tension a bit. "Well," he smiled gently, "I'm easy, if you change your mind just give me a call, OK?" He smiled with a friendly nod. He then left to go home for a shave and shower, and a change of clothes before going to the office.

She watched him go, but there was an empty feeling in her heart. He was so good to her, she hoped that she hadn't offended him by refusing, maybe he needed a break from the office, but she thought that he understood.

Alan had not been gone long when Michael Prescott phoned saying he had the photos to show her but they hadn't come out very well, but he would bring another camera and take some more. She said that she would not be there this morning as she was going shopping with Zena and could he make this afternoon.

He said no, he had some business to take care of, and they had agreed that he would come early that evening, to show her the photos and stay for dinner, and then take more photos another time when the light was right. She phoned Alan, he was pleased to come. "It's just a casual dinner, I'm not making a fuss."

There was not very much for Julie to buy, she'd still not worn half her wedding trousseau, and each time she put something on it brought on a few tears thinking that she had bought them with Gavin in mind, and now he would never see them.

Zena bought sandals, tee shirts, and shorts in the new Ralph Lauren shop. The new shopping centre all under cover, called Lime Grove, had not long been open and was a wonderful addition to Barbados, with Cartier, Michael Kors, and Louis Vuitton, not that they needed jewellery or expensive handbags but it also had a nice restaurant and was not too busy. "There's a super bar here in the evenings," Zena said over the table as the waitress brought them the menu, "It's always packed with hundreds of people, you must come down with us one evening." Knowing that Julie was still a bit down and not wanting to go out, Zena thought it would cheer her up, "I know it must be hard for you, but you have to get out and meet people, I don't mean looking for a man, I mean people, nice people." She smiled gently. "I'll introduce you to some nice friends."

Julie nodded, knowing she was right and she meant well, but she wasn't ready yet, and the thought of just going out without Gavin brought a few tears to her eyes.

Zena saw it, and felt sympathy in her heart, but said nothing more. They ordered, and Zena keeping the conversation going said, "We're going on holiday next month to Miami, you can come with us if you like, it would give you a break away from the island."

Julie shook her head with a smile, "No, it's very kind of you, Zena, but no. No thanks, not yet."

Both Alan and Michael arrived within minutes of each other, both keen to come for dinner after living for the best part of the week on Pizza Hut and Kentucky Fried food. They were in the gazebo, Charles had served them drinks and Michael was showing them the photos. "Look at this one, sorry it didn't come out very well, I think there's something wrong with my camera – I'll have to get it checked."

The photo of the whole drawing room was colourful with the red carpet and purple armchairs, and so well photographed it looked liked like a show room. But in the rocking chair there was a white misty shadow. Alarm bells rang as both Julie and Alan looked sharply at each other.

"I'm sure there was nothing in the room when I took the picture," said Michael, "I just can't make out what that is. It's also on this one that I took of the silver lady, LOOK!"

"It's him, it's a ghost," Julie said quietly, "It's him. Isn't it, Alan?"

Michael looked from one to the other and laughed, his mouth open, "Who? A ghost!"

"It's no joke," Alan arched his eyebrows and shook his head.

They told him of their experience in the drawing room with the rocking chair moving on its own. Michael was intrigued, "Well as a matter of fact it did move while I was trying to take the photo, but I thought it was the draught from the open doors, I blocked it to keep it still." He couldn't stop smiling to think that he had captured a ghost on film. They looked again at the photos of the silver lady, and they all then decided that the swirling mist around her was the ghostly figure of Honeybeck.

CHAPTER FIVE

The weeks went on and there had been no more activity from Honeybeck. Michael had gone back to Florida and life went on, Julie and Alan occasionally having dinner out and not being late as he had to work in the mornings. On Sundays they had lunch at the Silver Lady Cottage and after lunch they relaxed, sitting by the pool enjoying each other's company.

Alan had his eyes closed behind dark glasses, lying back on the deck bed shaded by a large green umbrella. "Nice breeze," he murmured as a cool wave drifted across the garden, rustling the leaves on the trees and rippling the water.

"Mmm," Julie smiled sleepily. She was also lying back behind dark glasses, enjoying the lazy afternoon and listening to the twittering of the birds. The wine with lunch had relaxed them both.

"Did Michael come back and take more photos?" Alan said, still with his eyes closed.

"Yes," she turned her head towards him, "but they came out the same. He's convinced that it's his camera, he can't believe the story of a ghost. But I guess Honeybeck's spirit is everywhere in the house, after all he did build it, but I haven't explored the whole house yet, *or* the garden either for that matter."

"Haven't you? What after being out here most of the time, I thought you were looking for treasure." He grinned. "You haven't found it have you and are keeping it quiet?" He raised his eyebrows with a smile.

She chuckled, "No *not yet, there's fourteen acres you know.*"

"*What! Fourteen acres of TREASURE?*" His voice rose playfully. He swung his long brown legs over the deck bed and sat up, slipping his feet into trainers and tying them up. "Come on," he said, standing to pull a tee shirt over his head, "let's explore the fourteen acres," holding a hand out to help her up, and putting a hand into his beige shorts, making sure his phone was still there, he rarely went anywhere without it, and then sticking his sunglasses on, "Come on, where shall we start? Let's take a walk around, we won't find treasure just lying here with our eyes closed."

She chuckled, "You'll be lucky to find treasure anyway, but I must say it's keeping my mind busy all the time, you never know. I'm still looking for the key to the safe. I wonder what's in there?" Putting on a matching wrap over the red and green flowered bikini and then slipping on red, flat, strappy sandals, "OK, let's go!"

They went up the rough greenish blackened and weather-beaten coral stone steps, shaded from the hot afternoon sun by the leafy mahogany trees and dotted with fallen crimson petals from the flamboyant, and made their way across the lawn. The garden was like a small park with the odd white painted iron seats here and there, and serene stone goddess-like statues with closed eyes and 'Mona Lisa' smiles. They came to the same mound again, they had already decided that it must be a grave – but whose, Honeybeck's? Or Thurgold's? Ambling slowly past the stone statues, and stopping to look at the serene and peaceful faces, they moved further on keeping as much as they could under the shade of the trees and following a very overgrown path that vanished into the thick undergrowth. They eventually came to a large barn, the old wood blackened with age, a few roof tiles missing, and the old and dry wooden door must have been all of ten feet high and had a rusty iron lock. Alan shook the door, the whole front of the barn rattled.

"Perhaps this is where old Gibbons keeps his gardening tools, I saw him with a motorized mower the other day," said Julie.

"No, this lock looks too rusty," said Alan, "shouldn't think it's been opened for years." He pulled hard at the door, and then shook it roughly again, and the whole front of the building shuddered. "Mmm, doesn't look too safe does it," as he pulled the door and the screws in the rusty lock just gave way. He pulled at the door again, the rusty hinges squeaking and grinding, it took all his strength to open it, the wood being old and splintering as it scraped and creaked at the bottom on the hard uneven dusty ground and then stuck fast and shuddered at the top. The gap was now wide enough for them to squeeze through.

It was darkish inside with no windows, but the sun sent shadows around the walls from the half open door. Thin shafts of sunlight came from the missing roof tiles, lighting up the thick grey cobwebs that hung like heavy drapes in the corners from having been shut up for so long and looped like pelmets from the rafters; it made Julie shiver, thinking of the big black spiders that must be lurking there. There was a heady smell of old hay or straw, and a pile of sugar cane and palm leaves now dried white and like paper; also a musty dampness from a rain shower in the night that had come through the roof, the barn had also weathered many rain showers and storms over the years. The warmth from the continual daily sun had dried the heap of rotting straw that they could just make out in the gloom at the far end high up in the loft, and the atmosphere was warm and clammy but there was also a dry dust in the air that irritated their throats. Birds twittered as they flew in and out and perched on the rafters. The wooden flooring that was sparsely covered with dry straw creaked under their tread and dust particles danced in the very thin shafts of yellow sunlight coming through the gaps in the roof.

On opening the door, and with their movements, dust clouds arose clogging their throats and making them cough. Their coughing disturbed a mongoose that scampered across the barn disappearing into the darkness and the straw, it had obviously found its way in through a hole in the wall, and two pigeons flew from the rafters with a loud flapping of wings sending more clouds of dust down upon them. To their right halfway along the wall there was an old and dusty saddle on the floor and beside it a heavy horse collar, above it a harness hung on a nail. To their left and at the far end, was an old wooden cart half full with straw, a large wooden cartwheel stood against the wall, and some iron farm equipment that they didn't recognize, probably part of a plough. Nearby there was an old shovel and a rusty old machete with a wooden handle and a broad blade used for cutting the cane. It seemed as if they had opened a grave, all was so still, apart from the birds, and all must have lain untouched like this for a century.

"I suppose Honeybeck kept horses, there must be a stable somewhere," Julie's voice broke the silence and a bird flapped its wings and flew across the rafters.

"Hmm! And the Turners I suppose, it was the only mode of transport in those days," said Alan, "yeah, there must be a stable. Farm equipment must have been kept in here, this used to be a sugar plantation, so I read in that book. I wonder how many staff old Honeybeck had here, or I suppose it was slave labour then."

"You know, I never thought about him having staff, I thought he was a pirate, and I suppose he must have been away at sea a lot of the time so he must have had quite a few staff to look after a house this size and a sugar plantation."

"Hmm," Alan nodded thoughtfully, "come on let's go and do a bit more exploring." He turned, taking a step towards the door and gave a shout as the floorboards cracked and gave way under his feet, and he stumbled heavily on his hands and knees. Julie went to help him up, then as he was about to get up a bit carefully, the floorboard creaked and cracked and gave way under his hands, and then seeing the gap in the floor while still on his hands and knees he looked through. "Could be a well," he said, "a bit too dark to see."

"Better get up quick then," said Julie, "A bit dangerous, you could have fallen right through. Maybe be that's why the barn has been locked up and not used."

He moved gingerly, sliding back in case it should go further, but luckily it didn't. Then his hand touched metal. He swished away some of the loose straw with a sweep of his hand, "There's hinges here, this is a trapdoor." He looked up at her in surprise. He got up, the floorboards were a bit bouncy under his weight, and stepped to the side, it seemed a bit firmer here. He wriggled the heavy rusty bolt which obviously had not been opened for years, the hinges creaked and squeaked as he lifted the trapdoor and opened it flat back and they both looked down into the gaping darkness of the hole – there was a ladder.

"Can't be a well," said Alan.

"Honeybeck's treasure do you think?" said Julie anxiously, "It would be exciting to find it wouldn't it?"

"Yeah," Alan chuckled, "only one way to find out. You stay here." He began to descend the ladder, "It's a bit rickety."

"Be careful," Julie called anxiously seeing him disappearing into the darkness.

Alan's voice came hollow from deep down, "It's a long way down." And then she saw a light, it was from his phone. "Can't see much, need a torch."

"I'll go and get one, wait a minute," she called back down, and went running across the garden. It took a few minutes to get back to the library, where she had left a torch in the drawer, and then she came haring back to the barn, "Hello are you there? Sorry if I was a long time," she called down, catching her breath, "I've got a torch." She shone it down seeing him on his way coming up the ladder, he got almost to the top taking the torch from her, "Can't see much down there, it's a cave I think, looks quite big."

"I'm coming down!"

"He said, "NO!" But she was climbing over on to the ladder, "Stay there, let me get to the bottom first it's a bit rickety." He reached the bottom, shining the light up for her as she made her descent very slowly. He shone the light around what appeared to be a large semi-circular area – there was nothing but sharp cold coral stone rock; going up the light caught a sconce on the wall – someone had had candles or a flaming torch, there were burn marks on the wall, and then the light caught drawings on the wall. "Hey look at *this*," Alan's voice rose in some surprise as he shone the torch – on the wall there were primitive drawings of men with bows and arrows, donkeys, fires and cooking pots, "this has got to be hundreds of years old," said Alan as he turned the light slowly around in a circle, "I would think this was done by the Arawak or Carib Indians, it said in *that script*, that they had lived on the island for up to a thousand years…" His voice trailed off as, if in wonderment, "Just fancy that! It's amazing isn't it?" As he moved the light around there was a gap in the rock; they moved towards it, Alan leaned in, shining the light – it was narrow and the walls were sharp on either side, and he had to duck his head as the rock was jagged and sharp above. "I think this is another cave," his voice echoed back to him, the words running into each other, "Come on."

Julie took a step carefully towards the light, not very sure-footed – it was dark below and the coral uneven. The light showed what looked to be a tunnel, Alan ducked his head and stepped forward.

"Are we going in?"

"Yes keep your head down."

She was a bit unsure as she followed closely behind him, and then felt for his hand in the darkness, the beam shining down and the torch showing a large round circle of light as he kept his right hand over his head for the uneven rock, and they moved slowly forward, one small and careful step at a time. The rock underfoot was very uneven and sharp beneath the thin soles of her sandals. He kicked his toe and almost stumbled and swore, "You alright?" she asked,

"Yeah I'm OK." They moved on, it proved to be just a short passageway and they found themselves in another cave. The torchlight showed more wall drawings of men with bows and arrows, mules, pigs and birds, men with knives, and women cooking over a fire, and children, and babes in arms.

"Can you believe that people once lived down here," Julie shivered, "it's very cold."

"Yes I expect that's why they lived here, to get out of the heat of the sun. But I wonder who built the barn over the top, and why?"

"Well to keep the farming gear in I expect," said Julie.

"Hmm, but why build a barn when you have a large and cool cave that could be used for the same purpose?" said Alan.

"Well I expect it was too deep to get the farm carts down here."

"Yeah," he splayed his hands, "Yeah! Could be. I would think Honeybeck used the cave for storage, perhaps at one time there was probably a rockfall, leaving a gaping great hole, perhaps that's why they built a barn over the top. I wonder if the whole house is built over the cave, I mean, there might be tunnels everywhere under the garden, even out to sea, maybe that's why Honeybeck built the house here, he must have been smuggling, and wanted to have somewhere to hide his ill-gotten gains, he must have had the authorities after him all the time, and then he could hide down here."

"Perhaps that's why he built the barn over the top because the treasure is hidden down here in the cave – no one would think to look under a barn for a cave would they?"

"Hmm, you've got a point there, but why leave a trapdoor exposed with just a covering of straw? Especially, *if,* there is a treasure hidden down *here.* No, I think the cave was used for cold storage. And the barn is not as old as the cave, I should think the Turners built the barn, it must be about a couple of hundred years old but not as old as the cave." Alan inclined his head, shining the torch slowly around the walls again, "but *if there is* any treasure, where could it be? There's nothing but solid coral stone rock."

"Well, there must be a door or an entrance somewhere," said Julie touching the wall, "there must be an entrance to the house, mustn't there?"

Alan grinned, "You're thinking of stately homes in the UK with secret passages, but why have the trapdoor in the barn?"

"Well," she said thoughtfully, "maybe it's an escape route, he obviously must have been pursued by the police." She frowned, "Did they have police in those days?" she went on, "He perhaps could get into the cave from the house and hide, and he could also escape through the trapdoor, or vice versa if he was in the garden when the cops came banging on the door." She arched her eyebrows, her eyes staying wide. Alan didn't comment. "Anyway, who is going to come into a barn and find a cave down here?"

"Us!" Alan chuckled. "But if I hadn't fallen through the floorboards we wouldn't have found it covered in straw – we wouldn't even have looked, would we?" His voice echoed back at him, as he swept the beam of light across the centre of the floor catching a pile of sticks and ashes where there had been a fire. He held the light closer, "Is that a bone?" He put the toe of his trainer into the dust.

"Probably the remains of some Stone Age Indian's dinner," Julie looked down into the circle of light.

"Yeah, I should think they were smoked out." He shone the torchlight up, it was too high and dark to see much, "They had flaming torches down here there's an iron bracket over there, and there must have been smoke."

Suddenly there was a loud bang that echoed through the hollowness, it startled them both and they looked toward the tunnel. The atmosphere rapidly changed and an icy draught swept from somewhere through the cavern disturbing the stillness, it seemed to whirl around them and they stood like statues. In a bikini and a cotton wrap Julie shivered.

Alan turned the torch on the tunnel, about to make the way back, but they were stunned as a white cloudy mist formed in the torchlight and filled the entrance.

Alarm bells rang in Alan's head, his first thought was a rockfall, the mist was dust, the entrance would be blocked... but then, to their amazement the mist was taking shape and a shadowy figure of a big man was slowly developing and filling the entranceway, then a gruff low and sinister-sounding chuckle echoed through the cavern.

As quick as it had formed, the figure then began to fade away. Julie cringed and shivered, "Ooh, Alan," it was a tearful shaky whisper, she clutched tightly at his arm.

He swallowed hard, holding the torch steady but there was nothing, there was no more movement, "I think it's gone now – come on, let's get out of here." He took her hand but she pulled back.

"But he might still be in the passageway." Her voice rose to a frightened squeak. Then in a slow and breathless whisper, "Was it Honeybeck?"

"Mmm, I should think so. Come on," he encouraged, squeezing her hand, "we've got to go through, it's the only way out." He moved a few steps forward and they stood at the entrance to the passage. The light shone on the coral stone – it looked clear, the atmosphere seemed back to normal, whatever that may mean, still cold but not freezing. But nevertheless Julie still shivered, feeling an icy chill on her skin as she stepped gingerly behind Alan, holding his hand, her heart racing. She expected any minute Honeybeck would loom up in front of them again, *and what if something blocked the entrance from behind and they were trapped in this narrow passageway?* She could feel the panic rising from within. Nothing happened but as they reached the ladder there came a low chuckle, they both spun around quickly wide-eyed into the darkness, but as Alan swung the torchlight an icy chill swirled around them again so cold that it could almost be seen – but they saw nothing. There was a wary feeling between them; they both swallowed hard. Alan shone the torchlight upwards, there was hardly any daylight showing through the small gaps in the wood, "Come on, hurry up, you go first," he said, steadying the ladder.

Julie scrambled up the ladder more than anxious to reach the top and going too fast for her own good and slipping, crying out in alarm and then regaining her footing again and clambering to the top, then struggling to open the trapdoor, "I can't move it," she called down, "it's closed tight."

"Come down and let me have a go, it's probably too heavy for you to push up."

She came down, "Put your foot on here and hold the ladder steady." Alan went up, leaving her in the dark. She could see the trapdoor in the torchlight and hear him up there banging, "Can't budge it," he called, "I think the bolt's got jammed. Is there anything down there I can use as a leaver or something to hammer it up, a piece of loose rock or something? I can't do it with the flat of my hand. I need something to punch it up hard, it might loosen the rusty screws," but he couldn't imagine how the trapdoor that he had opened and laid flat back could have closed – someone must have come in and slammed it down and bolted it.

An eerie chuckle echoed through the cave, again, "OOOH! ALAN!" Julie peered into the darkness behind her, she was scared, but there was nothing there.

'It's alright," Alan's echoed, "it can't hurt you. Did you find anything?"

"I don't know, wait a minute." She could see nothing in the very faint dimness that was coming from the upturned torch, it put all below into shadowed darkness, and she really felt afraid to move in case Honeybeck may be there watching.

"Find anything?" Alan's voice had a spooky echo and seemed to shatter the walls, he flashed the torchlight down.

"NO! There's nothing!" And just as he flashed it back up again, "OH! Wait a minute, yes. There's a long stick." She reached out and picked it up and handed it to him, "HERE! Is this any good – it's quite sturdy."

He took it from her, looking at it in the torchlight he frowned it was possibly an animal bone. He began hammering upwards thinking that it would dislodge the heavy iron bolt or splinter the wood but the trapdoor didn't move even though the wood was dry and seemed weak, and even the broken boards that he had fallen through seemed solid enough. He tried putting his hand up through them but he couldn't reach the bolt. He was about to come down, but with the shifting of his weight the top rungs of the ladder suddenly gave way under his feet. His loud shout of alarm echoed throughout the whole cavern, his hands slid down the sides of the ladder but he managed to hang on until his feet felt a solid rung and the stick and the torch came hurtling down, and Julie squealed dodging out of the way as they landed beside her. The torchlight went out.

"You alright?" she called anxiously. "what's happened?" she picked up torch, she could feel that the batteries had come out.

"Yeah! Bloody ladder gave way, but I'm OK. Shine the light."

"I can't, the batteries have come out." He was still gripping the side of the ladder his feet resting now on a more solid rung and getting his breath back. He then came back down beside her in the darkness, "Where's the torch?" He took it from her, and then switched on his phone light, it was very dim but she saw a battery on the floor and picked it up. Alan put it back into the torch and they had light, only one had come out. "Can't move the trapdoor," he said, "I think someone must have shut it. It couldn't possibly have shut on its own, and now the top bloody rungs of the ladder have broken away. I suppose the wood is rotten, and I can't even reach the trapdoor now, well not enough to put any pressure on it, even with this," he bent to pick up the stick shining the torch on it thinking then it was an animal bone, "Where did you find this anyway?"

"Just there," she said pointing behind the ladder. "I could barely see it. Why, what is it?"

"Looks like a human skeleton bone." He shone the torch behind the ladder and there it was sitting upright in the corner, its face drooped and pained, its knees together up under its chin. The torch wavered as Alan dropped the thigh bone quickly with a gasp, and Julie squealed, it gave them both a jolt.

Julie cringed, holding her hand to her mouth, then took it away quickly frowning with distaste, and quickly wiped her hand down her wrap – she had been holding a human bone – a cold shiver running right through her body. She wiped her hand down her wrap again, trying to rid herself of the smooth bone feeling, and watched in horror as Alan went a little closer and stood the thigh bone back in place. "It's a wonder that the whole thing didn't collapse when you took it," he said.

"Oh! Alan, how awful, I wonder who it is?"

"Who it *was*, you mean."

Julie's heart was thumping at the gruesome and alarming sight, it was a shock to her system knowing that she had been holding a human bone. It was even more scary than the eerie chuckle. She gradually calmed down then moved cautiously a little closer beside Alan, who was now squatting down in front of the white and fearful bones. Now in full light, they could see a small clay jar on the floor between the knees, "What's that?" she whispered.

"Don't know," said Alan." He was about to reach out for it, when out of the deadly silence the low and gruff chuckle came again. It made them both stand up and spin around. Her heart leaped so painfully her hands went to her breast, and she stood tight as if holding herself together.

Alan flashed the torch around the hard cold coral stone walls quickly, "Who's THERE?" His voice echoed back at them heavily then whined away into the distance, nothing moved but they could feel the icy air they saw nothing and *yet*, there was something there… Julie was wringing her hands tightly to her breast, her eyes wide and fearful staring into the darkness beyond the torchlight. *Was someone down here playing a scary trick?* And then there was loud and distant laughter, Ha, Ha, HA, haaaa… As if whoever it was, was walking away. They stood like statues, holding their breath for some long seconds, their hearts beating fast, their ears clogged with a cloudy sound of silence. Julie tightened her grip on Alan's arm, they were not sure if the voice came from outside. "HELLO!" Alan bellowed, his deep voice shattering the silence and echoing all around and reverberating off the walls and then whined away to dead silence. They listened, intently, both their hearts were racing and the beating in their ears drowned out any other sound, then the slightest touch of cold air filtered through from somewhere; Julie hoped it could be from the barn above and that it was not Honeybeck come back, or, the ghost of the skeleton – it made her hold her breath. She was hoping that *it was* someone having a joke and in a minute they would all be laughing. But it didn't happen, it was eerie and the cold seeped deep into her bones, and the deadly silence and the darkness was frightening.

Whatever it was passed. Alan let out his breath, he was sure it was gone.

"Whatever was that?" Julie whispered, afraid of her own voice, "it was outside, wasn't it?"

Alan inclined his head, then with hardly a movement of his right hand he moved the torchlight across the hard rock, turning slowly in a circle. All was still, all so deadly quiet but for the loud beating of his heart that thundered in his ears fogging his attempt to listen. The beam fell on the skeleton again, Julie felt a loud PANG! in her head as the ugly face leered at them. Alan stood motionless; the chilling thought that this thing had been sitting here for years so quietly waiting for rescue, it was scary, but he knew it couldn't happen to them – Rick or Charles would miss them – but it might be a long wait. He picked up the thigh bone and bent down in front of the skeleton, and although his movements were very slow it disturbed the air and the bones creaked, and a knife fell down and landed through the knees, knocking over the clay jar it cracked and silver coins spilled out. Alan quickly flinched back, still sitting on his heels, and then very carefully put out his hand to take some of the coins, and as he did so, a bony white arm was dislodged and the hand fell down with a chink of dry bones on to the coral covering the silver coins as if to stop him from taking them. It made him jump yet again in alarm, and Julie gasped a loud "OH!" and jumped back in fright. Her voice echoed eerily through the cavern. Alan picked up a few coins as the echo died away, leaving them with the deadly silence once again.

Julie, seeing the hand like a fossilized huge white spider covering the coins cried out, "Come on let's get out of here."

"We can't!" Alan shook his head, "the trapdoor is shut solid, I can't budge it!" He shone the torch on the few silver coins in his hand and put them in the pocket of his white shorts, then turned the torch back to the cracked clay jar that was now lying on its side, with more coins spilling out under the bony fingers, you could almost hear the thing breathing, *it's all mine*...

"Do you think that's Honeybeck's treasure? Is *that him?*" Julie grimaced, her voice a bit shaky.

"Dunno, could be part of the treasure, though! But I would have thought that a pirate's treasure would amount to much more. And, the book said he died on the patio of a sword wound. Wouldn't have thought that the staff would have dumped him down here though would you? After all, pirate or not, he was a captain, and the master of the house. This is more than lightly Thurgold, but whoever brought him down here must have sat him up, but I wouldn't think that anyone would have left him with a pot of money? So! Perhaps he wasn't dead at the time, and maybe they thought he was! And shut down here, he just starved. *Or*, maybe perhaps it's some other poor devil who came down here and thought he had hit the jackpot, and nobody knew he was here?"

"STUCK! Like we are?" she raised her eyebrows, wringing her hands again nervously.

"Hmm…" Alan twisted his mouth. "I've got the phone, I'll call Rick." She felt relieved. He tried, "There's no signal down here."

"Oh Alan! What are we going to do? Rick will come looking for us won't he, but I wonder if he knows where this old barn is, we only found it by chance didn't we."

"Well somebody knows where it is, I'm positive that the trapdoor couldn't have closed on its own. I laid it flat back on the floor." Just then the torch battery flickered and faded and went out, leaving them in total darkness!

"Oh, Alan!" It was a small cry of despair. Then, out of the darkness came a low gruff chuckle again and a long sort of drawn in satisfied breath.

"OH! ALAN!" She gripped his arm tightly looking around her in panic, but of course seeing nothing. The voice echoed as if in the far distance and an icy breath seemed to surround their heads. Goosebumps run down Julie's spine, she was frozen, holding her breath and feeling her breast swelling tight hard against the bikini bra, and imagining any minute something would grab her.

They were both staring wide-eyed into the darkness… But then, as their eyes became accustomed to the very faintest glimmer of light from the broken boards above, the cold seeped though the thin cotton beach wrap and Julie's hand went to her throat as they saw the white mist rising again. Alan had a quick intake of breath, she knew he was also scared.

"Come on." He suddenly felt for her hand on his arm as he moved, feeling his way along the wall.

"Where are we going?" It was a breathless whisper.

"Through to the other cave, here's the entrance to the passage – keep your head down and keep close behind me."

"You're joking, I'm not even going to let go."

He stepped carefully, feeling the uneven rock beneath his trainers, and keeping his head low. She carefully followed him, it was just a few steps but in complete darkness and deadly silence. The sound of their shallow breathing was frightening. She glanced behind her, she saw nothing, felt nothing, but it sent shivers down her spine.

Alan, no longer feeling the rock above him, knew they had made it through to the second cave, he straitened his shoulders and stood upright. "Look up there!" It was a soft whisper but it echoed off the walls, "See that pinprick of light?" The words ran into each other, "That's the sun. I knew there must be an opening, if there had been a fire, the smoke would have to go out somewhere. Now stay just there, sit down."

"Why? Where are you going!" Her eyes wide and anxious.

"I'm going to climb up there and find a way out."

"What in the dark?" she was flabbergasted

"Well there's no other choice. Now sit down, then you can't fall over anything," he gently pushed her to a sitting position. "You OK? Stay there!"

"Don't be long." It was a breathless whisper.

"I'll only be a few minutes." He turned from her, his arms outstretched at shoulder level in front of him, stepping slowly forward, it was like being suspended in mid-air. He caught his foot, scraping it along the coral, and knowing that it was the bone and ashes of the fire. He knew now that he was about in the centre of the cave and had about another five or so steps to cover; if he turned he would be disorientated. He moved on slowly, sliding one foot before the other until his hands reached the needle-sharp wall, he then reached as high as he could trying to lift himself up, but the coral was sharp and bit into his fingers, and climbing the wall wasn't easy. He felt around in the darkness to get a good grip, but it seemed that the first few feet of the wall was flat, and then he felt a bulge, and his hand went into something like a deep smooth crevasse, and he got more purchase on the rock. Then with the strong muscles of his arms he heaved himself up and was clinging on the rough indentations of the very needle-sharp coral that bit into his fingers making them bleed. But luckily now the toes of his size twelve trainers got a grip as the sharp coral gripped the rubber. Being tall he reached up a bit further and his hand felt a deeper indentation – he supposed another hole in the rock – and he pulled himself up finding a better grip for his feet on a small ledge, but then scraping his knees as he edged upwards to the pinprick of light.

Julie could hear his laboured breathing and cursing under his breath, as he scraped his body on upwards. She was sitting here now in the darkness with her knees up, she thought, *maybe the skeleton had sat here just like this, for days or even weeks just hoping that someone would come.* Although she could not see Alan she was looking in the right direction and the pinprick of light got wider as his hand moved part of the overgrown greenery and a bird's nest and bits of twigs and grass fell from above.

She could hear the birds twittering and Alan mumbling, "You alright?" she called.

"Yeah! Found the opening," his hollow voice came back breathless and muffled, "got a bit of light, but the hole's not big enough to get out." He was hanging on with one hand, supported now just by his toes and leaning his body hard into the rock while pushing away at tangled greenery, and then with relief he could see the sky. Obviously the barn did not cover this part of the cave, and the hole in the rock was no wider that a pipe, but at least now they had a little light.

Julie watched his shadow figure as he came down the rock a lot quicker than he went up, sliding most of the way not able to get a grip, and then sitting on the floor to get his breath back, and painfully rubbing his sore and badly blooded hands and his badly grazed knees. She dabbed them with her beach wrap, she could see his shorts and tee shirt were bloodstained, his chest badly scored. She sat down with him on the cold uneven floor in front of the cold fire ashes as she supposed a family of Arawak had done a thousand years before. She put her arms around him and he winced at the scratched wounds on his chest, "What else can we do?" She knew it was a silly question.

He smiled, "It's alright, Rick is on his way. Up there it was open to the sky and I managed to contact him on the phone. He didn't know about the cave but he knows where the barn is. So all we can do now is wait. We've been in the dark, but I got a light on my phone," he smiled flicking it on, "never gave it a thought before. We'd better get back into the other cave." Alan stood up stiffly with a groan and with a little help from her then leaning on the wall they made their way back very slowly to the first cave with the light from the phone, then sat in the darkness by the ladder. It was an eerie feeling knowing that the skeleton was just an arm's length away and had been sitting here waiting for years. And now the waiting seemed like hours, but was probably just about fifteen minutes, and then they heard voices, and they shouted hearing footsteps and the creaking of the wooden floorboards above them. Then the bolt was being drawn back to their great relief, and they saw Rick as the trapdoor was opened.

Julie went up the ladder, the top three rungs missing. She was pulled up by Rick and old Gibbons the gardener. Alan followed, and of course there was now all the explaining to do, Rick asking questions, nine to the dozen, that Alan said they would discuss it later, not wanting to tell about the ghost in front of old Gibbons.

It was later that evening after dinner, they were sitting in the drawing room, Julie had phoned Rick asking him to come down, and they told him how the floor in the barn had given way and of the ghostly activity.

Rick said he knew there *was* a cave somewhere on the land but didn't know where, and who would have thought that it would be under the barn. But he had never been in the barn anyway. When Sir Gabriel Anderson had bought the property, he was asked to find a surveyor, and Rick had walked around with John Coldridge, but then he couldn't find a key to the barn at that time, and John Coldridge had said that day to leave it until later, but it had never been mentioned again.

Rick had had a word with old Gibbons, who had said that years ago they had used the barn, but the floor wasn't safe and so it was locked up. He knew about the trapdoor, but Mr James Turner had forbidden any of the staff to go down there.

Rick was more than surprised when told that they had a ghost, in fact a bit sceptical – he couldn't really believe what he was hearing at first, and laughed, then realized that it wasn't a joke. It was then that he mentioned Mrs Anderson's hasty retreat from the drawing room the other evening, but when he'd gone into the drawing room, he'd seen nothing.

It was just at that very moment that the rocking chair plunged forward as if someone sat down in it and then it began to rock – it alarmed them all. Rick stood up abruptly with a gasp, his mouth stayed open, he felt the hairs on the back of his neck stand up, and his big brown eyes were wide with alarm. Both Julie and Alan looked at each other with a slight grin.

"I can't believe it!" said Rick, looking at Alan in amazement, "I know you said there was something in this room, Mrs Anderson, but I didn't really believe it." He looked at the window, "It's the draught, or the fan. Isn't it?" He frowned as his voice rose with uncertainty

Alan raised his eyebrows, "No, Rick, it's not the draught, it's Honeybeck. Can you smell the cigar smoke?"

"Yeah!" Rick stood trance-like, looking deep into the polished wood as the chair rocked gently back and forth then nodded to Alan, "Yeah." His brown eyes showing wide and white with alarm.

Alan looked keenly at Rick, "Please don't tell the staff about this or they might leave, and Mrs Anderson can't live in a place this size on her own."

"No, Sir!" Rick suddenly came back to life, "No, Sir, I understand, I won't say anything." Still staring at the rocking chair he tried to imagine a pirate sitting there, but the chair was empty and still rocking – it was eerie.

Alan suggested they go into the library, they left the chair rocking. "I knew there was a cave on this land," Rick went on as they came into the hallway, "do you think Honeybeck's treasure is down there in the cave?"

"Dunno, it was really too dark to see with just a torch, but this might be some of it," Alan showed him a few silver coins.

"WOW!" Rick was amazed picking up a coin, "Is this *really* pirates' treasure? Is it worth a fortune?"

"Hmm, not sure," Alan smiled, raising his eyebrows, "they are certainly old coins, I suppose they must be of some value. There's still a few more down there, they're in a clay jar and…" he dipped his chin and raised his eyebrows high, "They are guarded by a skeleton!"

"A *skeleton?*" Rick's brown eyes opened wide, "who is it – HONEYBECK?" His voice rose with great surprise.

"Dunno! He didn't say," Alan joked. "Can't see much, what we really needed was more light."

CHAPTER SIX

It was Saturday morning, a week had gone by and Alan was not at the office. Rick had got a new ladder and he'd also got a couple of bright lanterns. And they had agreed to explore the cave further.

Julie was sitting by the pool when Alan arrived, they had a cup of coffee together, she said that she didn't want to go down into the cave again.

At mid-morning Alan and Rick descended the ladder. Alan wearing jeans this time, his knees still sore from the last week's little episode.

Rick had told the staff that he would be out for the morning, he didn't say where, and they were only to phone him if it was an emergency. He had told old Gibbons who this morning was working over the other side of the garden, never to go into the barn again; it was too risky it might collapse on him – it wasn't true, after all it had stood storm damage over hundreds of years, but the old man was grateful for the warning, and knowing that the floor was unsafe he asked what was down there. Rick told him – nothing– it had been a cold storage room before they had fridges. It could also have been true.

Rick was amazed at the size of the cave, and also at the drawings on the wall of men with bows and arrows, and there were animals that looked like donkeys and dogs. Then Alan shone the light behind the ladder and showed him the skeleton, now with the brightness of the light it was an even more gruesome sight. Rick was a little shocked, and intrigued to see it sitting up against the wall with its knees up, "I suppose it's a man." He glanced curiously at Alan, who frowned, he hadn't thought of that, he just grimaced. The right thigh bone was lying in the front where Alan had left it. Alan inclined his head with a grin, "Good job Julie picked this up in the dark, she thought it was a stick," he chuckled, "and it was a wonder that the whole thing didn't collapse, if it had moved… Well…! Ha Ha." They chuckled together, their voices getting louder and echoing in the hollowness. "It's not a very nice thought though, holding someone's bones, is it, it made me cringe a bit," said Alan.

On closer inspection now with the bright light they could see that there was a small piece of rag at the side of the skeleton and they supposed that it had once been a shirt, and the leg still had a small fragment of cotton attached to the right thigh bone. There was a wide strip of leather on the stone floor and a rusty buckle; nearby the grey clay jar was tipped on its side between the legs near the ankles, and the hand that had fallen earlier when Alan had touched the jar looked eerier, and seemed to be guarding the silver like a great white hairless tarantula – it sent a chill down the spine. "Wonder who he was?" said Alan.

"Honeybeck?" Rick raised his brow, "protecting his treasure?"

"Could be," Alan arched his eyebrows, "but you said he died in the house, we read that he died on the patio of a sword wound, the staff surely would have buried him, wouldn't they?"

"Yeah?" Rick nodded. "Should think so. And, whoever put this guy down here wouldn't have left the silver would they?"

"Hmm, that's what I said," Alan nodded. "Maybe he wasn't dead when he came down here, maybe he got stuck here and couldn't get out and found the trapdoor closed like we did."

"Yeah," Rick nodded thoughtfully, "but someone must have locked the door to the barn, there's no key. I have a whole bunch of keys, I tried them all when I was here with the surveyor, before you came, but nothing fits."

"There's another cave through there," said Alan, walking towards the passageway. Whether a rock fall had caused it, or whether it had been manmade it was hard to say. Rick followed him into the other cave – it was wider than the first cave, the ashes of the fire showed up in the bright light, a bit spread now where Alan had caught his foot in the dark, and there were half burned pieces of wood, and bones obviously animal bones, probably the remains of an ancient Amerindian meal. He pointed up to the opening letting in a little light, "That's where I made the phone call to you, couldn't get a signal the other end – there's no barn over this bit as you can see."

"I wonder why a barn was built over a cave," said Rick, looking at more drawings on the wall of men with weapons, spears and knives – one had speared a pig, and there were dead chickens. On the opposite wall was a drawing of women with babies in arms and older children, and there was a boat, and nets with fish in it.

Suddenly there came a loud bang! They both looked up, "What was THAT!" Rick was startled.

"The trapdoor closed again," said Alan, "I hope it hasn't locked again."

"It can't possibly close on its own." Rick looked surprised.

"That's what I thought," Alan lifted his eyes with a nod, "but it can, and it does. What I can't figure out *is*, if someone shut it last time, *or*, if it was ghostly activity?'"

"Ghostly activity?" Rick rolled his eyes, then quickly said, "what's that!" Then, looking towards the passageway they both held their breath as a white mist swirled and appeared in the entrance of the arch. "FIRE!" Rick exclaimed in alarm.

Then he was stunned as it began to form into the shape of a human being, and even more unnerving was the gruff chuckle. He turned quickly to Alan, who of course was alarmed but he *had* seen it and heard it all before. And then it began to fade. "Wh-wh-what was THAT?" Rick pointed a finger turning to Alan.

"Ghostly activity?" Alan grinned.

Rick was stunned, *"Was that Honeybeck?"* his voice quivered. *"A ghost?"* He couldn't believe it!

"Dunno," Alan inclined his head, "could be the ghost of that poor devil out there, and I don't think *that's* Honeybeck! Although we heard the same chuckle before. It happened last week and now I'm sure the trapdoor *is* ghostly activity. Eerie, isn't it?"

"Y-yeah, yeah! What!" He frowned, "was it Honeybeck then that closed the trapdoor?"

"Well, dunno for sure, but I can't see how it can possibly close on its own. And why would anyone come in, and close it anyway?"

"Do you think we should called police?"

"No, I'm sure they can't help," Alan shook his head and wrinkled his nose, "I think we should contact an archaeologist to take a look at that skeleton don't you?"

"Yeah! Good idea," Rick nodded with a grimace, "I'll try and find someone. That's if we ever get out."

Alan lifted the lantern higher, "It's all clear, let's get go."

Rick cringed as he passed through the arch where the ghostly mist had been just minutes before, he felt nothing, there *was* nothing, but the thought was eerie and made him shiver. Back now in the first cave, they reached the ladder; Rick went up quickly, still having the ghostly image in his mind and he was anxious to get out. He pushed hard at the trapdoor, then gave it a really hard punch upwards, several times, "It's stuck," he called down to Alan. He tried putting his hand through the gap in the boards as Alan had done, before. "I can feel the bolt but I can't move it."

"Yeah I know, I couldn't move it either," Alan called up.

"Can't budge it." He gave it a really hard punch up, then winced and shook his hand with the pain, but it had lifted and inch or so, "I think I've got it." He gave it more hard punching with the flat of his hand, the strength coming from his powerful shoulder, and the screws in the bolt squeaked and loosened. He punched it hard again and it sprang open a few inches, "I got it!" One more punch and he flipped the trapdoor back with a loud crash. A little light came in from the broken floor boards, and dust poured down on them both.

"Hey! Come back down," Alan called, "come and look at this."

The light from above and the lantern light lit up a dark corner and near the skeleton there were two wooden boxes, Alan had not seen them in the dim light before and he was already investigating when Rick came down. There were also dusty grey clay flagons of wine in an open broken wooden box, and several empty flagons on the floor. Alan picked one up out of the box by the handle, "I bet this is Spanish wine," he opened it and sniffed into the narrow neck, "and I bet it's gone off by now," he poured a little drop into his left hand – it was brown and watery and bits of black sediment floated in his palm. He stood the flagon up against the wall and could see that the wine was no good but just had to taste it anyway – he dipped his finger in, and put it to his tongue, pulling a terrible face and wrinkling his nose with distaste, "Yeah! Ha, ha, it's OFF!"

"There's a date on here," said Rick, bending down to get a closer look at the box, "16 something, looks like... 1668 or 63, or could be 1560 something," he rubbed his hand over the scratched date, "anyway, it's been here a dammed long time." He put his toe to one of the empty flagons, "I should think this poor guy probably survived on the stuff for a few days wouldn't you?"

"Yeah maybe it was off then and that's what killed him. There's another box here," said Alan, he thought it was more wine and pulled at the broken lid, "HEY! Take a look at THIS!" He was waving a flintlock pistol; Rick looked up and stood up, in the light the handle was engraved with flowers and vines. Alan turned it over, "It's ivory isn't it? And is this the handle or is it the butt?"

"I don't know," Rick grimaced and shook his head, "I don't much about guns." He went back to the box and pulled out a rusty sword. "Look at THIS!"

Alan turned, weighing the gun in his hand. "It's quite heavy, feel the weight," he handed it to Rick and took the sword. Rick still bending down, picked up a wooden-handled knife.

Alan thrust his arm out charging the sword into the darkness, "This thing is heavy too, you'd have to be pretty strong to handle one of these." He weighed it in his hand, as he had done with the pistol.

"You know," Rick said, "I think, this guy came down here to steal the silver, and got caught at it, and probably didn't have time to get to his weapons. Although I don't know why they would be in a box do you? Somebody must have put them there after they had a fight down here?"

"No," Alan shook his head, "they didn't fight down here, and this guy didn't get caught with his hand in the cookie jar." He shook his head, "No one would have killed him and left him with a jar of silver would they? He was probably chucked down here, *after the fight*, DEAD! Or, left for dead! BUT, probably barely alive, then found the silver, and just sat down and died of starvation."

"Yeah, guess you're right, and nobody checked on him and he just died holding a fortune. Wonder how much it's worth?"

Alan inclined his head, "Dunno," he bent to scoop up a few more of the silver coins leaving what he couldn't reach, he didn't want to knock the skeleton over. "Come on, let's get out of here."

"Well what about the rest of the silver and the weapons?" said Rick.

"Leave it," Alan grimaced, "let's get some archaeology guys down here – they can sort it, they like to see it as it is." They mounted the ladder, coming out into bright sunlight with the shafts streaming through the roof of the barn. Rick closed the trapdoor and after being down in the dark for so long they both quickly put on their sunglasses. Then, Alan went to the pool to tell Julie what they'd found, and Rick went back to the office.

CHAPTER SEVEN

It was Wednesday, 10.30 in the morning, Julie left Rick in charge of showing the two archaeologists the cave. "They were most interested," so Rick had told Mrs Anderson after they had gone, "they took photographs of the drawings and also the skeleton and the weapons," said Rick, "then after a while they dismantled the skeleton and brought it up in a crate; they'll probably put it together again as it was down there. They also took the silver, the box of wine and the arms, which you haven't even seen yet, but they said they would let us know within the week."

Julie nodded, she was interested, but the thought of that hideous skeleton still made her cringe, "Did you tell them about the ghost of Honeybeck?"

"No," said Rick, "I didn't know whether to or not."

"Mmm," she nodded, "I wonder if we should get the Ghostbusters in?"

"I don't know if there is anyone on the island," said Rick, "but I'll check."

"Yes, check but don't call anyone yet, I'll have a word with Alan first."

"OK."

A whole ten days had gone by when Julie got a phone call from Jackson Verity an American doctor of archaeology from Charleston South Carolina, he said that he had been working here in Barbados for two years. She made arrangements to meet him at the college. Rick drove her, and she asked him to come in with her.

Jackson Verity was a big-built man and stood over six feet tall. He was about fifty years old, very upright with a military stance, his deep reddish suntanned skin a contrast to the shock of thick pure white straight hair; he had a keen forehead, with bright piercing china blue eyes behind square rimless specs which suited his broad face and strong chin. He wore a pale blue short-sleeved open-neck shirt and grey pants, giving him a very strong clean-cut appearance. He had a deep southern drawl as he bent his head politely, giving Julie a genuine smile and a warm firm handshake. She then introduced Rick Holland, her house manager.

They walked with him down to the laboratory, and to a long narrow room where there were several white-coated scientists working. He showed them into a side room, and introduced them to Travis Braithwaite. A very dark-skinned Barbadian man in his forties, he had lived here in Barbados all his life, and Merrill Harper a bone specialist, also a Bajan young woman aged about thirty with a very light brown skin.

The skeleton bones were sitting on a table and propped up against a board, as Julie had seen in it the cave but in the full light it was still a hideous sight. Merrill said that there was no doubt about the DNA – it was a man of African descent aged in his early twenties. "And I would say he's been dead for maybe two hundred years or more."

"Oh, not Honeybeck or Thurgold then – they were both English weren't they?" She turned enquiringly to Rick.

"How did he die?" Rick asked, "did he get locked in and just sit there and starved to death?"

"Well," Jackson inclined his head, "Possibly, but we think he was probably whipped, but we're not sure." He nodded at Merrill who carried on.

"Well," she pursed her lips, "there's a lot of broken bones, the contusions are significant with that of a severe whipping. You can see here," she pointed out, "these jagged marks on the edge of the bones, I would think is where he was whipped; the bones have been lacerated, in fact there is a minute fragment of something that *could be leather*, probably from a whip," she looked at Travis, he nodded in agreement and she went on, "I would think he was nearly stripped of all his flesh and then thrown down into the cave and left for dead. He has a broken back and a broken shin bone, but he was possibly still barely alive; also this rib bone looks like a knife – or possibly a sword – would have caused this chipped hole that is nearly through the bone, but that could have been an earlier wound, I can't tell. There was also a lot of dried blood in the cave around the body."

"We did find a rusty knife," said Julie. "It fell down from somewhere when Alan touched the clay jar," she looked at Rick

"From the photograph," Merrill inclined her head, "he looks as if he is holding a pot of coins. From this I would think that he must have sat himself up against the wall for support, but I can't imagine how he could possibly have done that, with so many broken bones, especially a broken back, he must have been a very strong man."

"But what *we did find*," Travis cut in with a smile, "are these," he held out his hand, with a sapphire and an emerald ring.

Julie looked at Rick, and they both looked at Travis and Jackson, in amazement. "A sapphire, and an emerald?" Julie raised her eyebrows.

Jackson nodded, "Yeah! We found them under the body, I would think he'd swallowed them, maybe that was the reason for the whipping." There was a long pause while Julie and Rick thought it over.

"What about the silver coin," said Rick, "is it very valuable?"

"Yes very valuable," said Jackson, "and it's not all silver, there are a few golden doubloons there too." He took a box from a side table and showed them to Rick and Julie, "These are quite rare, and this clay pot is extremely old, I should say about a thousand years."

"Wow!" Rick was really taken aback, "A thousand years? Must have been made by the Arawak." He looked at Julie.

Jackson nodded, "Quite possibly was. It should be in a museum."

"What even though it's cracked?" Julie looked surprised.

"Well, yes," Jackson smiled. "If I could keep it for a week or two, I could get it valued for you and possibly restored."

Julie looked at Rick, "Is it mine then?"

"Well yes it was on your land," Jackson smiled.

Julie looked at Rick, "I think we've found Honeybeck's treasure."

"You mean Desmond Honeybeck! The pirate?" said Travis.

"Yes he built my house," Julie smiled, "you know of him then?"

Travis nodded, "Yes, he's a well-known name on the island, he terrorized the settlers and stole everything. They say there is a treasure, it's never been found, at least not to my knowledge. I should like to come and look at your house sometime."

"Yes of course," Julie smiled, "make some arrangements with Rick." Travis nodded to Rick with a smile.

Jackson walked out with them to where they had parked the car, and said that he would be in touch. They thanked him and said their goodbyes and Rick drove back to the Silver Lady, he parked the car and then went back to his office at the side of the house while Julie went up to her room to change into a bikini and a wrap. Then taking her bag with suntan cream, a book, and the mobile phone and laptop, she made her way down to the pool. She was excited to tell Alan about meeting Jackson Verity, but when she phoned his secretary, Rebecca said that he was in a meeting; they were to have dinner in a restaurant that night, so she would have a lot to tell him then.

She was lying under the umbrella, the book open. Since losing Gavin she hadn't been able to concentrate on much, her mind kept going back to that awful day. *She could still hear Suzie's scream as she lost her grip, and their hands slipped from each other* she rubbed her fingers together still imagining the slippery grip, she closed her eyes trying to shut out the terrible scene of *Suzie sliding down the almost vertical deck and then the splash into the water, she could see now in her mind's eye the big black swell lifting and heaving and then clapping down on her, she waited but she didn't surface and they waves enclosed her forever, it all seemed to be happening in slow motion.* She shook her head it was all still so vivid, *it was my fault I should have hung on tighter*, she shook her head again trying to rid herself of the dreadful scene… *Gavin by then, was possibly already gone…* She shuddered at the thought, *what a bloody awful day it had been*, she felt the tears prick her eyes again and she tried to hold them back, she had already cried enough. She still wondered what she was going to do with her life, she loved it here, but should she go back to the UK? She would have to go back to her parents, because when she was going to live in Barbados she had let her flat go for a long-term rent. She had left the running of the beauty salon to Miranda, who had been in touch several times to let her know that things were going well but really again, she wasn't able to concentrate, and more or less just told Miranda to get on with it. She nodded; *she would go back some time.* But of course at the moment, she was still, in two minds; she was glad to have a friend in Alan Stone. Both still grieving, they got along well supporting each other, they knew very few people on the island. She knew from the way he talked that he missed Suzie very much, he was lonely, and they each knew how the other must be feeling, and they commiserated together; she missed Gavin more than she could say – *she missed his smile, his handsome face, his laughter, his loving and caring ways – she imagined now being enclosed in the warmth and strength of his arms,* and the tears were uncontrollable and running down her cheeks, and she grabbed blindly for the tissues, *she had never met anyone like him, and the heartache would never go away, she still looked out to the sea expecting him to suddenly be there waving to her with that wonderful smile, she could hear his voice calling her and for a moment it was all so real that she answered it. And yet she knew it was stupid and she must let go, but the images were bright in her mind. She knew it must be the same for Alan, but at least he did have a body, and know for sure that Suzie was gone. She, would be forever in the air waiting and wondering and yet never knowing…*

CHAPTER EIGHT

The funeral was quite small, Alan had flown the body home, and she and Alan had travelled back to the UK. There were a few relatives, Suzie's parents were devastated, and her mother had been quite ill since the day she was told of her daughter's death. Going back to the UK, Sir Gabriel and Lady Elizabeth had also arranged a church service for Gavin, and over a hundred people attended, including her parents and also Suzie's parents. It really was a week of sadness, both she and Alan relating the story of the catamaran disaster over and over again and hurting inside with every word. Then after two weeks she and Alan had met up at the airport and travelled back to Barbados, both thoroughly exhausted. But it had given Julie a chance to see Miranda at the salon, and also the opportunity to stay with her parents; they didn't want her to leave, but she said that she had got to get on with her life, and then it had been hard saying goodbye again.

Of course in her heart she knew that Gavin would never come back, but she couldn't rid herself of that hopeful waiting feeling, sort of expecting him to suddenly come in with a perfect explanation. She shook her head in despair, knowing that it was stupid thinking. Alan had tried to tell her to stop thinking and being hopeful so many times and he was right, she should put it out of her mind, it was never going to happen, *Gavin was GONE! Gone. Gone, out of her life, and she must start all over again.* She sniffed; but then, Alan had something to do, he was busy working, keeping his mind busy, but she had really nothing to occupy her time. *They thought they were coming to a small cottage and she was expecting to do the shopping and the cooking and the cleaning it would have kept her busy... But now, everywhere she looked she saw Gavin...* Then thinking back it had been such a wonderful surprise for them both just looking at the luxury here, of the Silver Lady, they couldn't believe it. And then Sir

Gabriel had phoned to say it was theirs. She'd had emails and phone calls from her mother asking how she was coping and also from Sir Gabriel and Elizabeth, and like her they would never get over the loss, of their son and *life would never be the same for any of them again…*

Her thoughts were interrupted by Charles bringing her a glass of ice cold lemonade, she quickly sniffed and perked up, not wanting him to see her crying, she sat up but kept her head down thanking him as he put it on to the side table and went away quietly. Her thoughts then went to Honeybeck. *I wonder what Gavin would have made of Honeybeck?* She never knew if he had believed in ghosts she hadn't thought much about it herself, and of course she never would know now what he would have thought. But thinking on it now, she did have something to occupy he mind. *Honeybeck's treasure*, she would concentrate on that, although it was probably all nonsense anyway, but it was keeping her mind busy and she would continue to look for it. *Fancy the silver coin and golden doubloons, she hadn't given a thought that they may be valuable, but then again, her mind was not really clear anyway.*

She'd had a letter from the lawyers, Briskers and Goodson, informing her of her good fortune left to her in her husband's will, *but what good was it without Gavin?* But then she already knew that Gavin had left her well provided for – they had gone through all that before the wedding, but of course neither of them knew it would all end so suddenly and so tragically, their plan was to sail along happily into old age… *Well don't all young couples entering into married bliss think it is going to last forever?* There she was again, thinking of what could have been, she must get it out of her mind… *That skeleton, that poor man the pain, the suffering he must have gone through, and the thought that he had just sat there and died and withered away she wondered for how long…*

At least Gavin wouldn't have suffered too much or too long, even though it was a terrible tragic thought and then in her mind's eye she could see and feel the terrible suffocation of the water closing over Gavin's head… But then of course she had felt it herself, but luckily she had managed to surface, and it could have happened to her had she not been thrown clear of the cat. The thoughts of that awful day came back, pictures clear in her mind, *the deep black swells, and the white splashes of the people struggling and screaming in the water, the woman and the child crying* she closed her eyes tight trying to shut out the awful scene, *but then, maybe they were back in the UK now and possibly, had lost her husband and a father*. She shook her head. The pictures were there again and so vivid, *the clinic waiting room was crowded with painful sniffing and crying and she could now recall the smell of damp clothing and wet bodies as the crowded cold air conditioned waiting room got warm as people piled in. Then seeing Alan Stone, the first face that she recognized, it was such a relief, he had given her his hand and they had clung together*. She closed her eyes tight again, trying to get rid of the awful scene... The skeleton came to mind again, *fancy just sitting there in the dark and in pain, a stone's throw from the house, he must have shouted, and no one came, and with a pot full of silver at his fingertips probably the most money he had ever seen in his life...* She wondered if he might have just died of fright after seeing or hearing the ghost of Honeybeck. The Turners obviously had not been down into the cave for years, if they had someone would surely have taken the silver coins and surely someone would have buried the poor devil. Perhaps the barn had been locked up and the key thrown away. Perhaps the Turners were away, but there would have been staff in the house. Wouldn't there? Someone must have missed him? Not unless he was a thief that had broken in, stolen the coins and couldn't get out, well he obviously couldn't get out, could he?' No, wait a minute, Jackson and his team said he was whipped to death! But he obviously wasn't *dead! Was he?*

She frowned and shook her head gently, trying to get it straight in her mind. She finished her lemonade, and sat wondering, *was that silver Honeybeck's treasure? Surly there would be more?* And then her thoughts went on to the Turners, *had they found the treasure? They were said to be a very rich family, maybe it was the treasure that had made them rich*. She wondered, *if they had experienced any of the ghostly activity, maybe that's why they left?*

The sun was hot and she was feeling sleepy, lazing here doing nothing just thinking, her mind going around and around in circles. She stood up and stretched, putting her wrap around her and slipping into her sandals. Still deep in thought, she made her way up the coral stone steps, a little walk would do her good she couldn't just lie there all day. Walking towards the gazebo, she stopped in front of the silver lady looking into the staring blue eyes, she whispered, "What *is* your secret, Madam?"

"What?" came a quick reply, "what did yer say, Mistress?"

Julie turned quickly, old Gibbons was there with a broom in his hand, "Oh, she said, "I was just asking the lady here what her secret is – I'm sure she holds some secret."

"Yeah, bet she could tell a few tales, eh? Yeah, a few 'unnndred yeeears she bin 'ere she 'as, Mam. Long before my time."

"Were you working here, Mr Gibbons, when the Turner family lived here?"

"Yeah, Mistress," he grinned widely, "they were 'ere since seventeenth century – father to son, father to son – and so on. They were 'ere right up to nineteen 'nnundred an' some'at. I worked for old Alfred then, I started at thirteen, 'ee was a character 'ee was, maaan in charge if the garden then, 'ee were. Young Denny," he pointed his thumb back over his shoulder, "'ee's bin 'ere about a yeeer," he inclined his head to the side where Denny Bell could be heard clipping with shears somewhere unseen through the bushes, "and it was Mr James Turner, when I first come 'ere but then he died shortly afterwards he didn't have a son so Mr Ronald his brother took over. They 'ad four kids, and when Mr Ronald died 'is son Mr Edward took over. Mr Edward was the last Turner, 'ee 'ad four kids too, all educated at university you know, but a bit wild, all the Turners were," he sort of winked. There was a pause. "Mr Edward was a scholar, wrote books... And then there was Mr Cedric, 'ees son, and his wife Emily, but they didn't stay long, she wanted her kids to be born in England..." He sort of paused as if thinking about it, "and Mr Edward stayed on 'ere. Course he eventually died... long time ago though."

Julie nodded thoughtfully, looking at the figurehead. "Not very glamorous is she?" she glanced at him with a smile.

"No," Gibbons grinned, twitching his nose.

"She gives me the creeps, I'm thinking of getting rid of her."

"Oh! NO! Mistress! NO!" Old Gibbons was alarmed, his brown eyes were white with fear, "She bin 'ere over three 'nnundred yeeeears. NO! Bad omen. Mistress. LEAVE 'ER…"

"Oh!" Julie glanced at him, a little startled, "I never thought of that, I never thought about it being unlucky, but she does give the garden an eerie feeling doesn't she? Especially at night."

"Mmm," Gibbons grimaced, he didn't comment but his thick lips bunched tightly together and he nodded, pulling a face thoughtfully.

"Do you think she holds the key to the treasure, I expect you've heard all the stories about Captain Honeybeck and the treasure haven't you?" She turned to Gibbons again.

"Oh yeah!" He had a slight grin and scratched the back of his neck, "Oh yeah!" He flashed yellowing broken teeth. There was a pause… "But I ain't dug nothin' up yet!" He chuckled.

Julie smiled, then taking a deep breath, "Well I mustn't keep you. I expect you are busy, Mr Gibbons, just keep digging." They chucked together and she moved to go. He bowed his head, "Yes, Mistress," and went away into the trees, his broom over his shoulder, and a wide grin on his old and wrinkled face.

Julie was still standing in front of the lady. *A bad omen? She had never thought about the lady being lucky or unlucky, but then, dismissed the thought of ever dispensing with her. Just in case. But she WAS eerie, especially glowing at night. But she felt that she held the key to the treasure. But then the Turners must have already thought about that, and even the bank people that had occupied the house over the years. It wasn't that she needed to find the treasure, it was just the thought of finding it! It would be so exiting. After all, how many people find buried treasure, not many, and who has ever found a pirate's treasure? Captain's Kid's treasure, just for instance, could be anywhere on the island. It brought thoughts of a chest brimming with gold cups and plates ruby necklaces and pearls, just like you see in children's books.* She wrung her hands together *wondering if pirate treasure was really like that? Whoever found a pirate's treasure anyway, did pirates really bury treasure? Did Captain Kidd, really bury treasure, or Black Beard or Henry Morgan, and did Honeybeck's treasure really exist? It might have done, if of course the Turner family had not already found it! They were said to be a very rich family? But then, had they found a treasure? Someone would have known surely? Especially pirates, buried treasure...* It conjured up diamonds and pearls again, she'd seen the film *Pirates of the Caribbean.* She smiled to herself... "Well!" She clapped her hand quietly together, *Honeybeck WAS a pirate of the Caribbean... wasn't he? And it was all fairy tales anyway. IF! Captain Kidd had buried a treasure here in Barbados, it had never been found even with all the digging and building of houses and hotels, and the tourists came for the sun and the sea – no one has time to dig up the hard dry ground looking for buried treasure, but whenever it's mentioned it gets people thinking and wondering and it could still be anywhere on the island. But Honeybeck's treasure? Well, that's a different thing, IF, it still exists? It could be right here in this garden...* "But where?" She clapped her hands again quietly to her lips and shook her head, then she got to thinking about the Turner family, a wild bunch old Gibbons had said, and Mr Edward wrote books! Then, there was probably something of their lives in the library seeing that they had lived here for generations there must be something. And maybe, a clue to the treasure?

She moved thoughtfully away from the lady, and walked slowly across the garden passing the gazebo. The French doors to library were wide open as usual, as were those of the drawing room; the maids opened them every morning to let the air in, when closed the old antiques gave off a musty smell. She entered the library and stood for a minute or two, and then walked around the room slowly looking at the bookshelves – there was a multi choice from floor to ceiling, they were in alphabetical order by author, but what was she looking for? TURNER, it would be on the other side of the room. She crossed the room, but nothing seemed to stand out. She walked back and forth, and then switched on the ceiling fan and sat down in one of the winged armchairs and sighed, exhausted by the heat of the day, *there must be something here?* Her elbows on the chair arms, her hands like a steeple touching her lips, and now feeling the coolness of the ceiling fan, her eyes scanned the books on the right side of the room thinking. *What were the Turners like, what kind of a family were they? Wild, according to old Gibbons. There were oil paintings out there lining the walls in the hall, maybe they were some of the Turners, they had to be after being here for so long but there were no names.* She sat scanning the books thoughtfully, and then right on the bottom shelf she saw a black cover, and a small hand-printed sticker that said Edward Turner. She got up and lifted it – it was quite a large volume and heavy, she took it to the desk, the front cover was hard, the name Edward Turner was handwritten on a torn scrap of card and stuck on the front. When she opened it the cover fell off and she found it was not bound, but just a stack of loose handwritten pages, all numbered from 1 to 460 where she noticed that it stopped in mid-sentence, she supposed that Edward Turner was interrupted… She turned the volume round and sat down in the desk chair, the hard black cover obviously belonged to something else. The first page of the beautifully handwritten script was headed:

THE FAMILY. By EDWARD TURNER.

She began to read:

The information that I am about to write, I have acquired from family members throughout the ages, family memorabilia from old documents, love letters, diaries and notebooks of generations of distant relatives left in old cupboards and drawers or hidden here in the house and garden, I have found it interestingly profound so far and I may write in more, as information comes into my possession. It was in the sixteenth to seventeenth century that Great-Great Grandfather, Sir George Turner a politician, and his wife Great-Great Grandmother Lady Louisa, and their three children Andrew, Emily and Mary sailed one foggy November morning from England's cold and wintery shores, to the warmth of the Caribbean. The journey had been long and hazardous so it's been told through the ages by family members. George had come to the warmer climate for his health. Sir George had been born of very wealthy parentage in Scotland, but had lived in London England for many years, and although he looked a robust man of strong stature he had suffered all his life with a weak chest in the cold damp and English climate, in winters on two occasions he almost died. He had been into politics for years and the opportunity came for him to take up a post in the British House of Assembly here on the island of Barbados. The voyage had taken weeks owing to stormy weather and hazardous Atlantic sea and they had all been violently seasick, but now weeks of warm sea air and the warmth of the Caribbean had expanded George's lungs and for the first time in his life he felt well. The island was populated mostly with English settlers. Barbados lies upwards of the main island arc, it is hard to attack from the sea, and has never been caught up in the colonial wars, there is no Dutch, French or Spanish influence to speak of in the language. The island was found by a Captain Henry Powell when his ship *The Olive Blossom* had been blown way off course in a violent tropical storm, the ship obviously damaged, he came ashore for fresh water. He found the island uninhabited, and claimed the island in the name of King James 1st of England, by sending some of his crew ashore, who carved on a fustic tree, 'this island is claimed by King James 1st of England in the year of our Lord, 1625'.

Sir George and Lady Louisa Turner moved in to the charming Silver Lady Cottage, that had been empty for several years. The house had been built by an Englishman, Captain Desmond Honeybeck, who had made his fortune by pirating on the high seas, and had been killed in a duel. The house was large and far from the suggestion of an English cottage, it was fully furnished with some priceless antiques and the bank had kept a few staff on to maintain it; the sugar crop which was part of the twenty acre estate, was still worked by slave labour.

It seemed that Sir George Turner was an ancestor of Oswald Turner, who had been the Boatswain on the ship *The Silver Lady*. And when Captain Honeybeck had died from a sword wound, the servants in the whole house were in confusion, especially when the ghost of Captain Honeybeck had been seen on the stairs and in the drawing room, it was then that Oswald Turner had taken charge with an iron hand but little else is known of him.

Sir George had soon employed a household staff of thirty, and many slaves had been brought in from West Africa to maintain the sugar crop that was expanding. Although having a privileged upbringing, George had, at a young age, made his own fortune in banking in London, this before he had gone into politics. And his son Andrew, who is some distant cousin of mine, at the age of twenty-four also went into banking, and the girls Mary and Emily, still in their teens had a private English governess.

The sugar plantation that was just a few acres when they first arrived grew to many acres and took many West African slaves to maintain it and eventually the house was left to Andrew, and with each generation the sugar crop has prospered.

The cane was harvested, and...

Julie thumbed through the pages, not wanting to read about sugar cane harvesting. There were no photographs, and then picking pages at random, she realized that Edward Turner was most probably an author, and had intended to get this story published. There seemed to be no date, but from his writing she thought it to have been written somewhere around the late seventeenth to eighteenth century.

There were paragraphs on several of the Turners, and on turning the pages she chose to read about Thomas Turner. Edward described Thomas as:

...a tall, strong and stately man, with long dark hair tied back with ribbon, and ruggedly handsome; he wore fine frock coats of silk brocade with golden buttons or velvet, in midnight blue or dark green, and matching breeches and polished knee boots with silver buckles. At his throat a lace cravat, and lace cuffs at his wrists. He was a bachelor, who had taken over the house and the family fortune somewhere around the mid-sixteenth century. Thomas was a good master but he stood no nonsense from his slaves, he ran the house with strict military precision. He enlarged the cane fields and marched through the slave quarters every morning at dawn when it was cooler and had the overseers have the slaves lined up for inspection outside their small chattel houses, before going to work in the fields. To my knowledge, I believe there were maybe four or six overseers, each on charge of so many acres.

Thomas was never seen without a whip in his right hand which he slapped against his black highly-polished leather boot menacingly, but rarely had he to use the whip, not one would dare to cross him, he ran his slaves like an army and looked after them well, with good food and time off at midday, the hottest part of the afternoon – he needed them well and fit for work this is how the fields prospered. He allowed them time off to do their own bidding to walk free to the village one day in a month, only two at a time, but if anyone of them did not return, the whole family would be flogged, from the father to the smallest child, it had only happened once, when a child aged 3 had died instantly after just one lash.

Thomas's downfall was drinking and gambling, he lost a lot of money playing cards with his wealthy friends, mostly sugar plantation owners like himself. He had then married Jane Lenard, an American widow; she had come to Barbados with her husband an American millionaire who traded in sugar cane, and molasses; they had three sons. They had rented a small house, for some long weeks, but while in Barbados her husband Francis Lenard fell ill and died of a fever. Jane was then left with three sons – James 10, Michael 8, and Philip 6. She was desperate to get back to California, but while waiting almost a year for a ship, she had met Thomas Turner at a house party. It had been a whirlwind affair, she needing comfort, and he seeing her as an attractive young woman but no great beauty, but her *money*, to him, was far more important than her looks. Although he *was* a reasonably well-to-do man, he squandered a lot of his money on gambling at cards and cock fights or dog fights and regularly spent lavishly on loose women, and now, was virtually in ruin. He was generous to Jane and had driven her in his carriage to many beautiful spots on the island. He had taken her sailing on the sea in a large yacht owned by a friend but he had lied, saying that it was his own, and he had also showered her with flowers and gifts of jewellery and hand-painted silken fans, and fine fabric of silk and lace from the Orient for her gowns that he purchased from incoming ships. He looked after her children like a father, but it was all show and done to impress her. He was also into stealing. She thinking he was a rich gentleman, they had married, but she soon found that her nights were lonely – he spent a lot of his time with his friends drinking and gambling, he was also a womanizer and had many affairs, he also had great charm that people, mostly women, found irresistible. He stole from these women after he had left them sleeping peacefully in their own beds, and he lied to his wife about business meetings that kept him out late. He had said that the plantation was not doing so well, and Jane innocently supplied him with more funds. She had heard snippets of conversation at house parties and seen women fluttering their eyes over fans, but dismissed it as nonsense knowing that Thomas was a handsome man with a charming manner and all women were attracted to him. But, what she didn't know was the other side of him – beneath all the charm and flattery, he was a compulsive gambler, a cheat, a trickster, a liar and ruthless in his business undertakings. He also had a six-year-old son, by a West Indian slave girl named Katie who worked in the house; the affair still went on and of course it was a secret that Jane knew nothing about. Anxious to keep it quiet Thomas had promised to marry the girl Katie, but really he had no intention of ever doing so, she was beautiful, but was there only for his amusement when he returned from his drunken nights out with his friends or rich women. Then of course when he had married Jane Lenard the girl Katie was furious, and she had threatened to expose him as the father of her son Joseph.

To keep Katie quiet, of course he supplied her with money, Jane's *money*... And promised to buy her a small house where he could still visit her, saying that he would always love her and be there for her. He also promised to give the boy Joseph the good education, but no one was to know his benefactor, and she agreed to say nothing, not knowing that his loving promises in the night were worthless. By day she still went quietly about her duties in the house.

CHAPTER NINE

Thomas, at Jane's request, had engaged a governess for her three boys.

Sarah Kilbride was Irish, she had left Ireland and come to Barbados with her family when she was twelve. She was now twenty-eight, unmarried and was proving to be a good teacher. She was fair-haired with delicate fair skin and big baby blue eyes, and Thomas found her Irish lilt a joy to his ears. She was a quiet well bred girl but she soon, like all women, had succumbed to his polite and roguish charms, and enjoyed the warm nights when they secretly met in the barn and rolled in the hay. He telling her how beautiful she was and that his wife didn't understand him and that one day soon he was thinking of divorce and they could be together always, with promises of marriage and she would be mistress of the house and this would be all hers – but again it was all just talk, he couldn't afford to divorce Jane.

The boys had lessons in the garden, they were all doing well. Jane looked from the window with a smile seeing her sons sitting under the mahogany trees listening to Sarah Kilbride who was there every morning at seven o'clock when the day was still cool. She found Sarah to be a very pleasant young woman, and they chatted regularly about her sons.

Then Jane saw a young native boy close by, hiding in the trees and listening. She had seen him there on several occasions – he had obviously come from the slave quarters. It was one morning, when Jane was there in the garden that she saw the boy's mother, Katie, come to scold him and take him away. But Jane had called to her and insisted that the boy stay, saying that he was welcome and it was good that he wanted to learn.

Katie was alarmed at the mistress's suggestion that her son, a slave, should join the class, and scowled at Jane's generosity;

inside she hated her for taking her man – why had Thomas so suddenly married her? But then on second thoughts it occurred to her that it would be a good thing for Joseph to learn and she accepted Jane's generous offer. Thomas had promised faithfully to do something about the boy's education; he was still promising, but had so far done nothing... She herself had never had the opportunity to learn to read and write.

Sarah Kilbride was quite happy to take on another pupil, but the other three boys could already read and write having been to school in America, and so with Joseph she had to start right from the beginning with A B C. Sarah found that Joseph was bright and he soon caught up. His mother, Katie, made him study in his free time from the cane fields, and egged him on anxiously every day.

Jane had found Katie to be a very pleasant young woman, on meeting sometimes while walking around the house and while the girl was cleaning or by chance in the garden. Jane engaged her in light and pleasant conversation about her son, and saying how well he was doing, and also apologizing for him having to go into the cane fields after lessons, but saying that it was the master's command, even though in her mind Jane didn't agree with slavery and thought it wrong for children of seven to have to work. But it was a way of life here on the island, and the cane field had to be maintained, and without these people where would they all be. But she was glad that Thomas did treat them well.

When Jane had commented on her son's progress, Katie had nodded but said nothing. In her heart she hated Jane and wanted revenge – Thomas had promised her marriage for years. She also felt that the Master's son should have privileges over his stepson's. But of course she couldn't say that to Jane even though she wanted to, but she was going to see that her SON, had the best in life, and one day she would tell this smarmy planter's wife that HER SON would be master here at the Silver Lady some day. And although Thomas still came to her at night she had noticed that things had not been the same since he married.

Katie had put Joseph to bed as usual in the little one-room wooden hut that Thomas had given her near the stable. Apart from the squalid and foul-smelling unsanitary slave quarters, it was barely furnished, with straw bedding on the floor, which she shared with Joseph late into the night after Thomas had gone back to his wife. There was also a small table, one wooden chair, a broken stool and a shelf with tin plates, and two tin cups hung on nails. The roof was so low, as were all the slave huts, that at five feet four inches tall she could barely stand up straight. There were no windows, glass was not available, and like most houses it faced west into the glare of the afternoon sun but away from the east trade winds. She cooked on an open fire outside the hut.

Thomas visited her every night, but not tonight, he had a business meeting. The hut was warm having had the sun on it all day, and she went to sit in an old armchair that was left outside. Here, it was much cooler, and she did this most evenings since having her son, which enabled him to sleep undisturbed, while half her nights were spent just next door in the stable with Master Thomas. She rested her head back on the chair looking up at the starry night sky, then closed her deep brown eyes with the long curling lashes with a feeling of peace and contentment. The slightest warm breeze disturbed the still warm night air, brushing her brown bronzed skin, and as usual the tropical night was alive with the sound of the tiny whistling tree frogs that were never seen in the daytime. There was a creaking and a rustle of leaves in the mahogany branches as the last bird fluttered its wings and settled for the night, and high above the tall coconut palms were silhouetted majestically still against the night sky with maybe the very slightest movement as a soft warm breeze disturbed the tranquil night air. Then the first quarter of a pale moon appeared from behind a fluffy grey cloud and then disappeared again, leaving her once again in the darkness under a magical starry sky. She breathed deeply, relaxing and taking in the smell of the grasses and the fragrant blossoms of the sweet scented frangipani, lady of the night, and jasmine, that hung heavily on the tropical night air and the softly shushing sound of the sea. She opened her eyes, looking up into the black velvet sky studded with a million stars, while the palest half moon came from an unseen cloud again and shone a silvery beam across the garden, turning the lawns and the trees to a soft shade of grey; it shimmered across the sea, sparkling like a million diamonds, and then disappeared again. Her hand went to her throat *imagining it just like the diamond necklace that Thomas had promised to buy her,* and she smiled at the thought, *seeing his handsome face in her mind's eye and feeling him so close.* His lovemaking made her feel so special, *his strong arms around her his hard body against hers, his roving hands over her flawless black silky skin and his tender kisses, his whispered promises, and his soft words of love whispered in her ear sent her into another world* with thoughts on becoming mistress of the house. He had promised her most sincerely that it would be soon, she would be a lady, and have servants of her own. She took a long deep breath, raising her shoulders to her ears and smiling in utter contentment. The night was warm *just like his caresses, and all so peaceful after a busy day cleaning in the house but she wouldn't have to do it for much longer, she imagined her days as a lady, probably sitting on the patio doing embroidery.* She looked down at her rough hands, *they would be smooth and clean and her nails would grow long and fine. And she would even keep that Sarah Kilbride on, she could teach her to read and write, she would have fine silk clothing, and feathers in her hair and smell of lavender and jasmine. She would have tea parties with other planters' wives, and they would discuss the events of the week, and their children and her son Joseph would be recognized.* And she smiled – *he would have a room of his own and would grow up a fine gentleman, and one day he would be Master of the Silver Lady Plantation.* She took a deep breath, *it was going to be OH, SO WONDERFUL. But she was to miss the romantic lovemaking and the strong arms of Thomas tonight, he having one of his many late business meetings. But missing one night would not matter, and maybe he would come even later after his meeting.* They had spent so many wonderful nights together in one of the empty stalls in the stable when he had come to her, way after midnight, and then she had more visions of when she was a lady – *their lovemaking would be in his large feather bed which she dreamed about every day as she made it up, smoothing her hand lovingly across the snow white pillow on his side of the bed where his head had lain just hours before.* She heaved a sigh, *she had never slept in a feather bed or lived or slept in a proper house, and it would be all so wonderful when the rain fell, it wouldn't drip through the roof, and when the wind blew it wouldn't rattle the door. Oh so wonderful. So very wonderful.* She shook her head gently and smiled dreamily into the night.

She raised her head and sat up quickly, disturbed by the fluttering wings of a bird that flew from one tree to the next, it was possibly disturbed by the sudden creak of the barn door a short distance away caught by the slight breeze that whispered across the garden. From where she sat the barn door could not be seen behind the trees but obviously it had been left open, and in the quietness the smallest sound carried it had happened before. Peering into the darkness, as the pale moon had disappeared again, she blinked as a grey shadow was moving across the lawn – it might have been an animal it was hard to tell, maybe a large stray dog or perhaps a mule got loose from the slave quarters, the darkness was deceiving. She stared hard into the shadows and the greyness of the night. All was still, then a sudden stronger breeze disturbed the leaves on the trees; she then thought that she must go and shut the barn door in case the dog, if it was a dog, wandered in there to sleep the night, and if the wind got stronger she knew the door would be creaking all night.

She got up, hesitating for a minute and listening, it might be a wild dog and it might attack her. She picked up a broom that was leaning against the wall of the hut and walked cautiously across the lawn towards the bushes and to the side of the barn door, ready with the broom in case the dog should pounce. All was quiet but for the hushed and almost silent step of her bare feet on the hard and dry ground. The barn door was open a few inches and as she came nearer whispered voices floated on the night air, she cocked her head frowning and listening hard, was it voices? She could be wrong, but it wasn't a dog, it could be just the sounds of the night the air the wind in the trees. But no! She frowned again, It was a woman's voice, probably one of the maids that she had seen crossing the lawn, possibly from the slave quarters. She was about to turn back, but then she was curious, and crept closer, frowning and listening harder – it definitely was a woman's voice. There were no windows in the barn and so, treading carefully and silently, she looked through the crack in the half open door – she could see nothing, and then the pale moon came out again and she stepped back in case she cast a shadow. Then a man's voice – it was a heavy toned whisper, it sounded like Thomas; she frowned, maybe he had come back early and had heard these two in there and gone to investigate. She opened the barn door a little more, very quietly, but the hinges squeaked and the man's voice came from the darkness, "Who's there?"

Katie, knowing it to be Thomas, opened the door wider and a very pale stream of moonlight shone in. They were lying in the hay, "THOMAS!" she exclaimed loudly in surprise.

"KATIE!" He stood up quickly, facing her in all his nakedness, alarmed! Shocked! "Katie?" Of course she was in shadow the moonlight behind her, but he recognized her voice.

The woman sat up attempting to cover herself... And as Katie charged forward with broom in hand, the woman started screaming.

CHAPTER TEN

The boys were waiting under the mahogany trees. Miss Kilbride was an hour late this morning, and James told his mother. So Jane told them to take out their books and read until Sarah Kilbride arrived.

That morning Joseph was late for lessons. He ran arriving breathlessly, saying that he was sorry to be late. James said that Miss Kilbride was late this morning too, and they had been told read until she arrived.

Jane had sent Henry the slave boy with a message, down to Miss Kilbride's house, in case she had been taken ill. The boy came back in fifteen minutes saying that he could not get an answer – there was no one there.

"Not even a maid?" Jane queried.

"No, Mistress, no one."

It was mid-morning when a messenger came at a full gallop down the drive, shunting the horse to a full stop and splaying the dry sandy gravel two feet up in front of it, the rider then jumping down running and almost tripping in his intense haste and calling urgently for the Master.

On hearing his name called, Thomas came quickly on to the patio to see what all the commotion was about. The messenger told him breathlessly that a woman's body had been found by fishermen – she had been drowned; it was Miss Kilbride, and could he come quickly to the beach.

"Well have you informed her family?" Thomas sounded quite surprised and anxious.

"No Sir, I not informed dem, dey all down dare on de beach now!" he replied anxiously, "dey is much confusion everyone crying, Sir, an' I tought you ought to know Masser Turner Sir, please come Master Turner! Please come quickly!"

Thomas told the man to wait; he went unhurriedly to the stable telling old Sam to saddle his horse, and then the two of them set off together at a trot.

The boys, seeing the messenger, all stood up and came a little closer; seeing the excitement, and overhearing the commotion, they were alarmed and surprised. Philip went to inform his mother that Miss Kilbride had been drowned, and Jane came quickly to the patio in all confusion, just in time to see her husband riding off with the messenger, feeling sure in her mind the boys must have been mistaken.

When Thomas arrived on the beach they tethered the horses to a bearded fig bush, and he and the messenger walked over the sand. He was alarmed to see a dozen or so people – it was a terrible sight; Mrs Kilbride, Sarah's mother, was on her knees and in floods of loud tears over her daughter's slim and naked body, the whole family sobbing and wailing in despair. The servants all confused, some crying into their aprons. The two fishermen alarmed and wide-eyed. She had been caught in their nets and dragged through the water, so one of them managed to tell Thomas in his distraught state, "We thought we had caught a big tuna, but then when we drew in the net…" The man splayed his hands then put them to his head in a hopeless gesture of sorrow and despair.

Thomas looked closely but then cringed turning away at the sad and horrible sight, the beautiful face was pale and bloated and distorted, the blue eyes wide and staring at the clear blue morning sky. He suggested that maybe she had been taking an early morning swim and had got entangled in their nets.

"NO! NO! Sir!" The fishermen shook their heads sadly and utterly bewildered. "There was no one out here, Master Thomas sir, when we come, it quiet every mornin', she been already under water when we threw out the nets."

"Never! NEVER!" Shamus Kilbride shook his head in despair at Thomas's very suggestion, "My daughter couldn't swim, and she would never had gone into the sea NAKED!" The man turned away, appalled at the suggestion, and quickly choked putting his hand to his streaming eyes.

The still anxious messenger was hovering, he grimaced, and turned away discreetly speaking from behind his hand, "Looks to me as if she be strangled, Masser Turner Sir."

Thomas turned to him in astonishment and drew in a deep breath; his mouth and eyes open wide, he didn't answer. Leaving the confusion on the beach, he mounted and rode back to the Silver Lady Cottage slowly, his head bowed, deep in thought.

Jane was very upset when Thomas told her the tragic news. The boys cried all day and Jane had tried to comfort them, they had grown so very fond of Miss Kilbride, and for days, they moped about sadly with nothing much to do, and then to keep their young minds busy, Jane began to give them lessons.

Thomas, being the employer, had agreed to pay for the funeral; it had all been very sad, losing a beautiful young woman so tragically. The small church was full, the Kilbrides having lived in Barbados for years had made many friends and the tragic news had passed quickly from village to village. Most had walked behind the coffin to the church, and Jane and Thomas had arrived at the last minute by carriage; the boys did not go.

It was five days afterwards that tragedy was to strike the Turner family again, when in the early hours of the morning a slave was banging on the front door. Alfred, the butler, was then urgently knocking on Master Thomas's bedroom door waking him from a deep sleep, which the man wished that he hadn't had to do, for the abuse that he got, and then telling the news that the body of Katie the housemaid had been found deep into the cane field at the back of the old barn.

It had appeared that the dog belonging to one of the sugar plantation's overseers had got loose, and the overseer Ben Watson was awakened by its frantic barking and jumping at the door; he got up and called to it but the dog turned in excited circles in front of him, begging him to follow, and so he had gone to investigate. All was quiet but for the shushing of the cane as he pushed forward, following the dog. At three in the morning the air was still and humid, and a bright full moon lit up the cane field like daylight. The dog, now barking furiously a short distance ahead of him, made him quicken his pace; he was shocked to see the naked body of Katie the housemaid now crawling with insects and maggots and a rat scampering away as the dog's continuous leaping and barking frightened it. Ben then grabbed the dog's collar and pulled him away. Revolted by the sight he was physically sick. He took off his belt and put it through the dog's collar and led him away back to his chattel house and locked the dog up. He then had two slugs of rum to steady himself of the horrible shock, and sat outside his house in the warm night air, breathing heavily, stunned and trying to compose himself. *Should he wake Master Thomas? Should he wait until the morning or not? It was urgent!* It was then that he heard a baby's cry coming from across the slave quarters and he saw Rufus the young father, a slave, trying to console the baby – he went to him and sent him to fetch Master Turner very urgently.

Losing the girls had worried Jane, two tragic deaths within a week of each other, it was thought that the girl Katie might have been strangled. And then there was unrest and a lot agitation among the slaves – they were like children, fearful, muttering and the men taking good care of their wives and daughters, all fearing that they could be next. Thomas, seeing their fear, cracked the whip which sharpened them up, and telling them that there was nothing to fear, only from his whip if they didn't get back to work. He also said that Katie had been attacked by a wild dog and he had since shot the dog and so there was no fear of it roaming through the plantation. After that the tension eased.

Jane now felt sorry for the boy Joseph, who was living in the little wooden hut alone. Why he had not told anyone that his mother was not there was a mystery, but she had heard this from her personal maid Anna. But now that people knew, two families had offered to take him in, but he had refused, preferring to live on his own, but he had come to Betsy's kitchen for his meals, she being a close friend of his mother's and she was also doing his washing.

Jane had then discussed this with Thomas who was surprised to hear that the boy had been attending the classes every day. He had promised Katie several times on their nightly romps to give him a good education, but he really had no interest in the boy at all – to him, he was just another dark-skinned boy like his mother, a slave that would grow up on the plantation working in the cane fields with little or no education. And now that Katie was gone, he dismissed the child from his mind.

CHAPTER ELEVEN

It was a kind of an adoption – Jane had taken Joseph under her wing seeing that he was eager to learn, and even with the tragic loss of his mother he was there on time for class every morning, and so she included him with her three boys again when the new German governess Fraulein Hildegard Hungerfort took up residence in the house. She was of middle age, stern and demanding and always wore black from head to toe – all she needed was a broomstick, said Michael. Fraulein Hildegard drilled the boys around, not only for lessons, but on their appearance, their deportment their speech at any time of the day whether in the house or the garden, she saying that they should appear to others including the staff well groomed, and set an example at any time of the day or night, as gentlemen, and that the staff should never see them otherwise.

The boys secretly called her a 'hatchet-faced old hag'; Jane was inclined to agree but chided them for saying such things. No one dared to disobey her, she always had a stern long face and rarely smiled. All were a little frightened of her, especially the house staff, even Jane was a little cautious when asking questions. And Thomas of course steered clear.

Fraulein Hungerfort abhorred slavery, and looked down her long thin nose at Thomas Turner, telling him in her stern no-nonsense manner just what she thought! He telling her in no uncertain terms that without the slaves he would not be able to grow his cane and *she* would not get paid. This soon put a stop to her aggression, and she kept out of his way.

Joseph was never late for class, his mother had always insisted on him being on time, and now he was always smartly dressed, guided by the Hag Hungerfort, wearing Philip's left-off shirts that Jane had given to Katie at different times, and now Betsy kept him clean.

The boys despised him, for his winning ways, as Fraulein Hungerfort favoured him knowing of his mother's tragic death, and knowing that he was born into slavery and was a boy with manners and great charm and most of all intelligence and willing to learn. Also, Jane quite often took his side in the many disputes that occurred with the boys daily. She also agreed like the boys on the hag being a witch, but kept her thoughts to herself.

During the growing years nothing changed and now into their teens, Joseph was still the underdog – fighting, lying and cheating his way through life – and although he spent much of his time with the boys he was never accepted. There were many disagreements, and fist fights broke out, much to the appalled disapproval of Fraulein Hungerfort, and Joseph quite often coming off worst when it was three to one, and much to the annoyance of Thomas – being now well educated he disrupted the working routine of the teenage slaves, talking to them, encouraging them to stand up for themselves and saying that they didn't want to be slaves all their lives, and this caused aggression.

Jane took pity on him when he came into the garden with a swollen eye or a cut lip or a bloody nose, she dressed his wounds, knowing that he had no mother to care for him. And she was taken in by his politeness and almost going on his knees to thank her for her kindness, knowing that would keep him in good stead with the family. And, this is why the boys despised him, they knew it was all show.

The boys were also now about to have fencing lessons with Eduardo Calpino, a Spaniard that Jane had met at a dinner party who had come to live in Barbados for a few months with his wife, son and daughter. He had been brought from Madrid by an Englishman, John Tippard, a well-to-do sugar planter, to teach his son Paul to fence. Jane had thought it a good idea and asked him to give her sons lessons in fencing; this of course included Joseph, who was a gambler and a cheat like his father, but of course in fencing he could not cheat, it was one man's skill against another!

The fierceness of the fencing lessons worried Hildegard Hungerfort, she thought they would kill each other. But Jane had watched and felt quite proud of all their performances and telling Hildegard not to worry, they had a long life to go though and at times it would be hard and there would be troubles and they would now be able to defend themselves.

CHAPTER TWELVE

In their later teens James, Michael and Philip still despised Joseph's artfulness and for playing up to their mother, knowing that most of his troubles were brought on by his own doing. They knew that he sneaked out at night and that he won a sizeable amount of money at cards with the local planters' sons, and then lost it all again playing with some of the village men, such as the overseers.

Joseph often felt irritable just trying to keep up with James Michael and Phillip – he knew he could never be quite like them, it took breeding; he admired their lifestyle, their dress sense, their culture, their sophistication and aloofness and also the social ability they had with other planters' sons and daughters. And he hoped that one day he would be like this, but most of his time was spent in the cane fields. However, he was trying to better himself, and spent a lot of that time trying to make money – you couldn't have the life of a gentleman without money... And he secretly thanked his mother's pushing him to learn. He did have an advantage over the other slaves, this is why he played up to Jane, he didn't want to lose that prestige and he was determined that he would one day be a free man. He was not going be a slave for ever.

The boys played a friendly game of cards with him knowing that he had not got a lot of money, but they lost, which of course didn't worry them they could afford to lose a little silver here and there, but not knowing that he cheated them.

But then suddenly one day he was flashing money about, wanting to bet Michael on two beetles running up a tree, or wanting to play cards or dice, and Jane's boys discussed this between themselves, wondering where this sudden source of wealth was coming from.

It was then discovered that their mother had lost some jewellery, and their suspicions were aroused. Thomas did allow his slaves free time, and they could go into the village only in the daytime if they asked the overseer for permission, but their time was limited to only one hour once a month, and no more than two could go at a time.

Knowing that Joseph had not left the premises in the day, the boys watched him escaping one night from a hidden spot in the slave quarters, where of course *they* were not supposed to be, and then secretly followed him down to the dockside, where they saw him in a tavern dealing, and money was exchanged for something that they couldn't see, but they surmised that it was jewellery. Then he got to drinking with rough low-class seamen, and kissing raunchy bawdy serving wenches that screamed with delight at his young roving hands and his vulgar ways. The boys, leading a sheltered life, were appalled by this behaviour. And they saw him taking a pocket watch by sleight of hand from a well-dressed stranger. He also cheated at drinking while distracting his pals – he poured his drink into their tankards and while they got very drunk he stayed sober, then robbing them of their purses and the jewellery that they wore, such as a ring or a gold chain or a silver pocket watch, sometimes even a diamond earring, and also relieving them of the jewellery of which he had only just sold them. They now knew that this was how Joseph lived, by cheating his way through life – he was quick and agile and they had to admire him, but on this particular night, one of his drinking pals wasn't so drunk, and Joseph got caught and then a fierce fight broke out between them all, and from this he ran. The boys were unable to help him, all they could do was watch as the sailors caught up with him and beat him and shanghaied him on to a Spanish ship called the *Magdalene*.

When Philip told his mother what they had seen, she wept. Thomas asked her why she was weeping, she said that Joseph had gone to sea. He'd been shanghaied.

"GOOD! It will straighten him up! Teach him a lesson!" But wondered how he had got down into the village at night. The boys did not tell on him, but Thomas wanted to know how they knew, and they had said that a friend had told them that he had seen it all happening.

Thomas liked to think that the boys were honest but he was not sure about this, but he would tell the overseers to tighten the security. He also felt relieved that he would no longer be reminded every day of the girl Katie.

CHAPTER THIRTEEN

When Joseph awoke he was in the dark and dim hold of the ship, lying face down on a pile of old and damp sacking; there was a pungent smell of decay, and bilge water sloshed around him. He had a headache and was in a lot of pain from a large gash on the back of this head, there was blood on the sacking and it had run and congealed down the back of his neck. His left eye was badly swollen and almost closed, and his nose had been bleeding. His whole body ached as he moved stiffly, and he cried silently with the pain, and it was now that he missed the kindness of Jane Turner, something that he had never really appreciated, it was just the means to an end. Also the old Hag Hildegard Hungerfort had a kind side to her stern nature. Suddenly he looked up blinking through tearful blurry eyes, as light suddenly streamed into the hold, someone was near but he couldn't focus. He cried out in pain as a bucket of cold water was thrown over him, and a harsh voice told him to get up off his backside and get up on deck; and then he was seized by the scruff of his neck and roughly flung across the hold to the steps and he crawled up very painfully and very slowly. Up on deck the brilliant sunshine hurt his eyes and for a few minutes he was blinded; he was pushed roughly in the back and fell on his knees, a bucket and scrubbing brush was pushed into his hands – the tone of the language was bitter, harsh, and swearing although he could not understand a word of it, but by the action knowing that he was expected to start scrubbing the deck.

Life for weeks aboard the *Magdalene* was hard, not many spoke English, the first mate *was* English, and the captain – Alonso Garcia – a short and podgy Spaniard, spoke a little English. Over the weeks the captain had noticed that Joseph was not lazy and any given task he did it well, he was also taken in by his charming and polite good manners, and surprised to find the black boy was well educated, and well above the intelligence of other members of his crew. He also found that he was a trouble maker and a fist fighter, and handy with a sword – when one of the crew suddenly surprised the captain in his cabin, putting a sword to his throat, Joseph grabbed a sword and was there ready to defend him. The man was thrown to the sharks. But now, knowing him to be a good guard, he put him in charge of the ship finances, much to Joseph's delight, and he did manage to curb his dishonesty for some months. He played cards with the crew members; they found him friendly, the language a bit of a problem, but having access to money made him popular and his cheating made him rich. But after checking and finding that the books did not tally, with some cargo, and also finding that he had been robbed of his personal belongs, and a few of the precious stones that he had kept hidden in his cabin, the captain had Joseph flogged and then set adrift in and open boat.

He drifted for days, dying of hunger and thirst under a blazing sun and had collapsed, eventually waking in a state of delirium to a torrential rain storm and finding every limb stiff, his skin burning his lips and eyes blistered. In his weak and almost lifeless state, he found that the boat had landed on a beach, he clambered feebly and exhausted over the side, splashing head first in to the shallow rushing waves which brought a little spark of life. Leaving the boat washing in the heavy surf, he struggled and crawled ashore seeing trees through misted vision that were swaying and being battered by the elements. In his weakened state he was mowed down by the wind and heavy rain, and lay face down on the sand.

He had no idea of how long he had stayed there, but awoke as lightning lit up the darkened skies and thunder roared. He crawled weakly on all fours, dragging himself towards the trees for shelter. The rain revived him and catching the rain water in large leaves he drank thirstily. The thunderstorm raged through the night and Joseph drifted off into a deep sleep and awoke to sunlight, and focused his bleary eyes on waving palms high above. He could hear the birds calling and twittering and the shushing of the sea; he sat up, and then got unsteadily to his feet, his legs so weak he stumbled forward like a baby just learning to walk and then fell over, then, remembering the boat he crawled the few feet to the beach – the boat had gone. Crawling back to the cool shelter of the trees, hunger pains gripped his stomach; he found a few large leaves that still held rainwater, and then on regaining a little strength, and exploring, he found that he was on a remote island he supposed, somewhere, in the Caribbean. He found a mango tree – the fruit on the ground was rotten and had been pecked heavily by the birds but what was left he ate hungrily, his sun-blistered lips smarting on the acid; and then looking up the tree and finding that the fruit was too high for him to reach, he found a long stick and managed to knock two down. This exhausted him and he then found some more leaves that held a little water, and sat down to rest.

From there on he lost count of the days and the months, and maybe years that went by, surviving on fish that he caught with a wooden spear that he had made, and coconut milk to drink keeping the shells for catching rainwater. He lived on fruit – bananas, mangoes and sea grapes that grew along the beach. He made a small shelter from branches and leaves, and laid out a fire in readiness to signal a passing ship; but the days and the nights went on, and when a ship eventually appeared on the horizon he tried desperately to light the fire with a piece of glass bottle that he had found on the beach, trying to catch the hot rays of the sun playing on to dried grasses, but the greenery was still damp from a light rain shower the night before and by the time the flame eventually caught and he had smoke the ship was gone. From then on he kept the fire going day and night, hoping to be seen, and also afraid that there might be wild animals lurking in the undergrowth, but after weeks of exploring every inch of the island he found that it was totally uninhabited – he was there completely alone with the mosquitoes the ants and the birds. His only clothing was trousers now in rags, and he beat the fibres from the banana trees into soft linen-like cloth to make a sarong. It had taken a long time for his black skin to heal, and now he kept as much as he could to the shade.

He had dreams of Thomas Turner, and dreams of Jane Turner and her sons, they probably all thinking that he was dead, but he was determined to return to the Silver Lady Cottage one day, but he had no desire to go back into slavery and what would Master Turner do, after all this time punish him? At lease here, he was free... He marked strokes on a tree, keeping account of every single day. Eventually, after four years, he was picked up by a passing fishing boat manned by just four native men from the island of St Lucia. The natives were sailing to Trinidad, where they dropped him off, and on that very first night they all went to a tavern together, where for Joseph it was pure luxury to eat chicken and drink rum. And then, while they drank, he sneaked away and stole their boat intending to sail to Barbados, but he was caught and put in jail, from which he escaped after a month by charming the guard to play cards, and then killing him. He lived rough, hiding in the trees, something that he was used to, but now chased and hounded by men of the watch; and then, after two days, finding his way to a remote village where a kindly widow took him in and cared for him, feeding him and giving him clothes. She turned out to be a rich woman, and he worked for her for a month, then left her one night after stealing money and a ruby necklace. He made his way to the port and was going to stow away on a boat, but outside a tavern he heard a crew playing cards and mentioned their sail to Barbados, and asked if he could join their card game. He had money jingling in his pocket, and he had not lost his charming manner and they let him join in the game. He found that they were from a fishing vessel called the *Starlight*, and that in the early hours of the morning they were to catch the tide and leave for Barbados. He couldn't believe his luck, and asked the captain to take him. The captain said that he needed an extra hand, and Joseph joined the crew.

CHAPTER FOURTEEN

It was Old Sam the stable man, who saw a strange man coming out of the hut, and went hurrying across the garden to find the Master. On his way he bumped into Hildegard Hungerfort, and alerted her of a wild man. Although no longer needed as a governess, she had stayed on at the Silver Lady Cottage and become a sort of secretary/right-hand *man* to Master Turner, although he avoided her as much as he could, but he needed someone of intelligence to run the finances of the sugar plantation.

She saw the dirty slovenly stranger with the long black beard and a mop of frizzy filthy, curly hair, his clothes in rags, coming towards her, and she ran calling anxiously for the Master. But it was Jane who came rushing to her aid, a shotgun in hand.

The two woman stood by the door looking at the wild man. Jane raised the gun as he was coming towards them and she told him to stop!

He shouted, putting up his arms in defence, but even then the two women were a little wary of him. Then the Hag demanded loudly wanting to know who he was and what he wanted.

It was Michael who heard the commotion and came rushing to his mother's side with a drawn sword, and demanding to know what this creature was doing on their property. But when the wild man spoke saying that he was Joseph, they were all surprised, and Jane lowered the shotgun and was more than pleased to see him again and would have gone to put her arms around him, had not Michael stopped her from going near the filthy creature.

But then after he had gone to the little hut, and cleaned himself up, he shaved his ugly beard and most of his head. Jane had found him a clean shirt and pants, and he appeared on the patio before them – they were all amazed to find that the twenty-two year old had grown into a six foot tall, handsome, young dark-skinned man.

He pulled an expensive ruby necklace from his pocket, that made them all hold their breath, he then gave it to Jane telling her that he acquired it especially for her, from his travels.

Thomas was not pleased to see him back at the Silver Lady Cottage, but found that he grown into a fine figure of a young man, and it did touch his heart; in a way he felt proud, but of course didn't show it.

Travelling had educated Joseph even more, and Thomas felt that he could no longer treat him as a slave, although he did not officially give him his freedom. He severely questioned him, telling him the penalty for leaving the plantation was flogging, as he already knew, and threatened to do so, but then saying much to his annoyance that he had been gone so long and that he had no family to take in to consideration and now what would be the point. Then telling him in no uncertain terms that he should be ready for the cane field early in the morning and if he was a minute late he would get the flogging of his life! He had then walked away in disgust at seeing the boy again.

Thomas was most surprised to find that Joseph was there in line, and on time for inspection like the others, and he went off to the cane fields each day as he had done a few years ago. The overseer told the master that he had worked well, and that he was different to all the other workers, he was methodical and he was thorough. It was then that Thomas had told the overseer to find him a different job, and the next morning he was called out of the line, and was sent into the small chattel house that was used as an office and put in charge of the paperwork that the overseer usually did, keeping the books for the daily quota of the cane that was cut and sold, and the weekly quota of wood required for burning that kept the vats boiling to produce molasses. From then on Thomas rarely saw him, it brought back thoughts of the slave girl Katie, that he would rather forget.

James, Michael and Philip, now grown men, and all working in Bridgetown – James a lawyer, Michael and Philip into banking – had put away their differences. All four now sat on the patio that very first night with a glass of wine, and Joseph entertained them and intrigued them with his adventures at sea, telling them that he was shanghaied, of which they knew but said nothing, for of course *they* could have done nothing to help him. He spoke of other islands, that they knew nothing about, and of his terrible experience of being on a deserted island all alone for four years, but of course he had lied and said he was shipwrecked, and not saying that he was cast adrift. He told them of America, their mother's country. James said that he'd thought to go to America one day and really make his fortune.

To which Joseph replied in surprise, "FORTUNE! You already have a fortune! You've always had a fortune. And, you will always have a fortune!"

"Yes," James raised his eyebrows, "and you have NOTHING! And you will always have nothing!"

Joseph grinned, "Don't be so sure, I'm trying. I don't intend to be a slave forever."

Joseph had moved back into the small wooden hut, he had cleaned it and furnished it with a table a chair and a bed, but most evenings he had joined the boys on the patio and they related their days at the office, and then they played cards and enjoyed a glass of wine. When he played honestly he quite often lost money, much to the delight of the boys. And now the substantial amount of money that he had stolen from people and ships along the way, was dwindling fast… Joseph had not joined them to play cards for a week or two, and when asked why, he joked that they had won all his money, and he would have to find a job before they could take his money again.

The overseer told Master Thomas that the slave Joseph, had been missing for a few days and nights and no one knew where he was.

Thomas thought that there was really nothing he could do about it, the boy was too intelligent to be working in the fields and he guessed after seeing some of the world, the boy would need to get out, and he would get out anyway. And he would want to make some money, so he washed his hands of him. The overseer, never having been through a situation like this was so confused, and when Joseph continued to come and go he just let the matter drop.

CHAPTER FIFTEEN

One evening Jane was in tears, while getting ready for a party that was to be held at the Tappards' house. She found that some of her jewellery was missing – a sapphire ring and emerald ring, and the beautiful ruby necklace that Joseph had given to her was gone!

Thomas had harshly questioned the household staff, leaving the maids in tears, and the young men nervously aware of being suspected; but one young slave, Herbert, was whipped for insolence, telling the Master that he no right to suspect and distrust any of them when they had worked for so long in the house. But no one had any knowledge of the lost jewels.

When Joseph came back after being missing for a few days, Thomas severely reprimanded him. But then he had been through all this with Joseph before, and as he had no family there was not much point in carrying out the normal severe punishment. But he had to make an example of him and so he told the overseers to put him in chains for the whole of the day out in the blazing sun, without food or water and that night there was a torrential rain storm. In the morning Joseph was released from the chains, his arms and legs stiff and painful, and he was tired from having no sleep having been worried by insects and mosquitoes. He was in line early in the morning for inspection and Thomas ordered him a day working in the cane field, and when the others stopped for a break he was given a little water but no food all day. The next day he was sent back to his job in the small office, but his back hurt and he could hardly move his painful arms after swinging a machete all day.

It was several evenings later when he had got his strength back that Joseph came to the patio. The boys were playing cards, and he was smiling and joking now that he could play cards again as he had been working on a fishing boat and had money, and so they let him in on the game. He was very concerned when James told him of the theft of his mother's jewellery, and that the ruby necklace was gone. He couldn't believe that this had all happened while he was away on the fishing boat; he wanted to know how anyone could have broken in, and was determined to find out who had done this. He charged into the slave quarters, backed up by James, Michael and Philip, causing a rumpus, and a fierce fight had then broken out with a dozen or so men and one young slave boy was severely injured.

Thomas was enraged by this news although he was strict with his salves, he looked after them and treated them well, he needed them fit and happy for work in the cane fields, not disruptive and aggressive.

All four boys had bruises, cut lips and black eyes, as did many of the slaves, and one older man in charge of mending fencing, had a broken arm and was unable to work. They had gained nothing by fighting, and Thomas gave all four of them a severe dressing down, and for once Jane was in agreement. Then Thomas took Joseph aside into the trees where he thought they could not be heard, he then accused him of instigating the trouble. Harsh words were exchanged and overheard by Jane and her sons, and Hildegard, as they stood at the open library door. Thomas accused Joseph of stealing the necklace, that Joseph most profusely denied it, saying that he wasn't even here.

"NO!" Thomas was heard to say, "you most probably took it with you *or,* came sneaking back in the night, to steal it! *unseen*! Of course, so you couldn't be accused!" he lifted his eyebrows with a sharp nod, and then Joseph's enraged voice rose accusing Thomas, "Well, you've been stealing from her for years to pay your gambling debts! and for your loose women! You only married her for her money! My mother told me!"

Jane and her sons caught their breath and looked at each other.

Thomas, of course enraged, denied it. And Joseph countered with, "And you are not only a thief, you're a murderer! I saw you that night strangle Sarah Kilbride in the barn, I heard a scream and saw my mother going in to the barn, and I followed her. I was there when my mother attacked you with the broom, and Sarah Kilbride was screaming and you had to shut her up. You hit her hard and she screamed more and tried to run away from you – you couldn't have her telling anyone could you! You were both naked. I saw you. Then my mother was screaming at you, accusing you of cheating on her, and then both women were attacking you, you threw my mother off, and she hit her head on the iron machinery and lay very still, and then you grabbed Sarah Kilbride because she was screaming to tell your wife! You shook her by the neck until she collapsed dead at your feet! My mother woke up to the terrible scene and she was scared and in tears but said she would never tell. I saw the two of you carry Sarah Kilbride out to the cart and you hitched up the oxen. I ran behind in the dark to see what you were going to do and saw the two of you throw her over the cliff into the sea!… I came back quickly and got into bed, and then what happened? Did you also strangle my mother too and then throw her body in the cane field, because she knew too much and you didn't trust her enough not to tell anyone did you? But she never would have, she loved you! She would have given her life for you, even though she hated you for marrying Jane, but even then she never would have let you down! She also hated Jane for taking you away from her, but in all the years she never complained did she? She believed all the false promises that you gave her about divorcing Jane and marrying her and she being mistress of the house! The promise of a diamond necklace, that *you* couldn't even afford, without Jane's money. You couldn't afford to divorce Jane, she's kept you since the day you married her, you only married *her* for her *money!* there's no love in you, you're no good to any woman… or, any man for that matter. You've lied and cheated all your life! You cheat your wife, and your mistress, even your own family! You treat the boys like sons but you only pretend to be like a father because there's money behind it! You just don't know *how* to treat people especially women. You're just no bloody good!"

Thomas, taken aback by this outburst, was so enraged that he lunged forward grabbing Joseph by the throat and slamming his back up against a tree, "HOW DARE YOU, HOW DARE YOU, ACCUSE ME!" he roared, like an angry lion. "I EDUCATED YOU!"

"No you didn't, Jane did!" Joseph, the stronger of the two shook him off, and laughed. "What now eh? You gonna kill me? you gonna kill me, you gonna strangle me like you did them, because I know you're a murdering cheating swine and no good to any man or woman. Come on then, just try it. I'll deliver *you* to your wife on the ox cart in a crumpled heap then chuck you over the cliff like you did to Sarah Kilbride, *your loving wife* who trusts you and who loves *you*, and *thinks* you're a gentleman! but I know you to be a sadistic old sod, but she doesn't know you like I do. *Faarrtheer.*"

Thomas's voice was loud and venomous, "I should have strangled you at birth!" he spat out the words, "your mother was a whore, I'm ashamed to call you my son…"

"But I am," he smiled, "aren't I, *Faaatheeer?* And they are all whores in your eyes *aren't they, Faaatheer?* How many more sons have you got lurking in the slave quarters? You've never been a father to me, you treat me just like any other slave! You promised my mother everything – marriage! A home! My education! But you lied and cheated her, just like you do to all women. Does your *wife* know where your late night business meetings take place? I do… other men's beds, and *they think* you're *their friend.*" Suddenly there was thump and a loud gasp…

Jane semi collapsed, holding her hand to her heart. Michael steadied her to a chair, where she sat dumfounded, with her hand clamped hard over her mouth. Michael again joined James standing by the window, they exchanged glances at such a harsh confrontation, and then they heard more sounds of punching and gasps of pain as a fight broke out, and leaves and trees shook violently, the aggression unseen. Then all went quiet and Joseph was marching away in the direction of his little hut, opening and clenching his fists, a determined and angry look on his face, and then a few minutes later Thomas staggered out of the trees holding his hand to his face his eye steaming with blood.

Old Sam, hovering in the trees, had heard every word. He was shocked and worried, his big brown eyes showing white with fear; no one had ever talked to the Master like that before and he not wanting to be caught eavesdropping hurried away back to the stable, almost at a run, and close on Joseph's heels but not wanting to be seen. He'd known about the affair with the girl Katie, he'd almost stumbled in on them one night when the horses had been restless, and had guessed for many years about Joseph being the Master's son, but he had never dared to say a word.

Later that afternoon when Thomas eventually came back to the house, Jane at the sight of his mutilated face was shocked at what Joseph had done, but told him that he had deserved it – she had heard every word of the heated argument – and that she was leaving him, accusing him of cheating on her for years, and for not telling her that Joseph was his son, and saying what a fool she had made of herself, with that poor girl Katie, and then fell with tears over the lovely Sarah Kilbride. She said that she had already sent James down to the harbour to find the first available ship going to America. "You will never get another dollar out of me! I'm leaving this house!"

Thomas, still enraged, shouted, "SHUT UP, WOMAN, you're not leaving, you are *my wife* and you obey me or I'll—"

"What? Kill me like you did the others? Oh no, no!" she chuckled, "you can't afford to kill me! You need *my money!*"

"Oh, get out of my sight, woman!" He lashed out, smacking her in the face and sending her flying and sprawling on her back across the room smashing into a chair and breaking a small table and ornaments.

James had just returned, he was telling Michael about the ship… Then on hearing the shouting and then a thump and the breakage they both came bursting into the room, and both jumped on Thomas. They beat him to within an inch of his life; he fought back but was no match for two strong and younger men. Expensive porcelain and glass was smashed and antique furniture broken, as they tumbled and lunged at each other with vicious blows. Thomas half managed to get up and crawl away before their hard boots kicked him out onto the patio, in front of some of the bewildered servants who had come to see what all the noise was about, and never expecting to see the *Master* thrown to the ground in such a state. Blooded and bruised, and for the first time without his whip, he struggled to get to his feet, holding his broken ribs, his breath taken from his body but he managed to growl at them, sending them running back to work and screaming for their lives like children.

James and Michael rubbed their hands and pulled at their clothing, straitening themselves up, and smiled at each other feeling that they had done a good job.

Philip came in at the last minute; seeing the fight and his mother on the floor took her into another room and sat down with her, and of course asking what had happened. Still hearing the rumpus that was going on, Jane was worrying that her boys were taking a beating that they didn't deserve. Then when James and Michael came in with hardly a scratch, Jane was so relieved. Philip was holding her hand, and Anna her maid was bathing a cut across her eye where Thomas's ring had caught her. Then Philip went to his brothers, asking what it was all about and they quickly explained.

"Where is he?" Jane asked timidly.

"We threw him out," said James.

"He'll have a headache," chuckled Michael.

James chuckled, "Among other things. He might not even come back."

Jane still tearful, nodded, she also had a headache, but she wasn't really hurt although shaking and unnerved. "How did you get on down at the harbour?" she asked James.

He shook his head, "There won't be a ship available for about a month, until the *Santa Maria* comes in – she's a Spanish vessel on her way from the Americas now, and she will be returning within a week of her arrival. She's a cargo ship, but can take eight passengers so they told me. So I told them to reserve a passage for four of us."

Jane nodded, rubbing her hands nervously, thinking that she couldn't stay here for another month, she would find another place to live, "You will come with us, Anna."

Anna nodded gratefully, "Yes Mam."

The boys had not mentioned that they'd witnessed the big argument, but Joseph knew that Jane and the boys were preparing to leave and that *they knew* about Thomas being his father, and also about the murders. He also knew that it had been whispered among the house servants, and throughout the slave quarters; but life more or less went on as usual, although Joseph did not go into the cane fields again, he spent most days working on the fishing boats along the shore. And when the overseer had mentioned that the boy Joseph was missing again, Thomas told him not to worry about it, and dismissed it from his mind once again. He couldn't keep imposing punishment on him, but the boy *was* making a fool of him. He concentrated on the cane fields, as usual, and at night seeing his mistress Lucy down in the slave quarters; and now having separate rooms, Jane didn't know if he ever came into the house at night at all.

James, Michael and Philip, were playing cards on the patio, when Joseph came by and said that he had been working and had money and wanted to play, and so the boys let him join in on the game. But Joseph was in one of his cheating moods, and won a lot of money off Michael. They agreed to play again the next night, hoping to win their money back, but Joseph won again. It was then that Michael caught him cheating and accused him, with harsh words, and also accused him of having fixed the dice in another game, just a week ago. Of course Joseph denied it both times and an argument broke out, which was nothing unusual – it was just like old times. Michael also asked him how much he got for his mother's ruby necklace. Joseph was taken aback, stunned for a moment, but then as always ready with an answer denied it again, saying that he was not even here when it was stolen, in the night. "How do you know it was stolen *in the night*?" Joseph was again stunned, and then Michael saying he was like his father *a liar*, and a cheat! And they almost came to blows on the patio but both James and Philip intervened. But tempers had not cooled down and Michael challenged Joseph to a duel.

Joseph laughed heartily "A DUEL…?" Then realized that Michael was serious.

The time was set at two in the morning in the old barn. James and Philip were there, to see fair play, and also two young men from the slave quarters, Samuel and Henry were there to support Joseph.

All four boys were accomplished swordsmen, having had lessons when they were younger, with Eduardo Calpino from Spain. Also Joseph on his exploits had got into many scrapes and was much more experienced than Michael.

A few young lads from the slave quarters had heard about the duel and had crept away in the night to watch.

The barn was in deep eerie shadow from the candles that had been placed around and now there may have been about a dozen young men gathered there. Michael shed his green frock coat, and Joseph loosened the gold buttons on his blue waistcoat and rolled up the full sleeves of his fine white cotton blouse, and then took up his sword; both had a stern look as the duel began with a soft sound of steel blades gently touching as they honoured each other, they had agreed to stop when one of them drew first blood. There was silence in the barn and deep concentration from them all. The only sound now was the shuffling of their feet as they circled each other warily in the flickering candlelight, each man eyeing the other, and weighing the weapon in his hand, waiting for the other to strike first. Then there was the first clash of steel and a gasp from the spectators as Joseph suddenly lunged forward, and Michael defended himself and backed away. They moved slowly and carefully, the blades glinting in the candlelight, the atmosphere was tense and then suddenly Michael lashed out and Joseph retaliated sharply driving Michael back. It began to get more aggressive, and the steel clashed fast and often as each man defended himself, and then retaliated, lunging forward and driving back and the youths egged them on, and the hard and sharp clash of steel rang out across the garden into the darkness of the night.

Thomas, coming across the garden from the slave quarters after one his many drunken evening with the girl Lucy, heard sounds coming from the barn. He stopped. Swayed. And Listened. Frowning, and then coming closer and hearing steel he was astounded, it sobered him up, he pulled open the door and exclaimed loudly "BOYS!"

Michael was taken off guard and turned at the sound of the stern voice, just as Joseph lunged forward, stabbing him through the heart!

Michael slid slowly to the floor holding his chest with a painful groan, lying very still the sword falling from his hand with a clatter as blood covered the wide sleeves of the silken white shirt, and the green velvet waistcoat. All stood holding their breath, still and stunned and flabbergasted. The deadly silence that clouded everyone's ears could have been cut with a knife, it was like the calm after the storm – no one dared to move, and then James moved slowly, trance-like, breaking the traumatic tension and then was followed by Philip. They went on their knees at Michael's side, but it was too late – he had died almost instantly.

Thomas just stood looking down at Michael, stunned and shocked at the scene before him, then stared in utter bewilderment at Joseph who was transfixed, standing like a statue, the sharp blade still raised and glinting in the flickering candlelight steady in his hand, and stained with Michael's blood. He was stunned, and lowered the sword slowly as if in a trance, suddenly realizing what he had done.

Thomas then roared like an enraged lion at Joseph, "YOOOU!" He unleashed the whip in his hand.

Joseph ducked as the whip lashed out, "It was YOUR FAULT," he shouted at Thomas, "I DIDN'T MEAN TO DO IT."

In a flash the whip lashed out again catching Joseph across his right shoulder and neck, it cut into his flesh so fiercely that his whole body shuddered, and he staggered and put his hand up as blood spouted from his neck, then recovering he lunged at his father with the sword, not too steady on his feet, and as Thomas turned lifting the whip again Joseph caught him on the ear with the blade.

The frightened wide brown eyes of the spectators looked at each other in the dim light, the whole scene of the horror so great that no one dared to breathe. The slaves stepped back slowly and gently into the shadows, and those nearer to the door ran for their lives. And then a minute later there was loud wailing from James, just as Philip jumped to his feet grabbing at the whip and drawing it swiftly through Thomas's hand and lashing out at Joseph, who stumbled losing his grip on the sword and it fell with a clatter on to the wooden floorboards as he made a quick exit, stumbling out of the barn door – Phillip close on his heels and lashing out at him.

Thomas had tears in his eyes as he went down on his knees beside James, utterly deflated. Thomas, holding his ear, the blood streaming though his fingers and dripping on the floor, he looked sadly at James who shook his head and burst into tears.

There was now just the sound of their quiet weeping, as all others had fled. James got to his feet wearily leaving Thomas still on his knees with Michael, there was nothing he could do, and walked sadly and slowly outside the barn without an ounce of energy into the warm night air, where he saw Philip lashing in the darkness at Joseph who was crumpled up on the ground like a ball, trying to protect himself and squealing in terror with every lash. This straitened James up and as he approached, Philip turned and hesitated and Joseph then seized the opportunity and got speedily to his feet and ran off into the darkness, both James and Philip dashing after him, he just one step ahead of Philip who was still lashing out and catching him with the whip…

James and Philip carried their dead brother back to the house and took him to his room and sat with him for the rest of the night. They were reluctant to wake their mother, and decided that the best thing would be to tell her in the morning.

Jane was devastated when told and collapsed in a chair in floods of tears, she couldn't believe that Joseph had been involved in killing her son. But the boys did have to admit that it really was an accident, no one had ever expected such a tragedy but it had happened so quickly. It took Jane a long time to recover from that first moment, and she knew she would never really recover from the loss of her darling boy. But then she asked about Joseph, knowing that he too must be devastated at such a tragic happening. She went to his little hut to talk to him, but Joseph was not there. Joseph, was never seen again.

Three weeks after the tragedy Jane, James and Philip boarded the *Santa Maria*, and sailed for America, taking Anna with them.

It was later reported that the *Santa Maria* sank with all hands.

CHAPTER SIXTEEN

Julie feeling a little sad turned the pages; there was plenty more to read but she'd had enough. She checked her watch 5.45, and looked up as Alan came in to the library. "Oh! Hello. You're early."

'Yeah!" He sighed heavily, "just left another board meeting, glad to get away."

She smiled, "You need a drink, come on let's go to the gazebo, I've had enough in here anyway, I've been reading about the Turners. Glass of white wine?" She lifted her eyebrows. He nodded, she phoned Charles.

"Yeah that would be great." They walked across the garden, the sky was still bright with a flaming sunset and the humidity was high. "Hey what do you think, there's a new guy at the office named Trevor Thurgold."

"Oh! Really? Any relation do you think?"

"Dunno," he smiled, "but quite a coincidence, eh? All we need is a relation to a *pirate* working in a bank! Ha ha!"

Julie smiled. The table was already laid for two, but they sat in the easy chairs. "I've been in the library most of the afternoon finding out about the Turners. The skeleton is definitely Joseph Turner, well he was never really given a surname, even though he was the son of Thomas Turner." She told him about the duel and of Michael's death. "And I think that it was his half brothers that killed him, whipping him to death."

Charles brought the drinks, and they clinked glasses. And Alan sipped, gratefully, taking a deep breath and letting it go, "Oh, I needed this."

"There is so much to read," said Julie, "but from what, *I have read,* I think this Thomas Turner was a bit of a bad lot. Drinking and…"

"Like us?" Alan smiled raising his glass and arching his eyebrows comically. "When did he live here then?"

"About seventeen something, and he was a gambler and a womanizer. This Joseph, was his illegitimate son and took after him, or so it seems, at least for cheating and gambling."

"Oh the archaeologists were right then; he has been there for a few hundred years. I'll phone Jackson Verity in the morning – he'd be pleased to know who the skeleton really is. What was his name, Joseph Turner? All sounds quite interesting, I should like to have a look at this book."

"Well it isn't really a book, it's a script, a pile of loose pages handwritten– beautifully written I might add – by an Edward Turner, I would think years later."

"Not published then?"

"No but I'm sure he had intended to get it published, writing so much, but I looked at the last page, and it just stopped in mid-sentence – I would think he was interrupted, by surprise."

Charles came with a large tray held shoulder high and said the dinner was served. They got up and sat at the table, and Charles replenished their glasses. All through dinner they discussed the house and Honeybeck's treasure, and then got back to the Turners again. It was after nine when they finished dinner, and the wind started to blow and the rain fell heavily blowing in on them and they laughed and held up the linen napkins in front of their faces to shelter from the spray, laughing at their own silly antics. Charles came up quickly, caught halfway across the garden by a strong gust of wind and the slanting rain and was followed by a dog – a golden Labrador – who ran up the steps on to the gazebo looking for shelter. It happened in the islands, a squally shower could come suddenly out of nowhere and last a few minutes and then just stop abruptly, but this seemed in for the night, and they were getting quite wet. Julie patted the dog who had gone under the table, and Charles shouting above the hammering of the rain on the roof, saying that the dog Eddie, belonged to Ben Carding, who lived a few yards down the road, he must have got out.

Alan suggested that they go into the house. Charles said he would go and get them an umbrella. But Alan laughed and said no, they'd make a run for it, and he took Julie by the hand and they scooted giggling across the garden, Eddie the dog following them in under the arches of the patio where it was drier. But then a warm gust of wind sprayed the rain in, and they slipped in through the open door at the side of the house, where Charles had come in and out from the kitchen, the door being on the far end of the long blue carpeted hallway that led off from the far end of the main circular hall. They were giggling and shaking their hands and Julie shaking her hair, the rain was warm but being quite wet they shivered, and the dog shook himself and they laughed again, hunching their shoulders, getting wet again from the spray. As they were near the library, Alan said he'd like to take a look at this manuscript. Julie switched on the lights, and they went in, the dog not wanting to be left out ran ahead and found a comfortable spot under the desk. The library felt warm after having the sun on it all day, and Julie switched on the ceiling fan, and phoned Charles for another drink.

Alan found it interesting thumbing through the written pages, "My," he inclined his head, "there's quite a bit of it isn't there?" They learned more as Alan continued to read out loud. – John Turner had been in jail, for fraud. Anthony Turner, found a golden cup, and was chased by the ghost of Honeybeck who they say killed him with a sword. They looked at each other sceptically, "I find that a bit hard to believe, perhaps somebody with a sword, but not a ghost," Alan grimaced.

Ben Turner lived to 98, and had three wives and eleven children who had all lived in the house at different times; there were some happily married some divorced, some widowed. Albert jailed and then hung for murder of his wife Martha. His son Clement jailed for poisoning *his* wife Emily, but he managed to escape and was chased and killed by hunting dogs. Then there was Harold and Elizabeth, who were killed when their carriage turned over, they were racing away from the scandal of their daughter Isobel's pregnancy, she being unmarried. But the biggest disaster of all time was – it seemed that she was walking in the fields and was caught and raped by a horseman riding by, and the story went on that it was a phantom headless horseman. This set the whole village talking, and so afraid that they all closed and barred their doors and windows; some barricaded themselves in the church afraid to go outside at night and even in the daylight, saying that they had seen the headless horseman; and John Moresley, the priest, had gathered the whole village into the church and said prayers. And then there was more scandal as the baby was born without a head, which proved to be untrue as the boy Henry grew up to be the village idiot. And then as the years went on, it seemed that the stories of the headless horseman, were all untrue and that he was none other than the lover of Isobel, and a lowly stable lad, Finlay MacLennan, who had rode with his head covered so as not to be recognised. And then there was a Cedric Turner who was hanged for killing a fellow sugar planter over the price of a few barrels of molasses, by deliberately pushing him in to a boiling vat. And then Peter Turner who was lost at sea leaving a family of nine children and a wife Ellen who remarried Peter's brother James and had two more children. Then in 1780 there was a terrible hurricane, when twins Lillian and Lydia were lost, and then again in 1831 another hurricane that killed family members – children aged 5, 7 and 16 – all running for shelter when a tree crashed down on them. And then there was the terrible cholera outbreak in 1854, when the whole island was in turmoil and several of the Turner family lost their lives, and all but three of Ellen and Peter's children died, and half the slave population. It seemed through the years a real mix-up, several children had died, but generally there seemed to be a bad streak running through the whole of the Turner family. It seemed that in all the years money was never a real problem, but Jack Turner was killed in a duel for not paying his gambling debts, and of course Thomas who gambled a fortune away, and then there was Harold Turner who owed money everywhere, and was eventually shot by a plantation owner, who later killed himself.

Alan flipped over a hundred or so pages, and came to a paragraph headed CAPTAIN HONEYBECK. "It seemed that all through the ages the family had searched and searched for this supposed treasure. Edward Turner had written... I found this bit of information in a letter written to Alfred Turner it read... 'We found at times traces of silver coins, not much, considering it is supposed to be pirate treasure. And there were several hauntings by Honeybeck after some silver was found near the Silver Lady. Also it was Great-Great Grandfather Anthony, who had moved the golden cup from the library where it had stood for years... No one has ever touched it since...'" Both Julie and Alan looked up and around the spacious room.

"I suppose that's it," said Julie pointing to a small gold cup, in an alcove near the portrait of Honeybeck.

Alan nodded and went back to the page, "He was found in the garden, run through with a sword, the golden cup lying close by. It is said that he found Honeybeck's treasure and the ghost of Captain Honeybeck killed him. This legend has been told for over a hundred years, but it can't be true, in my own opinion, he may have found some treasure, and someone killed him. But I doubt if it was Honeybeck's ghost? There I told you." Alan looked up, and then went on reading. "'To my knowledge the treasure has never been found.' The letter goes on but there is no signature."

"No," Alan shook his head, "no one would have killed him and left the gold cup just lying there in the garden beside the body would they? But somebody did. Probably one of the Turners, they didn't need money or riches, and it made it look as if Honeybeck had killed him."

"Well why didn't one of the servants pick it up?" said Julie.

"Afraid to go near the body, I expect, and in any case if they were caught with a golden cup, they would have been killed anyway, wouldn't they?"

"Honeybeck? Might have given him a fright, seeing a ghost," Julie arched her eyebrows, "and then someone stabbed him and killed him."

Alan wrinkled his nose, "Possibly, but what for, if they didn't take the cup?" He splayed his hand haphazardly.

Julie went over and picked up the highly polished small golden cup, "Feel it, it's quite heavy, solid gold do you think?" She handed it to Alan, "Doesn't say where in the garden they found the body, does it? In any case why would Anthony Turner want to take a golden cup, from here out into the garden."

"Probably picked it up, and Honeybeck appeared and he ran out in fright," said Alan. "*Or*, maybe he was attacked for it and then someone killed him and ran off without it?"

Suddenly at that moment, a draught blew through the room it startled them a bit, and then the door opened and closed again. Alan was quick on his feet, he rushed to the door and out into the hall expecting to see someone, but there was no one. Julie set the cup down on the desk and was close on his heels and they saw the door at the other end of the hall just closing. Looking at each other in surprise, they ran down the hall followed by Eddie the dog.

Alan opened the hall door with great gusto, but the circular hall was bare.

They stood near the round table looking up the stairs, there was nothing to see but Eddie was barking ferociously, and they heard the sound of heavy footsteps, mounting the stairs. "Honeybeck! Do you think?" said Alan. Julie looked wide-eyed and shook her head.

Eddie's loud barking brought both Charles and Oliver up from the basement wondering what all the noise was about, Charles was surprised to see the dog still there.

Julie stroked Eddie's head, and he suddenly stopped barking, stood back with a little whine then bolted back down the hall as if afraid. While Alan explained to both Charles and Oliver that they thought they heard someone go up the stairs, Alan saying that they must have been mistaken, not wanting to mention a ghost. And Charles and Oliver made their way down the back stairs to the basement again

It was now well past midnight and when Alan went back to the library to let the dog out he found Eddie under the desk. He called him and tried to let him out of the French windows, but the dog cowered away and wouldn't budge so Julie, who had followed Alan, suggested leaving him there until the morning. It was late and Alan had decided to stay the night. They came back to the main circular hall, and went up the stairs cautiously, hoping that Honeybeck was gone. But Julie turned to look behind her just in case, having an eerie feeling, wondering if he *was* still there?

At Alan's door they stopped, he gave her a friendly kiss on the cheek, asking if she would be alright; she nodded, they said goodnight, he watched her to the end of the hall, then called goodnight again. She turned and waved her hand, then both doors closed.

Julie switched off the bedside light, and lay listening to the sounds of the night, the loud whistling of the tree frogs, and the crickets. A dog barked somewhere in the distance and then there was the soft pitter-patter of rain at the window pane and on the roof; it got harder, hammering on the roof with a loud shushing sound, lasted just a minute and then stopped abruptly as if switched off! It happened like this a lot of the time in the islands, and then the palest light from the half moon came across the top of the drapes.

Her thoughts suddenly went to *Gavin out there somewhere in the dark cold depths of the sea, she imagined him struggling to get to the surface – he was a strong swimmer, so probably he had been knocked unconscious, she imagined him now floating down to the sea bed, his strong and athletic body just lying there, and now, possibly eaten by a shark. Oh, God, where were you to let this happen?* She screwed up her eyes tightly. *Oh what a terrible thought,* tears pricked her eyes and she shook her head trying to clear the horrible scene, *but it was all possibly very true, and she must try hard to stop thinking about it, he couldn't have suffered for long. She thought of him here beside her, they had only shared this bed for four nights,* the thought brought more hot tears, it was to have been a lifetime, *why was life so cruel?*

Suddenly there was loud laughter, a "HA, HA, HA" that rang from every corner of the house. She sat bolt upright and then jumped out of bed, grabbing her pink satin dressing gown from the chair. Eddie was barking ferociously again, she opened the door, quickly, Alan was already there in the shadows of the upper hall, she ran to him alarmed, "What is it?" Eddie was at the top of the stairs barking downwards, the loud laughter came again, "HA, HA, HA," the dog was frantic, and Charles and Oliver came from below stairs up into the main hall again, all were dumbfounded to see the white silhouette halfway up the stairs, and then it vanished. The house still shook with the echoing sounds of distant laughter that seemed to filled every nook and cranny before fading away then suddenly – it stopped! And a deadly silence clouded their ears… Even the dog stopped its frantic barking and stood like a statue waiting, puzzled like they all were, his tail just slowly wagging, his ears pricked, his eyes bright and staring, his back stiff – just waiting and ready to pounce should anything move. Then they all saw a slight flutter of something – it was so quick and no one knew what it was, but Eddie gave a sharp bark and went rushing down the stairs like a rocket and was sniffing around, but disappointed to find his prey was gone.

Julie was still gripping hard at the banisters. Alan was the first to move, "I'm sorry," he said again as he came quickly down the stairs, to face Charles and Oliver, who were both dumbfounded yet again, "We've seen it before, but I'm sure he can't harm anyone." Alan nodded and screwed up his face, "*It is* unnerving *I know*…" He took a deep breath, "It's late, try and get some sleep."

"It's Captain Honeybeck, isn't it?" said Oliver, with a curious deep frown. "We've seen it before."

Alan was surprised, "Well, yes, I guess it is Honeybeck, and it's a bit disturbing but we didn't want to worry you, we'll sort it out in the morning."

They both nodded, a little bewildered, and then Charles seeing Julie for the first time at the top of the stairs called up "Can I get you anything, Mrs Anderson?"

"No thank you, Charles, but Mr Stone is right, *it is disturbing*, but I'm sure he won't come back, try and get some sleep."

Eddie was sitting by the door. Charles said, "Shall I let the dog out, Mam?"

"Yes please."

Alan nodded and as he turned to go back up stairs the head of the serpent made him start, it seemed to leer viciously at him in the dim light from the chandelier, and then his own footsteps echoed eerily as he mounted the polished wooden staircase.

Charles walked warily across the open hall, his brown eyes darting from side to side, scanning every dark corner. He opened the front door cautiously just a few inches, and Eddie slipped out through the gap; he closed the door again quickly and locked it against the strong wind and rain.

Alan looked up as a voice came from above, it was Lucy and Rosalie the maids looking over the banisters from the attic, "What's happening?"

"Nothing, to worry about. A dog got locked in by mistake and was barking to go out."

"Oh," said Lucy, "I thought someone was laughing."

"Yes it was me, sorry to wake you. Go back to bed."

Alan and Julie now stood on the upper landing alone, looking down onto the main hall below, lit by the low light of the candelabra. Everyone else had gone back to bed and in the quietness the loud and slow tick, tick, tick, of the grandfather clock added to the eerie atmosphere…

The next morning at breakfast, the sun was bright, after the storm but the garden was a mess with branches and leaves strewn everywhere, and a huge mahogany tree lay forlornly across the garden, the chairs in the gazebo still damp and Charles had put towels on them. Then Eddie the dog came bounding up onto the gazebo, and greeted them with an excited wagging tail and a wide doggy grin.

Then Rick came up to the gazebo, saying that the staff were still talking about last night, and Alan filled him in about what had actually happened, and told Rick to explain to the staff about Honeybeck – he hoped that they would not leave.

"They already know," said Rick, "they are all local and apparently there had been talk in the village for years, in fact most of the island knows about the pirate, but I don't think any of them have ever experienced anything. Charles told me what happened. The maids were pretty scared but I think they will stay on." He looked around, "The garden is a mess, but the men will be here later to saw up the tree and take the logs away, they'll soon have everything back to normal."

"Thank you, Rick, it was a terrible storm wasn't it? And what with Honeybeck, it was quite scary," said Julie.

Alan didn't work on Saturdays and although sun was trying to come through, the day was dull and damp, and so they spent some more time in the library looking through Edward Turner's manuscript, again. There was some more on Desmond Honeybeck – it seemed he was a ladies' man, and had appeared to many of the Turner ladies, and Helen Turner claimed that she was on the stairs and that he had put an arm around her, and she had been so frightened that she had fled from the house leaving her husband Frederick and six children, and the very next day boarded a ship to England with a Mr George Mackleson a pig farmer from Holetown. "Sounds to me as if it was a good excuse to run away," Alan grinned. "By the way, did Rick find those paranormal people?"

"Don't know," Julie shook her head, "he didn't say, I'll ask him, might be a good idea to give them a try."

The phone was ringing, Julie answered it, Charles put it through – it was Michael Prescott, "Mellissa and I arrived on the island last night, what a storm it was a bit of a dodgy landing but it's wonderful to be here. Just wondered if you and Alan would like to come out for dinner tonight, short notice again I know, but we are only here for a couple of days – Mellissa has got to get back."

"Just a minute, Alan is here – it's Michael, they came in last night, do we want to go out for dinner tonight?"

Alan nodded, "Yes if you want to."

"Yes Michael, that would be lovely."

"OK. Meet you at Sandy Lane 7.30."

It was a nice evening. Michael and Mellissa were amazed to hear about Honeybeck on the stairs and the heavy laughter.

"Must be quite frightening," said Mellissa who now that she had got to know them a bit better had lost some of her aloofness, "I don't think I could sleep if I thought there was a ghost in the house."

"Well it's not a very happy situation," said Julie, "it is a bit frightening, but I don't think he can do any harm, do you Alan?"

Alan shook his head, and pulled a face, "No, but *it is unnerving* when he's there, and once he's gone, you can feel the atmosphere change, and luckily it doesn't happen every night, does it?" He glanced at Julie who shook her head, "Although, *we have heard footsteps* on the stairs and then found that there's no one there, but that laughter last night, was a bit daunting," he grimaced and raised his eyebrows with a nod at Michael.

"You still looking for that treasure?" Michael mused.

"Yes," Alan nodded with a chuckle, "we've found an old manuscript," he grinned, "and it's quite interesting. But we haven't located the treasure yet."

Michael grinned, "I wish you luck. But if you find it, let me take some photographs. *Please.* "

"I guess if this pirate is still hovering around," said Mellissa, "he must be buried there somewhere in the garden – have you found a grave?"

"Why?" Michael frowned at her.

"Well any ghost story I've ever read, it always seems that the ghost comes back to protect something. This pirate is afraid you'll find his treasure, and he can't rest. Perhaps the treasure is hidden in the grave with him?"

"Er… No! Haven't found a grave," said Julie, "but there is a cave, you could be right."

"A *cave?* You can bet your life the treasure is down there." Michael nodded, "and the body."

"Mmm," Alan rubbed his hands together, "didn't find much, except the skeleton, protecting a few silver coins, and some wine and weapons.

"Skeleton!" Mellissa gasped, her blue eyes wide open in amazement. She almost jumped off the chair, "you found a *skeleton?"* She looked at them all. "Well that's it then, he's not at rest, and that's why he's haunting the house."

"No, we've had the archaeologist in," said Alan, "and Julie, while reading through the manuscript, has found out that the skeleton is a native."

"Well it could be the pirate couldn't it?"

"No, Honeybeck was English, we've been reading all about it," said Julie.

"I should like to explore that cave," Michael said eagerly.

"There's nothing down there," Alan shook his head. "Except a few drawings on the wall, left by the Arawak Indians."

Michael's eyes lit up, "Arawak? God how old is *that?* I'd like to get a couple of shots of that, I could add that to the antique's mag. Did the archaeological people come back with any results?"

"Yes," Alan nodded, "the skeleton was about seventeenth-century, and we have just found out from reading in the manuscript, that it was the illegitimate son of one of the Turners, Thomas I think it was. Wasn't it, Julie? They were the people who lived in the house for generations after Honeybeck died. There is a mention of Honeybeck, I think he has haunted the house for years."

"Well, *did they* bury Honeybeck in the garden *then?"* Mellissa frowned curiously.

"We don't know, we haven't found anything about that yet, but this manuscript is very interesting."

"What about that other guy," said Michael, "Thurgold, you told me about him the last time I was here, what happened to him?"

"They probably buried them both together," said Mellissa. "After all, they killed each other didn't they?"

"Yes, as far as we know. We'll have to look further into our manuscript." Alan nodded at Julie, "it might even tell us where the grave is; we're not really reading it through, we are just dodging about, and finding different things of interest – it's about 460 pages. I guess we'll have to go exploring again."

"Can we come too?" Michael, sounded anxious, "I'd like to get a few photos of those Arawak drawings."

Julie was a bit reluctant, after getting stuck down there the last time, but they hadn't mentioned that, and she could see that Michael was really anxious to photograph the drawings. "Well yes, if you are only here for a couple of days, we can make it tomorrow," she nodded for Alan's approval, "OK, come tomorrow about midday – we'll have a drink, a light lunch, and then go exploring."

Michael chuckled happily, but Mellissa pulled a face, "OH! I *don't think* I want to go exploring a *cave*," she said indignantly, shrugging her right shoulder and looking at Michael in surprise, to think that *he,* would expect *her* to go exploring underground in a dirty cave. She shrugged her shoulders again, appalled at the very idea as her long red fingernails pushed back a wisp of blonde hair, and she give Michael a look of absolute disgust.

Julie could read her thoughts, *she wouldn't want to get her hands dirty or break a nail.* Although she herself wasn't relishing the thought of going into the cave again, and she couldn't really say no, or they would want to know why.

It had been an enjoyable evening, and was about 11.30 when Alan had driven Julie home to the Silver Lady Cottage. He got out of the car and held her hand to steady her as she stepped daintily, in high heels, on the uneven pathway through the bushes. They were suddenly surprised to see the staff all out on the patio. Rick and his girlfriend Chrystal, Charles and Oliver Lucy and Rosalie were all there together, with the two security guards and the German Shepherd Buddy.

Julie and Alan both anxiously asked, "What's happened?"

"It's Honeybeck," Rick was anxious, "he's been roaring through the house, things have been thrown about. The library is a mess."

"He came through the kitchen," said Oliver, his eyes wide with a worried look, "giving jumbled orders and whipped a saucepan of boiling water right across the kitchen, he wasn't ghostly, I thought it was some crank all dressed up in red, and then he disappeared... Young Robbie ran for his life I haven't seen him since... I was stunned..."

Alan was about to go in.

Rick caught his arm, "I don't think it's safe."

"No!" Ben Calder inclined his head, "we just came out even the dog was wary."

Alan stepped inside the circular hall, the flowers on the round table were knocked over and the water was running and dripping on the polished floor, he stood the vase up, and was then closely followed by Rick, Elliot, Calder and the dog. They made their way down the long panelled hall to the library where on opening the door, they all stopped dead still – books were on the floor, and the manuscript pages scattered all over the desk and the floor and on the chairs. They entered. There was a presence, they all felt it, something or someone was there; they stood stock still, the German Shepherd whined and would have turned back if Ben Calder had not pulled him close. "HONEYBECK!" Alan shouted, "HONEYBECK!"

There was a kind of low growl, they all looked at the dog, but it wasn't him, it got louder and filled the room. Then to their amazement a heavy glass ashtray just lifted and was thrown towards the door. Julie squealed and ducked as she just got to the door as the ashtray came flying through with great force, hitting the opposite wall and being smashed in half, she went quickly to Alan's side and stood open-mouthed at the mess.

"CAPTAIN HONEYBECK! WHAT IS THE MEANING OF THIS?" she commanded. All the men turned their heads sharply. It was having a lot to drink that made her sound brave – but she never expected to get a sign.

A definite cold chill filled the room and all eyes widened at the white mist and ghostly shadow that was barely visible as the gold cup on the desk lifted; all eyes were glued in astonishment to see it sail slowly on air across the room to the alcove near the portrait of Honeybeck, and was set down carefully by an unseen hand. They all held their breath, the air got colder and it was deadly quiet, but for the anxious panting of the dog.

"You didn't put it back," Alan whispered sideways to Julie. "That's what happened to Anthony. And he's DEAD!"

"Hummm," it came from all corners of the room, and they all glanced at each other, it was as if a long-drawn breath was taken in, you could almost imagine the chest expanding, and then the air blowing down the nose as the misty almost invisible shadow was fading. The dog growled, its ears pricked and alert, its head forward and as Dan Calder tightened the leash the forepaws left the floor and Buddy would have leaped forward.

Alan scanned the room his eyes darting from left to right, "HONEYBECK? HONEYBECK!" he called boldly, making all their hearts leap at the sudden explosion of his voice... The silence hung heavily in the room... Honeybeck was gone

"Fancy hearing a reply!" Rick was astonished. "It was a reply wasn't it?"

"Well, fancy the gold cup moving," Dan Calder's eyes were wide, as he let the long leash out, and the dog ran forward sniffing eagerly around the desk, but he was disappointed.

"A *ghost!*" Bill Elliot's big brown eyes showed white with surprise. He shook his head, "I would never have believed it, if I'd not seen it with my own eyes."

"What are we going to do?" Rick inclined his head with a frown.

Alan took a long breath and let it out loudly with a nod of his head, his shoulders deflating, "Dunno! I just dunno," he shook his head. "Did you contact those paranormal people?"

"Yeah, I found a group, but I said I'd let 'em know."

"Better get them in. Don't you think so, Julie?" She nodded to Rick.

Rick turned to Charles and Oliver, who had joined them and the security guards, "I rather you didn't talk too much about this, especially to the maids, I guess they know, but we don't want to scare them too much." The men all nodded, understanding. Then they made their way back down the long hall, to the girls who were still waiting on the patio, Alan and Julie stayed in the library.

Rick told the maids, "There nothing to worry about, it looks as if we've had had a break-in." They nodded, knowing it was more, and then made their way back up to the attic feeling uneasy.

The security men went back on duty, both staring more cautiously into the darkness around the garden and watching their backs.

Alan and Julie were still in the library, when Rick rejoined them with Chrystal.

"What a mess," said Julie, picking up some of the script.

"Don't do that now," Alan wrinkled his nose, "the maids can do it in the morning."

"All this done by a ghost? It's unbelievable," Chrystal was astonished, Rick had told her quickly something of what had happened but he hadn't told her yet about the gold cup moving. She shook her head, "Seems unbelievable."

Julie nodded, "I know."

"What *are these pages?*" Rick screwed up his eyes, referring to the hundreds of pages all over the floor, on the desk, and on the chairs, books lying open as if they had been flung from one side of the room to the other.

"It's a manuscript written by Edward Turner," said Julie, "I would think he was about the last of the Turners. There might have been more, but it finishes at 460 pages a bit abruptly. I think he intended to get it published. It's very interesting, isn't it Alan? The gold cup for instance, was found by the body of one, Anthony Turner, he was said to have been killed by Honeybeck."

"Yeah," Alan nodded, his eyebrows arched. "And, it seems obvious that Honeybeck doesn't like anyone touching his things," his eyebrows still raised. "Did you tell her?" He nodded to Rick.

Rick shook his head and turned to Chrystal. "That gold cup over there just moved from the desk on its own," he grimaced.

"Really?" Chrystal was alarmed, her voice rose, "it's weird."

"Yeah," Alan sighed, "but there's nothing we can do tonight," he looked at his watch it was nearly one o'clock, he looked at Julie, "I think I'd better stay the night again, not unless you want to go to a hotel?"

She shook her head, "No not if you stay."

Rick and Chrystal left, Rick saying that if they needed him in the night just to give him a call.

CHAPTER SEVENTEEN

The night had been uneventful and in the morning, after breakfast, Alan and Julie spent time in the library where the maids had piled the papers up on the desk, and now they had to put them back into numerical order. Over coffee, they chatted about the small golden cup, and saying that they would not touch it again and they had decided not to mention it to Michael and Mellissa, who were to arrive at midday. By then, Alan and Julie were by the pool, and Charles opened a bottle of white wine before lunch, which they all enjoyed. They had a light chicken salad down by the pool – the first time that they had eaten there.

Michael had brought his camera and took some photos of Julie and Alan together, while Mellissa sat in different poses model-like under the palms around the rocky pool, but then that was her job anyway. Michael soon finished the photographing, he was very anxious to go down and take some photos in the cave. Julie had said that she didn't really want to go down into the cave again, but since last night Michael had persuaded Mellissa into going with them, saying that he wanted to get some shots of her in the cave and that no other model would ever get the chance to be photographed with prehistoric drawings. Therefore she agreed, and so Julie knew that she must go with them anyway.

Michael was amazed at the drawings on the wall, he had brought an arc light with him but hadn't realized that there was no electricity down in the cave but the bright lanterns held by Alan and Julie were enough to do the job.

Mellissa shivered in the darkness, looking around at the cold grey coral stone walls. She didn't like being here and the drawings were of no interest to her. But Michael was enthralled to think that they were over a thousand years old, he would put them in the antiques magazine in a few weeks' time, he was sure that the editor would be pleased. They went through the archway into the next cave, and he took many more photographs. Both Julie and Alan smiled at his enthusiasm, he was excited and couldn't stop talking, but Mellissa was tight-lipped and annoyed, and stood her arms wrapped around her, shivering with thoughts of why she had let Michael talk her into coming down into this miserable, dark, damp and creepy place. Then suddenly there was a loud bang that echoed through the darkness, and made them all jump.

"What the *hell*, was that?" Michael looked alarmed.

"The trapdoor shut again," said Alan casually, but looking warily in the shadowed light at Julie who took a breath and bit her lip. Alan had put a heavy stone on top of the open door this time to keep it open.

Julie held her breath, thinking of the last time they were trapped in here, but she said nothing. There came a gruff chuckle, Mellissa grabbed Michael's arm, and gasped as the mist began to form in the archway. "WHAT IS IT! WHAT IS IT? WHAT'S DOWN HERE?" She squealed in a tiny high-pitched tone of alarm.

Julie felt the icy cold atmosphere gripping her arms again, seeing the white mist forming once more into the faded almost invisible image of a large man in a three-cornered hat – she held her breath.

"Is *that him?*" Michael whispered, his fingers fumbling nervously and clumsily with the camera that he was so used to handling and not taking his eyes off the misty image. Finally the camera flashed several times but the mist was fading quickly, and a low chuckle filled the cave.

Mellissa held her breath, "*Oh my god!*" she gasped, "was that a *ghost? Oh my god!* Is that what you're living with?" She turned to Julie.

"Yes," Julie's hushed whisper came out of the shadows, every bit as breathless and nervous, "we've seen it before, I don't think there is any harm, but I don't like it." She didn't mention that they had been trapped down here, but she was wondering just how long it would be before Rick realised that they were all missing, and then she remembered that he always left early on a Saturday, and they could be down here for the whole weekend. And had Alan got his phone, and would he have to climb the wall again? At least this time they were not alone and Michael was here to help, but she could see that Mellissa was a nervous wreck.

"Yes," Alan suddenly said now the mist had cleared, "we think it was the ghost of Honeybeck, and I think he shuts that trapdoor, that's why I put the stone on it and laid it flat back so it couldn't possibly shut, like it did the last time."

"OH MY GOD!" Mellissa put a hand to her throat as if she was stifled, "you've been stuck down here before?"

Alan turned to Julie, "Maybe it was him that shut that skeleton down here?"

"OH!" Mellissa gasped, "don't say that! Where is it?" She looked around her nervously.

"Oh, don't worry, it's not here now they've removed it."

"Thank god!" Mellissa breathed again, sounding quite weak.

"Don't you collapse on us," Alan warned.

"It's alright," Julie patted her arm, gently, "if we don't show up Rick will guess where we are."

"You mean we are really trapped down here? With the *ghost* of a *pirate?*" Michael gasped, "Do you think I'll get some more shots? I'm hoping that these will come out OK." There was excitement in his voice as if he just couldn't wait.

"Oh MY GOD!" Mellissa burst, putting a hand to her head. "For God's sake shut up. Is that all you can think about – getting a bloody good shot of a ghost? We're trapped down here, Michael!"

"Well darling, these opportunities don't come very often."

"Thank God, they DON'T! What are we going to do, and what good will your blasted pictures be if we are trapped down here?"

"I don't think we are," said Alan, "the bolt was loosened when Rick and I were down here a week or so ago."

"You mean you've been trapped down here TWICE BEFORE?" Michael was astonished. Mellissa groaned and caught her breath.

Alan kept his fingers crossed and his hand automatically felt for the cell phone, "Yes, but we got out both times. We had better make our way back."

"What through there, where, IT'S BEEN!" Mellissa's voice echoed back a high-pitched screech and she shook her head, "I'm not going back through there."

"We have to," Alan nodded, "There's no other way out, and it's alright he's gone now, come on." They made their way back through the arch, both girls shivering at the thought of going through where the mist had been, there was nothing, but they were looking for something, and automatically felt a chill.

Alan climbed the ladder and punched hard at the trapdoor – it was as he suspected, closed tight. He shouted back down, "Can't budge it!" Then with a bit of a chuckle he said, "Hey Julie, you can't find another one of those skeleton legs can you?"

"Oh Alan, *don't!*" He chuckled.

Michael, was holding the lantern, and they watched helplessly as Alan was banging away. Mellissa, although standing quietly with her arms wrapped tightly around her was feeling frantic inside, her heart thumping away and shivering not only with the cold but with her nerves.

Julie was wringing her hands, she knew Rick would come, but how long would they have to wait until he realized they were missing, Charles wouldn't miss them until six o'clock for cocktails, which she had arranged earlier and she was beginning to feel anxious, and then that rough chuckle came again and they all stopped to look around but saw nothing in the lantern light. Mellissa went into floods of tears, and Julie put an arm around her, telling her not to worry, it would be alright, even though she was worried herself.

"Oh shut up, Mellissa!" Michael's voice came sharply out of the shadows, "do you think we are stuck down here forever, don't be so stupid."

"It's so cold," she wailed, "and with that *horrible* ghost."

"HORRIBLE?" A distorted low hollow deep voice came out of the darkness, and they all stopped, looking around in alarm.

"Who said *that*?" Alan was looking down from up the ladder. They all shook their heads no one answered. Their nerves were tight with tension, and the deadly silence loud in their ears like a high-pitched whistle. But it had stopped Mellissa wailing for a moment and then she burst into tears again. Julie felt the cold on her arms, knowing it was the icy chill – Honeybeck was there.

Alan went on with his hammering, when suddenly they heard a voice, "OK, OK, I'm comin'!" At first Julie thought it was Honeybeck. And then to their relief the bolt was being pulled back and the trapdoor opened to shafts of sunlight, and the smiling gold tooth of old Gibbons, "Got stuck again did yer? You're lucky I don't usually work in this part of the garden on a Saturday, but then I jest got 'ere and 'eard yer bangin'!"

Mellissa was more than relieved, she covered her face with her hands, which was just as well, because black mascara was streaming down her cheeks, one false eyelash was hanging and she was now crying tears of relief. Michael put an arm around her trying to jolly her along, but it was not a loving comforting arm, "Come cheer up, you're not hurt."

They left almost immediately, Michael thanking Julie for drinks and lunch, and said he couldn't wait to see the photos. Mellissa gave him a disgusted look as they waved goodbye.

A few days had gone by, Michael had phoned disappointed – his ghostly photos had been a failure, but the drawings were good. Julie spent her days sunbathing, and reading by the pool, vowing never to go into that cave again. Most afternoons and evenings she and Alan spent in the library; the maids had cleaned the room of broken china and glass and put the books back, although not in order, and Edward Turner's manuscript was now back in numerical order and on the desk again. Alan had taken her out for dinner in the week and had come to the Silver Lady for Sunday lunch, with an enormous bunch of ginger lilies. She gave him a kiss on the cheek and thanked him, and then they had spent the rest of the day by the pool. Still living with their grief, but life was somewhat back to normal, and there had been no more trouble with Honeybeck.

A week later was pretty much the same – Zena and Perry had come for dinner, telling her what a fabulous holiday they'd had. The golf club had had a dinner, and she and Alan had gone with Zena and Perry; and now Alan was thinking of joining the golf club – he played when in the UK but since being here in Barbados he had not had the time what with the new job, and of course losing Suzie, he was only just beginning to get interested in life again.

Julie was once again flipping back and forth through the pages of Edward Turner's manuscript and the last chapter was on Desmond Honeybeck. It started with…

'Captain Desmond Honeybeck, so I have been told, and also have read in an old diary, had sailed the Caribbean waters for several years, his ship the *Silver Lady* was feared when seen on the horizon off the island of Barbados, and more feared when the crew came ashore. Cruelty aboard ship was a daily occurrence, according to the diary that had belonged I suppose to an old seaman, it seemed that his grandfather had been part of the crew. For just the slightest transgression, or disobeying the smallest order, was death by flogging up to a hundred strokes most men died before twenty strokes. For instigating a fight, keel hauling in shark infested waters was the rule, and for one poor soul Adam Shawcroft, for just speaking a polite word of good day to the captain's mistress who had just come aboard, he was tied to the figurehead of the *Silver Lady* for three days in the heat of the blazing sun, the salt spray drying his sunburned skin as the ship dipped continuously into a rough sea, and on a wild and stormy night his face was smashed and unrecognizable the next morning where it had continually dived into rough waves. And of course he was drowned. The *Silver Lady* was feared by seamen, she rammed ships and boarded them, robbing them of their cargo of gold and silver precious stones, silks, from the Orient, and precious spices used for the persevering food, they stole anything and everything. Then slaughtering the captain and the officers, and taking over the ship, and the crew forced to maintain it. On seeing the *Silver Lady* flag flying, she was often fired upon by other ships, or some ships would run from her. From the shore, the lookout from Mount Standfast here on the west coast of the island, on seeing her on the horizon, made ready the cannon and a warning signal of drums was sounded right around the island. The settlers hid their valuables, their food, their wine, and if possible their livestock, chickens pigs and goats. Wives and daughters ran to hide in the hills, and the villages were completely ransacked. After an attack many people were left dead, or dying; young men taken for slavery and woman quite often found and taken for pleasure and handed round to all members of the crew. There were competitions on the deck in front of the whole crew, screaming drunk and whistling to see who could last the longest, and then when the women were worn and broken they were thrown haphazardly to the sharks. The *Silver Lady* was feared throughout the Caribbean waters and known as the death ship, most mariners on board had been shanghaied, and most didn't live long. And when she sailed into Carlyle Bay quite often under cannon fire from the shore, the whole of the island was on alert. And everything and anything was given up without a whim. Honeybeck had acquired furnishing for this lavish house by just asking very politely for it, no one ever dared to refuse it meant torture and death. The rocking chair in the drawing room was his prize possession, he acquired it from the Governor General, after cutting the throat of his aid for no reason at all. The rocking chair to this day still rocks with a ghostly presence, and I do not know of one of the family who has ever dared to sit in it. I should correct myself here, there was a Clarence Turner a boy aged twelve who sat in the rocking chair and he was unexpectedly dead the next day! The diary also talks of chests containing silver and gold coins, precious gems, rubies, emeralds and sapphires, diamonds and pearls, that had been seen by secret eyes and carried up the beach and carted to the house by mule in the dead of night, then carried through the house. After this, none of the carriers survived to see the next day, their bodies never found. Even Thurgold had no idea of the enormity of the hoard or where it was hidden, and Honeybeck, even on their many drunken nights, gave no clues.

How the source of *this information* came about, I do not know. I found it scribbled on a treasure map tucked inside the diary, but it proved to be useless, and maybe the treasure itself is even a myth…'

Julie read that bit again, carried through the passage – *So! The treasure was, if of course it did exist, in the passage? Wherever that was? And if of course those that had transported the treasure were killed they had found no more skeletons.* She frowned and then read on.

It seemed that Honeybeck liked the ladies, many mistresses, she read, '…had passed though the Silver Lady Cottage and graced his bed, one especially beautiful Italian girl, the Contessa Maria Delores Consuela Cappolini, wife of Mario Eduardo Cappolini and captain of a galleon called *The Morannia*, who had been run through with a sword several times by Honeybeck, while hanging by his feet from the yardarm of his ship after it had been boarded by the *Silver Lady* cut-throats. Captain Cappolini did not reveal the whereabouts of the precious stones his ship was carrying, but they were found hidden in his cabin, and then his beautiful wife Maria, kidnapped, and eventually brought back to the Silver Lady Cottage with no means of escape. This next piece of information I had found in and old and faded letter at the back of a drawer in the desk in the library, it was written in Italian, there was no signature – it had been torn off. I had it translated. It seemed that Honeybeck, in one of his drunken stupors, had talked in his sleep, revealing the whereabouts of his treasure. The Contessa Maria had given Thurgold this information and in return he had promise to help her escape...'

The diary went on...

'It was after one of the many drunken evenings, that Honeybeck was suspicious of Thurgold's unusual behaviour, asking questions that he normally never asked, and it seemed then, that the captain had caught Thurgold in the early dawn going for the treasure, and Honeybeck had drawn his sword. Thurgold had also drawn his sword, but with Honeybeck's raging he had run, chased by Honeybeck on to the patio. Both men were excellent swordsmen and the fight lasted well into the daylight, both men exhausted and barely able to stand but then Honeybeck had the advantage and lashed out, catching Thurgold in the belly and he fell with a shout of great pain and lay very still. Honeybeck then getting his breath back stood exhausted looking down on him and then feeling a little sad, they had come a long way together, and fought many a battle side by side on the high seas, and then afterwards drinking and laughing at their conquest trusting each other, until the greed of the treasure came between them.

Honeybeck felt saddened thinking that he had killed his long-time friend and he knelt down beside him, then Thurgold with his last ounce of energy surprised Honeybeck by thrusting the sword in his the chest near his heart. And Honeybeck fell backwards, both men now dishevelled, their clothing cut and in ribbons, their bodies maimed and blooded and their faces pained, now lay very still in a pool of their own blood... As the sun rose to another clear and warm and sunny day the watching house servants and slaves that had been aroused in the early dawn by the sounds of the captain's rage and the clash of steel, looked on from windows and from behind trees and bushes with wide and frightened eyes afraid to move or go near, only the twittering of the birds broke the deadly silence of the new day... It was obvious that somebody had to take charge, but even two of the officers, John Webster and George Gossamund who were staying at the house until the next voyage, looked on in absolute stunned bewilderment to see their captain and first officer both dead! It was at that moment that Oswald Turner the ship's boatswain, a giant of a man, who just happened to have walked three miles from the ship to the house with a message for the captain, stepped on to the patio; he was also stunned, but then, seeing the situation and being used to giving orders and getting things done aboard ship, he took charge. A rough, and red-haired Scotsman, he suddenly roared orders to the dumbfounded slaves who suddenly came alive and fled to the cane fields, even the overseers were at a lost as to what to do, but Oswald soon took charge. The officers still shocked and bewildered were glad to allow Oswald to carry on.

Oswald Turner found that Thurgold was dead, and that Honeybeck was barely alive, he got the servants to take the Captain to his room, and ordered the female staff to tend his wounds, but Honeybeck only lasted for three days.

The two officers had now gone back to take charge of the ship, Webster acting as captain, and leaving Oswald in charge of the house.

Oswald, was a rough and hard man, he had been a seaman all his life, he was used to dealing with the roughneck crew, and for the next few weeks he took charge of the house, and the sugar plantation, and it was said that he proved to be a good master. It is also said that he took a wife and had children, but it is not known if it was the dark-haired beauty Contessa Maria Cappolini. But after Oswald's death by the sword some years later at sea, the house had been empty for years, nothing is known of his wife or his family. But a skeleton staff was appointed to maintain the house and the antiques. It was then that Sir George Turner and his wife Lady Louisa, came from England, to take up residence in the house, around the mid-seventeenth century. I would imagine that Sir George was a son or a relation of Oswald Turner I don't know for sure, there seems to be no record of this. But the Turners had occupied the Silver Lady Cottage for generations. Being a wealthy family, most, like myself, having had a good education in London England. Whether the family's great wealth originally came from Honeybeck's treasure, I don't know. To my, knowledge, the treasure has never been found. But the ghost of Desmond Honeybeck still lurks in the shadows, believed to be protecting his treasure and that is why the family eventually left the house; he became a threat, he was a violent and powerfully malicious man, especially to women, I have already sent my family to England.

It is months now since I have continued my writing, and now in my old age I spend my long days here alone, quietly in the library while the ghost of Captain Desmond Honeybeck still haunts the house and the garden to this very day. I have the feeling that I am forever watched, and the days are getting worse. But now I am thrilled and delighted to say that after searching for many years, I, Edward Turner, have this very morning, located the passage. I have not yet explored, but I am sure it will lead to the long lost treasure... It is now a warm and sunny mid-afternoon, I have waited this long to be alone. But... Wait! NO! Honeybeck is here again! Hovering close by, and NOW, a roaring and raging powerful voice is floating on the air, daring me to touch his treasure, books are falling from the shelves by unseen hands and the whole house is filled with the giant shadow of his presence, so now the treasure must wait a while. For months I have lived in fea...'

There was a long squiggle of ink across the paper, the last few words on page 460 seemed to be scribbled as if in haste, as if he was in a hurry to get them down, Julie was sure that the last word was meant to be 'fear'. It sent a shiver down her spine. There was also a wide brown smudge right down the paper, she wondered if Edward Turner had been surprised by Honeybeck while in mid-sentence, or could someone else have struck him from behind?

Julie sat spellbound, her elbows on the desk gripping her hands tightly together. Edward Turner, while writing this very manuscript, must have been sitting right here, as she was now. It sent a shiver through her body. He *had found* the passage? what passage? *and where... where was the passage?*... She glanced from side to side and then around the room, imagining the terror of books being flung across the room, but it didn't say the passage was in *this* very room. Then her thoughts were of

185

Edward Turner, *he had died right here in this very chair with the manuscript in front of him just as she was now*, this sent goosebumps down her spine again and she glanced behind her. *Was Honeybeck watching her now? Did he know she was also looking for his treasure, how could he possibly know?* She felt another shiver go down her spine. Could the ghost of Desmond Honeybeck really *kill...*?

She got up and went out onto the patio, feeling edgy, *better away from the house, or was it?* The staff were there if she called. Edward Turner must have had staff, but he said he was alone... Feeling nervous she decided to phone Alan and went back into the library, looking around her warily expecting Honeybeck to be there. Looking at his portrait on the wall gave her the creeps. She was about to sit at the desk again, and then decided to stand, cringing as she saw the brown smudge on the page 460 and thinking again that Edward had died right here. She dialled the number and Alan's secretary, Rebecca Childs, said that he was not in the office, and she left a message asking him to phone her as soon as he came in.

She turned to go out into the garden again, when the phone rang – it was Alan, he'd just walked into the office; she told him a little and asked him to come for dinner as she had a lot tell him. She had not seen him for nearly a week, he had been busy at the office.

Later that evening they sat in the gazebo and she talked all through dinner, saying that she felt more scared after reading the manuscript, "Do you think a ghost can *kill?*"

Alan twisted his lips, he could see that she was worried, but felt that she really had nothing to fear from a ghost. But of course he couldn't be really sure and suggested that Rick call the paranormal people.

"Well I haven't had any more trouble since the last time," she told him, "but after reading Edward Turner's report... And, there's a big smudge over the last page as if he was interrupted. It could have been Honeybeck? Come and have a look."

They went back to the library, she went in warily, the chilly feeling had gone. She showed Alan the pages, there was a long squiggle of the pen and a splodge of ink where the nib had caught the paper, and a wide brown smudge, "*Alan*, do you think that could be *blood?*"

He ran his finger over the smudge, raising his eyebrows, "Yeah! Could be! Perhaps somebody hit him from behind. It certainly does look strange but I can't believe it was a ghost, can you?"

Two evenings afterwards, a paranormal group arrived, Alan and Rick were there, and they all spent an hour or so discussing Honeybeck. Julie showed them Edward Turner's manuscript, and showed them what she thought was a bloodstain.

There were five of them, all American, Harry Shore the leader of the group. Steve Gilson was in charge of setting up the cameras and the computer, to which they would all be in contact, and John Simpson was a physic, Margie Kelly and Pam Western, made up the group. It was dark by seven o'clock, they suggested switching off the lights and lighting candles in the drawing room where most of the activity seemed to be and in the main hall, also each one had a torch.

Steve had set up his computer in one of the other drawing rooms which was rarely used; Julie, Alan and Rick sat with him watching the screen. He had set up the cameras and could see into the drawing room, the library and the main hall. Margie was there in the circular hall facing the stairs; also Charles, Oliver, Lucy and Rosalie the maids – they all stood quietly in the shadowed hallway watching. It was eerie as always and especially now as the only source of light throughout the house was candlelight. Julie had the thought that it must have been like this when Edward Turner was here.

Pam was upstairs in the guest bedroom, the one with the patchwork bedcover where Julie had seen the door close on several occasions.

John had been in the library but was now in the TV drawing room, with Harry. John shone the torch around and said that he could feel a presence; there was a click and both men turned and were on the alert, but nothing moved, Harry's whispered voice came through, "Did you hear that, Steve?"

"Yes, the rocking chair is showing red, and there was a sigh, on the monitor, did you hear it?"

"No." Harry's whispered reply came through the screen. Then, "CAPTAIN HONEYBECK?" Harry asked in a bold voice, "are you here? Can you make your presence known to us?" All was silent. "Can you move something?" Both had their torches on the rocking chair. Nothing moved, "Can you talk to us?" They waited. All was quiet, the rocking chair had not moved, there seemed to be no activity, and they stopped after midnight.

Alan thanked them for coming, and Harry said that they would come back tomorrow evening.

It had been into the early hours of the morning, after the paranormal group had left, that Rick finally left. The rest of the staff had already gone to bed. Alan was to stay the night. Outside his room, he gave Julie a peck on the cheek and said goodnight, watching as she went further down the hall to her room, he called "goodnight," and she turned and waved before she went into the room and closed the door. He closed the door, the house was quiet...

Harry Shore had mentioned something about her being under stress, she told him of losing her husband, Harry had said that Honeybeck could be drawing on her energy and if she could try to be a little calmer maybe he would go away. But of course, her mind was on Gavin and the disastrous tragedy every day. But looking for the treasure did help to keep her mind busy.

It was almost 6.15, and Charles told her that the paranormal group had arrived and were setting up their equipment again. Tonight, she had arranged dinner for them all; Alan had left the office early, and now Charles was serving them all cocktails in the gazebo.

"What's that glowing in the garden?" Harry Shore had suddenly noticed the glowing lady.

"Oh, that's the Silver Lady the figurehead of the ship," said Alan. He explained what they had read about Honeybeck and the figurehead rising to the surface of the water and saving the pirate's life. They were interested and all wandered down the garden with drinks in hand, and gathered around the silver lady.

"I can feel a lot of energy here," said John, "why do you light her up like that?"

"Don't know," Julie smiled, "I don't know why she glows, I think it is some sort of special paint."

John frowned, and shook his head, he looked puzzled, "No, it's not that, she's sort of singing inside, can't you hear it?"

They all frowned and shook their heads, "I can't hear anything," said Harry.

"Neither can I," Alan grimaced, and the girls shook their heads. It was then that Charles announced that the dinner was being served.

"Well do you know why she glows?" Julie asked as she walked across the garden with John.

"I don't really know much, but it could be a mixture of coral and salt crystals, probably a build-up after hundreds of years. I read somewhere that granite deep in the earth gets hot and when it cools it forms crystals – maybe it does with coral stone – and after so many years the wood must be porous, perhaps the sunlight gets in and heats the crystals through the day." He inclined his head, "It's strange, I really don't understand it."

Julie smiled, "I was going to have it removed but the old gardener told me it would be unlucky, so I've had second thoughts on it now," she chuckled.

"He may be right, if it's been there three hundred years," John smiled.

After dinner in the gazebo, they gathered in the drawing room, and then the paranormal group took themselves off to the same positions as before. It was almost 11.30, Harry contacted Steve, asking if he had got any reaction on the computer.

Steve said something about a red glow in the rocking chair again and that it was a sign of activity, but the rocking chair had not moved.

Julie, sitting very tense with Alan and Rick in the drawing room, suddenly jumped as Harry spoke to the empty rocking chair, "Captain Honeybeck, are you there? Captain? Captain?" He raised his voice, "CAPTAIN! I ask you to leave this house, you are not welcome here, leave these people in peace. GO! I order you to go! In the name of Jesus Christ, go! Leave this house! You are not welcome here!" There was a low growl, which made them all look up.

Then there was a click, all their ears pricked up again, and Harry quickly spoke to Steve on the intercom, "Did you hear that! See anything?"

"Yeah, heard it, something fluttered but it's gone now, all's seems clear."

Then Margie's voice came through the speaker, "There's footsteps going up the stairs, can't see anything."

Harry and John left the drawing room quickly, followed by Alan, Julie and Rick. As they reached the hall a door opened and shut upstairs. Alan and Julie glanced at each other, just as a squeal came on the intercom from Pam – she said somebody was on the bed beside her. Harry and John rushed up the stairs, but Pam was sitting on the bed alone, she said that the atmosphere had changed, it was cold. Steve's voice came through the intercom he said that he saw the bed move, and there was an indentation as if someone was lying there, John said he could feel a strong presence, and then suddenly it was gone.

CHAPTER EIGHTEEN

The days and weeks went on and there had been no more ghostly activity. Julie was convinced that the paranormal group had solved the problem. She was beginning to relax and life seemed to be getting back to somewhere near normal. Eddie the dog came and sat with her by the pool, and he was company, she talked to him and he seemed to understand, and she had taken him back to his home. Now she had made a friend of Loretta Carding and her husband Ben, they had a nice house a mile or so down the road from the Silver Lady. Ben apologized for Eddie, saying that he had put up a fence but he just jumped it and he couldn't keep him in, and that he didn't think it fair to tie him up all day. And Julie had said not to worry, as she enjoyed having him.

Loretta was Bajan, and Dan was English, he had been on the island for thirty-six years, and they had been married for thirty-four, and had a son and daughter at college in America. They were sad to hear Julie's story of losing Gavin. They of course had heard about the catamaran disaster.

Loretta said that she did a lot of charity work, for the dogs' home, and they needed drivers to pick up animals and take them mostly to the vet; some people could not drive or were housebound, or sometimes stray dogs wandered into people's gardens, and they needed to be transported to the Animal Shelter.

Julie said that she would be willing to help out, but she didn't want a full-time job; although if they were stuck for a driver she was willing to take a turn. During the month she met a lot of nice people and a lot of friendly dogs, and at last she felt as if she belonged. It also helped her to cope, keeping her mind busy. She had emailed her mother and told her of the Pet Life Organization and this made her mother feel better, knowing that she was at last doing something and making friends. She also kept in touch with Gavin's parents, and they were, like her, coming to terms with their loss.

A strong breeze blew across the garden, although the atmosphere was very humid. Eddie pricked up his ears and sat up, a large grey cloud came over, and a few spots of rain, she told Eddie anxiously to "come on." He immediately got up and they rushed up the coral stone steps, the dog bounding in front of her, but before they were halfway up, the rain poured down and the wind nearly took her off her feet. They ran to the gazebo but the wind blew the rain in, and she made another quick dash to the arched patio, Eddie passing her at speed his tail wagging excitedly as they both slipped in through the drawing room. She was almost soaked to the skin, then Eddie shook himself and she squealed getting even more wet. The rain hammered noisily on the roof and the wind rattled the louvered doors setting the rocking chair in motion; Eddie barked and growled at the chair, Julie thought it was the wind, Eddie was sure that it wasn't and he ran out of the door with a squeal as if his tail was on fire. On the patio he turned and waited for her, then barked telling her to come. Julie, taking the hint from him, went out onto the patio and quickly into the library.

It was warm in the library, the doors were wide open as usual, and Eddie followed her through. The wind rattled the door and was blowing the drapes but the rain didn't spray in. Usually the heavy shower only lasted a few minutes, it could come from one large cloud passing over, but this storm seemed to have come raging in and so quickly, the wind seemed at gale force, and so she decided to busy herself with Edward Turner's manuscript again. Flipping haphazardly through the pages she suddenly saw, 'passage way'. She turned back a few pages, and there it was, Edward had written, 'I found a book written by Ben Turner.' Julie frowned, "But, *what*? What passageway?" Edward had mentioned the passageway before on page 460, but Edward was now dead! She wished now that she had read the whole manuscript from the beginning instead of dodging about, she read on…

'It was on the 16th December 1648 and Daniel Turner's 12th birthday, he had found the key to the passageway, he was excited, thinking that he had found Honeybeck's treasure, and he had run to tell his younger brother Benjamin who was nine. The passageway was dark when they looked inside and so they both got a candelabra with three tall candles each to light their way. Daniel ventured in holding the candelabra high, Benjamin following. The twisted rough coral stone steps were deep and they went down and they proceeded cautiously, the flickering candles making shadows on the coral stone walls. It was spooky and quiet, and Benjamin giggled and they were laughing at the echo of their voices, so Benjamin had told his father later, and Daniel turned to speak and missed a step and was tumbling down the steps, the flaming candelabra falling from his hand. Benjamin said he shouted, and ran down after him, he was very still, and he shook Daniel but he was unconscious, and he was alarmed to see in the shadowed light that blood was running from his head and his nose. He said he was frightened, not knowing what to do, and then rushed back up the steps, to get help, and to find his father. In his haste he said he stood the candelabra down at the top of the stone steps and rushed out through the house calling his father. When John his father, and the butler and the footmen got to the passageway the flames were bright, the candelabra that Benjamin had set down had toppled down the steps, knocking the candelabra that Daniel had dropped halfway down the steps, and the fire had caught Daniel's clothing and he was engulfed in flames. The men quickly took off their coats to douse the flames, and by the time Benjamin had run through the house again to alert the servants and they had come with buckets of water, it was too late, Daniel had burned to death...

Of course the house was in mourning, the passage was locked up and Benjamin put back the key, and to my knowledge the passage was never opened again. Whether others in the family know of this I couldn't say, I have never heard it mentioned, I found this information in an old diary.'

Julie looked around – the *key?* Benjamin had put back the key. But where? In here? Where? She had looked so many times for the safe key, and she couldn't find it, *so now there was also a key to the passage,* she screwed up her face, "What passage?" she muttered, shaking her head thoughtfully, *must be a secret passage, and what room was it in? This Daniel had thought to find Honeybeck's treasure. So! Was this Honeybeck's revenge? Killing the boy?*

CHAPTER NINETEEN

Alan phoned to say that he couldn't make it for dinner; he was halfway through Holetown and the road had been flooded by the storm that had now subsided, but it was still raining, and there were trees down. He had also tried the highway, and the a car had come to grief – a tree had fallen on it, people were injured may even have been killed, and the police were turning people back, and so he had gone back to his little house. "What's it like your end?"

"Well I don't really know, about the roads but it's still raining, terrible storm wasn't it?"

Julie had dinner early, alone on the arched patio, the humidity was high, and the rain was just drizzling now; it was the first time that the patio dining area had been used; the night was very still, and now everything was damp and sticky, and in the semi-darkness and by the low security lights she could see that the garden was a mess with leaves and branches strewn all over the place. Her mind was still on *the passageway, and the key.* A dog barked somewhere, it distracted her – maybe it was Eddie. She sat quietly sipping a glass of wine, and she wished Eddie was here with her now, he was good company and she hadn't seen him leave.

It was just about eight o'clock, and she moved back into the library, not wanting to sit in the spooky drawing room watching the TV on her own, not that there was much to watch anyway. The house was quiet, and the pale blue shaded table lamps made spooky shadows in the corners; she would arrange with Rick to put a radio in here tomorrow, she seemed to be spending more time in here than anywhere else. Walking around the spacious room even the soft rustle of her silk skirt and the soft sound of her heels flapping on the leather mules seemed to thunder in the silence, and tonight her nerves felt on edge. She stood by the desk, Edward

Turner's manuscript still open as she had left it. She looked at it, Benjamin had put the key back, her thoughts again were, *But where did you put it, Ben? Was it in this room? She couldn't even find the key to the safe! And now there was another key to be found.* She opened the covers of a few books at random that were on the shelf near to the safe, hoping perhaps the key would drop out, and even more anxious now, hoping to find the key to the passage, she felt excitement rise within her but then if she did find the key, then she would have to find the passage, and that could be anywhere in the whole house, she grimaced, and sighed with that thought, the excitement was draining away. "And, I wonder *is* the passage the key to the treasure?" she muttered to herself, tapping her fingernails on the manuscript. "Yes, it has to be." Then she went though the desk again for the umpteenth time, muttering, "There must be a secret drawer here somewhere."

Rick tapped on the louvered patio door interrupting her mutterings and poked his head inside; it made her jump, "Are you alright, Mrs Anderson? I saw the light on, I'm just leaving."

"Oh!" She looked up in surprise, "I thought you'd gone! Mr Stone couldn't even get here the roads are all flooded and blocked."

"Yes I know, that's why I'm late leaving, and I'm walking home, can't chance the car, not that it's any distance anyway. I've just had a walk around the garden, there are tiles off the roof, and a big mahogany tree down right across the garden."

"Oh, I didn't know," she shook her head, "terrible storm wasn't it?"

"Yes, we do get them sometimes. I've phoned Tommy Miles, he's sending his workmen out here in the morning to saw up the tree – it looks huge, but can't see much now in the dark. I expect it will take a few days to really clear it up and cart it away." He nodded, "Well, I'll be going then."

"Thanks Rick, goodnight, see you tomorrow."

"Good night, Mrs Anderson, Mam."

She went back to the manuscript.

Alan phoned again, said that he was back home, and asking if she was alright. She told him about the passageway and that she was still looking for the key. And then he asked if she would like to go out to dinner tomorrow evening and said he would pick her up at 7.30.

The restaurant was full as it was every Friday night, buzzing with people, and good music, waiters rushing around with good food and wine. Alan said he needed a drink after a busy day in the office, and they sat watching the sea rolling up on to the sandy beach just a few yards away. The lights of a cruise ship twinkled out into the darkness, the sky still cloudy after the storm. She was telling him about the passageway, and saying that she had looked everywhere for a key, "I think Honeybeck must have been obsessed with keys – there was no key to the barn, no key to the safe and now there's this passage with a missing key, but then, if I find it, I still don't know where the passage is anyway." They laughed together. As the weeks had gone by they were both feeling more relaxed in each other's company and it was good to laugh again.

"But still it gave you something to do while the storm was raging. Did the guys come to saw up the tree this morning?"'

"Yes they've done some, but it's huge, it will take about a week to really finish it. But my whole day seems to have revolved around these keys."

He smiled, "Well I'll come and help you tomorrow." He drove her home and walked with her to the front door, and giving her a friendly kiss on the cheek, he asked, "Will you be alright?"

She smiled, nodding up at him, thanking him for a nice evening, then opened the door. The chandelier was on low, and Charles came to the top of the stairs, he had heard the car, and said, "Goodnight, Sir," and closed and bolted the door.

Alan stood for a minute or two and then walked back through the narrow path to his car, saying goodnight to the two security guards as they wandered past checking on his car. He sat for some long minutes, with the window open, listening in case she should call out. He wondered why he was doing this, but he worried about her – she was so small and very feminine, but he could see that she was really determined not to give in to Honeybeck, but he knew that it scared her, although even *he* himself felt uneasy when in the drawing room. He didn't like to think that she was alone in the house, but then, he didn't like to push himself to keep staying the night. But sometimes he wished that they were a little closer; over the months spent together he realized that he cared for her a lot, in fact, loved her, but then, thought it a little too soon to air his feelings. Of course he would never forget his darling Suzie, he'd loved her so very much, it hurt just thinking about her, and visions of her pale calm face as he had last seen her brought a tear to his eye. He missed her happy smile and her musical laughter, he smiled softly seeing her beautiful face before him alive and bright as she had always been, and tears pricked his eyes again – *why was life so cruel?* They'd had so many romantic evenings, and had been very happy together, and he had thought that she was the only girl in the world for him, he thought he could never love again. They had never lived together, and they were so looking forward to having their own home and spending their lives together... But now, all the hopes and dreams were gone... He took a deep breath... Now, here he was, with a good job making good money and living on a romantic paradise island, and for the first time in his whole life, he was now living alone, even Ted and Greg, who he had shared a house with had only been in touch once – he had last seen them at his wedding, he remembered his bachelor night, a week before the wedding, they had all got so drunk, and it had taken him two days to shake the hangover. He took another deep breath... But life had to go on, he couldn't mourn forever. He was lucky that he and Julie had kept good friends, they could easily have gone their separate ways, but they had supported each other through the hard months... and life was getting a little easier.

He inclined his head towards the open window, all seemed quiet and he knew that she had the security men close on hand. He wiped away the tears and turned the key with a sigh, the engine burst into life, and he drove away.

The headlights shone down the long and narrow road high with sugar cane on either side, it was like driving through a tunnel. He found his mind wandering as he turned a narrow bend, and a car with full headlights came towards him and narrowly passed, the lights dazzled in his eyes and he slowed a little, his mind was on Julie, *he knew that he loved her, but was it too soon to say? They had found happiness in each other's company, they had helped each other to cope, he didn't know how she felt, but now he didn't want to live without her,* and he kept thinking, *was it too soon to air his feelings,* and suddenly on a bend the car spun off the road and he lost control – he was in the ditch, his head hit the steering wheel and the air bag did not release. He was stunned and his nose started to pour with blood, the car was on its left side and he was hanging to his left in the seat belt; he tried to release it but he hadn't the strength in his hand, then suddenly it released and he fell to the passenger seat to his left. He then reached up, pulling himself up on his knees, holding on to the steering wheel, and tried to open the door on the driver's side but the automatic locking system was jammed. The engine was still running so he turned it off and the headlight went out leaving him in darkness. His head was spinning and blood was running from his nose, and the strength in his arm was failing as he clung on to the steering wheel. The leather seat under his knees was slippery and at a steep angle; the window on the driver's side was wide open and he managed with difficulty to pull himself up and then finding the wheels on the driver's side were high in the air, he slid out of the widow head first down the door, and fell onto the road. On standing up he found that his knee hurt and he felt dizzy, he judged that he was about three miles from the Silver Lady Cottage, and he started to walk back along the quiet and narrow country lane, but his knee was painful, and he sat down on the side of the road, his head spinning, then fumbled in his pocket for his phone.

Rick had transferred the late night phone calls to his house, and now was on his way to pick him up, Bill Elliot the security guard, went with him. They found Alan lying on the side of the road, a gash on his head and a bit disorientated, and covered in blood from a severe nose bleed, they took him straight to Holetown Clinic.

The next morning at breakfast, Rick came up in to the Gazebo, and explained to Julie about the accident, and said not to worry it wasn't serious, but the doctor had kept him in overnight. He had phoned the clinic earlier this morning, and he was going down to pick him up from the clinic at eleven o'clock.

"I'll come with you," Julie was anxious, "We'll bring him back here he can't stay on his own, in his little house. What about the car?" said Julie.

"Well I've got it under control, the garage is picking it up this morning, it's in the ditch, but I don't think it's too bad. There's no need for you to come, I'll go and collect him."

She sat, and poured herself more coffee, worried now and wondering, *how Alan was, and what would she do if she lost him. They had become good friends, he wasn't Gavin, but he had been such a comfort to her from the very first day, even though he was in mourning himself. And she loved him, how could she not love him, he had been such a consolation, he was handsome, sensible, strong,* and *attentive, and he had been so supportive, and she didn't know now what she would do without him. And she had to put Gavin out of her mind, she couldn't dwell on it forever, Gavin was gone, and nothing was ever going to bring him back,* she wiped the tears from her eyes, with the table napkin, just as Charles came to clear the table, and she moved away not wanting him to see her crying.

It had taken Alan three days to recover, he said he had a shocking headache, and there was a nasty gash on his forehead above his right eye and across the bridge of his nose, and he was limping. She suggested that he go to bed, but he said he would feel better up and about. Although wearing dark glasses the sunlight hurt his eyes, he rested quietly by the pool, under the shade of the umbrella and the trees and had early nights.

Cleo had phoned, asking Rick Holland if he had seen Mr Stone, as he had not been home from the office at all and she was worried, and then of course Rick told her about the accident, and apologized for not letting her know.

CHAPTER TWENTY

It was a bright sunny Saturday morning, and they were sitting by the pool. Alan had not gone into the office all the week. The gash on his head was healing, and he was now feeling a lot better.

The car had been repaired, and brought back to the Silver Lady Cottage, and although it had all been a terrible shock, on the whole, it was not that bad.

A dark cloud came over and the sun went in, the wind blew strongly lifting the green umbrellas, and a few spots of rain turned into a shower. Then the rain was pelting down, they screwed their legs up into a ball under the umbrellas and laughed holding towels up to save the spray. But they were getting very wet and then Charles came quickly down the coral stone steps with umbrellas, and all three made a hasty retreat to the gazebo where Charles had already left a tray of coffee and poured it.

It was almost lunchtime and the rain was relentless, Charles brought them smoked salmon and salad under a large umbrella. The wind was getting stronger and blowing the spray in on them; and then after lunch they made a quick dash with the umbrellas, giggling like children as they came on to the arched patio and into the library. And Julie was anxious to show him Edward Turner's pages on the key.

Alan looked over the manuscript, "It doesn't say where the passage is," he grimaced, "I suppose it could be anywhere. Benjamin leaving his brother's side, and Daniel burning to death – but there are no clues."

It's a horrible thought, isn't it?" Julie frowned, "imagine the scene… I wonder if he fell down the stairs because he saw Honeybeck."

"Mmm, could be. I shouldn't think anywhere in this house is safe from Honeybeck. You haven't seen him walking through a wall or anything have you?" said Alan with a smile.

"No, but I am looking behind me all the time now, at first I wasn't really *scared*, but now I am. It seems that anyone on the trail of this treasure is dead! But now I can't stop looking, and if I ever find it, I'll be ready to fight Honeybeck."

"Mmm," Alan joked, "what are you going to do, kill him?" He inclined his head jerkily and raised his eyebrows comically, "I bet that passage is in here behind these books, seems to be an age-old thing to have a bookcase that swings out into a secret passage, you've seen it enough times in films."

"Yes but they didn't have films in the seventeenth century."

"Well you know what I mean… I bet the films were copied from old houses, they all had secret passages."

"Mmm, well, just think, the whole house could have burned down couldn't it, and fancy kids walking around with candles." Her voice rose, "Where were the parents?"

"Well obviously not near, young Ben had to go and find his father. And, I guess it was the only means of light – they didn't even have a torch."

The wide-open louvered door rattled and they both looked up in alarm, their nerves on edge with the thought of Honeybeck. But it was Eddie who came bounding in, his high waving tail catching the large iron key that was flung from the lock and went down onto the coral stone patio with a loud clatter as he came excitedly to Julie, his mouth open in a happy doggy grin, his tail wagging. She happy to see him gave him a friendly pat telling him, "You're a lovely boy."

Alan went to pick up the key, and the blustery wind whipped the rain in onto the patio and he got wet and came back in quickly. "Well I've found a key," he chuckled, "it weighs a ton, fancy carrying this around in your pocket, these old locks are still in use after hundreds of years, and you think somebody would have put a Yale on them by now wouldn't you?" He held the key on the flat of his hand, it was about six inches long, black and thick heavy iron.

Julie smiled, "Well now, at last, we *have a key!* Let's try it in the safe."

"Oh don't be stupid, a key this size?" He grinned, weighing it in his hand, but to please her, he went to the safe. "WELL! What do you know! It FITS!" His voice rose in great surprise. He turned, looking over his shoulder giving her an astonished look.

Having that frightened excited feeling when the world seems to stop for a second, she came quickly across the room. His hand holding the large and heavy key in position, they looked at each other, she nodded a sort of unsaid 'go on' and he turned the key – it grated in the lock, he kept turning winding it like a clock until it stopped! Then, they both held their breath, and looked at each other, and he pulled the key, expecting the safe to open, but the whole section of the bookshelf swung out and a doorway about five foot high opened up. They stared in amazement into a dark coral stone passage... *"The passage!"* Julie gasped, her eyes shining bright with amazement. Eddie came and sniffed at the musty dusty air, and sneezed, and then ran away out onto the patio again.

"Good God!" Julie exclaimed, coughing as the dry dust seemed to clog her throat and she waved her hand in front of her face. Alan clamped his hand over his nose and mouth. "Gosh!" She looked, "Who would have thought it? And what a place to hide a key in full view and used every day on the outside door. I suppose any one of these door keys would have fit, they all look the same, and to think I've searched everywhere."

He looked at her equally surprised, and with a comical grin, "Well, are we going in?"

She looked at him wide-eyed, "Oh, do you think we should?"

"Well, don't tell me after all this searching and hunting, that *now* you don't want to take a *look!* Aren't you curious?"

She looked cautiously into the dark cold passage, "Yes, but I'm a bit scared of meeting Honeybeck in here. Is *this* where that boy burned to death?"

"Guess so! Come on, get a light! Not a candelabrum," he joked, with a grin, as she went to the desk. She came back and he took the torch from her. "Haven't you got one of those lanterns?"

"No they are both in the barn."

"Come on." They ventured in, hand-in-hand, very slowly. Even when just inside, the cold coral stone seeped in Julie's bones – it was like stepping into the fridge after the very warm humidity. "Wait a minute, do you think Honeybeck could be watching us now, I think we should prop the door open don't you?"

"Well I've got the key, but it might be a good idea." He propped the door open with a pile of books. "Come on," he put out his hand to her.

The torchlight was dim and made eerie shadows on the cold coral stone walls, it smelled dusty and dank and old. There were steps that went down, they were rough and uneven underfoot and very steep and they twisted to the left. They took each step extremely slowly and very carefully, feeling their way down the wall and the strong and musty smell got stronger as they ventured deeper and deeper into the unknown darkness.

Eddie watched them go from the doorway, and then came back and sniffed into the passageway, his nose knocking the books inside and the door closed with a quiet click. The library was filled with a low chuckle, but drowned out by Eddie's loud barking. He turned, sensing something in the room and with a painful frightened whine he dashed under the desk – his ears down, his tail between his legs – and lay with his head between his paws, his sharp brown doggie eyes scanning the room and feeling the vibration as unseen feet paced the floor. The wind rattled the open door, and he got up and ran out into the pouring rain.

Reaching the end of the steps, the passage went both left and right, Alan suggested right. It was very narrow and claustrophobic and seemed long, the torch beam showing just a yard in front of them, and at some points Alan had to duck his head as they moved on taking one slow step at a time, their movements making the dust rise and their throats felt dry.

"Eerie isn't it," Julie whispered behind him, "do you think there *is* a pirate's chest down here?"

"Maybe, if the treasure really does exist, I should think this is where it would be."

"I wonder how old Edward Turner was when he died? It said in the manuscript 'I lived into old age alone'."

Alan shook his head in the dark, "Dunno," he stopped and put out a warning arm, "more steps here! Down, don't want to go the same way as Daniel." Five or six coral stone steps led them down to another narrow passage, but it was just a few feet long and they came to a coral stone wall.

Julie frowned, "That's funny, why would steps lead to a blank wall?"

"Because," Alan turned to her in the dark, "this wall must be a door, an entrance way to something." He shone the torch around, then shook his head, "No handles or hinges or anything, it's just coral stone." He shook his head again.

Julie was pressing around the wall, "There must be a trigger somewhere."

"Can't see anything," Alan was flashing the light up and down and around the wall. And he stood back a bit alarmed as a rusty creaking sound echoed through the passage, he spun around shining the torch on her, "What did you *do?*"

"I don't know, I put my hand on this sconce up here on the wall, and it moved a bit," she lifted her shoulders with glee. "Well it's opening – look."

"Yeah!" He grinned in surprise, turning back to the now open wall and shining the torch, "This is interesting, this is a wooden frame, the coral stone must be cemented on, looks like a solid wall," he was wondering how it worked. "Come on," he held out his hand to her and they entered. The torch shone on Arawak drawings on the wall and they were surprised to find themselves in the cave a few feet from the ladder under the barn. Alan looked up; there was just the faintest glimmer of light coming through the broken boards where he had fallen through, "This must have been Honeybeck's escape route."

"Yes but if that trapdoor is still shut how did he get out?"

Alan pulled a face, "Perhaps there's another way out," he shone the torch around, there was nothing but coral stone, "there's another sconce here." Reaching up, it twisted with a rusty grating sound and the door began to close. "Fancy these things still working after three hundred years, needs a bit of oil though," he grinned.

"So! What do we do now," Julie raised her eyes comically, "look for another sconce to open up the treasure?" they chuckled together.

"Well there's nothing else down here," Alan inclined his head with a dubious grin, "You never know there might be one that opens the treasure," he shone the light up the wall "there's one here." Julie reached up, it was a bit high for her, "It's rusty like the others but, it's turning," they were surprised to hear a grating noise echoing through the quietness, they didn't know where it was coming from, and then Alan shone the torch through the archway – he stepped through, then jumped back quickly feeling the coral stone move under his feet. Shining the light down they saw a large oblong panel sliding along the floor, "Thank God you saw it in time," said Julie. He took a step nearer, and could see that there were steps going down, "Come and look at this." She came up beside him. "Come on," he took her hand, "let's go down."

"No," she pulled away nervously, "you go, and I'll stay here in case it shuts, we might both get stuck down there and no one will ever find us."

"OK," he nodded, "Good thinking," he started carefully down the steps, "Christ they're steep, and there's no wall or handrail to hold on to," he wobbled a bit, the coral was very uneven beneath his shoes, he spread his arms feeling the empty darkness on either side and he then leaned back, holding on to the step behind him to steady himself.

The light then disappeared, leaving her in complete darkness; she put her hand out onto the wall not daring to move, then as her eyes got accustomed to the darkness there was just the dim glimmer of light from the broken boards above the ladder. "Anything?" she called, but there was no answer, "Alan? ALAN!" Panic rose in the throat, and then the light shone up, and his voice echoed from the deep, "Julie you've got to come down and see this..."

It was still raining, and the strong force wind swept over the garden; the men could not finish cutting up the fallen tree, some of the branches had crushed through the roof of the barn, and they had left after telling Rick that they would be back tomorrow. Rick faced the elements, and went to check – there was a large plank of wood from the barn swinging in the wind and clapping on the tree and while he was there another piece of board came loose and the wind whisked it across the lawn. Rick thought it was dangerous, and got Denny Bell to go and try to dislodge it and get it down. Denny was in his thirties, quite agile and willing to do anything; he ran across the garden in a hooded jacket and swung himself up easily on to the branches. The rain in his face made it hard to see, but he hammered away at part of the wooden roof, he managed to free it, and the wind so strong that it whipped it from his and hands and it went down with some of the tree branches with a thunderous clatter into the barn.

Julie ducked, thinking the roof was caving in as dirt and dust came down through the floorboards. The vibration knocked the ladder sideways and she was choking in the dust; she heard Alan shout, and a grating sound, and the next thing she was in complete darkness – the light from the torch was gone, the floor panel had closed and Alan was down in the lower cave. She screamed his name, but of course he could not hear her. She was frantically feeling around in the dark, she was scared and she bumped to the ladder and fell to her knees, and sat there in pain crying, knowing that she must get to the sconce, she stood up feeling for it in the darkness. There was no glimmer of light now from the floorboards above, something was blocking it. She eventually found the sconce, but she could feel the ladder had jammed on to it and she could not turn it. Struggling with the long ladder was impossible in the darkness, the rungs had got entangled with the rusty metal, and it was stuck solid. In panic she shook the ladder as hard as she could, not knowing which way to free it, then… she felt it move, but it was still locked solid. The sconce was a bit high for her and she couldn't get a good grip on it. She was screaming for help, and then realized that it was still wet and windy out there so no one would be in the garden to hear her. She shook the ladder again and again and suddenly it came free, it was a mighty struggle to get it back to the trapdoor, it was much too heavy for her, but she managed drag it along the wall and rest it up against the wall, somewhere near as she thought to the trapdoor. Although she could see nothing she climbed up, and began banging and screaming, on what she thought was the trapdoor, not knowing that half the roof of the barn was on top of it.

Denny Bell heard the screaming and banging and came down from the tree branches very quickly, and ran back across the lawn in panic and rushed into the staff room glad to see Alf Gibbons there having a beer, "What's the matter with you, you look as if you've seen a ghost."

"I have! I have!" He nodded frantically, "Well not actually seen it but heard it," the whites of his brown eyes showed fear, even his black skin seemed to have paled. "It was screaming and banging."

"Well I don't expect that old Honeybeck likes this weather either," said Oliver with a grin as he put a cup of coffee down in front of him.

"I'll have a rum as well," said Denny, his eyes still wide and scared.

"Oooh! It really did give you a fright, didn't it? It was probably the wind whistling through the trees." Knowing that Denny rarely drank rum, Gibbons and Oliver watched him down it quickly, and glanced at each other with surprise.

'Oh, yeah, it could have bin the wind, but I never heard the wind like thaaa a fore, it sounded reeeeal, eerie maaan," he raised his shoulders with a shiver. But thinking about it being the wind, did make him feel a little easier and he drank the coffee.

Rick was still in the office, Charles phoned him, asking if Mrs Anderson was coming back for dinner, and was Mr Stone to stay for dinner. Rick said that she had not said that she was going out.

Charles was surprised, "Well I haven't seen either of them since lunchtime, I usually take Mrs Anderson a glass of champagne, at six o'clock, I think they went into the library, but they're not there now and that dog is still in there, he wouldn't go out and he's barking a lot so I've left the French doors open." Rick frowned and said that he would come down.

Alan was sitting waiting at the top of the steps, he could do nothing, he could hear nothing. He'd tried phoning Rick but there was no signal, he supposed he was too deep. He had been calling Julie and banging on the overhead panel – he couldn't think why she had been so long in opening the panel, and why had she shut it anyway. The torch was fading. Perhaps the mechanism had gone wrong and she couldn't open the panel, she had obviously gone to get Rick, *or*, maybe they were there now trying to open it. He sat down on the steps, there was nothing he could do, but wait. He switched off the fading torchlight, he may need it later, and sat in complete darkness, knowing that there was nothing there but it was eerie, he sighed, thinking, *well they had eventually found the treasure, and now here he was locked in with it, and just hoping that it would not be three hundred years before it was opened again.* He had thoughts of the skeleton sitting there in the pitch darkness, with that deadly buzzing silence in his ears, the deadly silence so noisy that he could hear nothing of the outside world; this gave him a nervous feeling. Although he knew he would get out, it was just a case of waiting and the time seemed endless; he looked at his watch – just a few minutes had gone by but seemed like hours, he wondered *if it had been just like this for the skeleton, but then maybe, no one knew he was there, and the poor devil must have been in great pain.* He screwed up his hands in to tight fists, glad that Julie had not come down with him. It was just a case of waiting, he did have hope, *Julie would get him out, he was in no doubt. Not unless... She was trapped too, and maybe, she couldn't get out to get any help... No, no, stop thinking like that.* But the thoughts kept coming, *it was the darkness...* He switched on the torch, the light was dim, three minutes had passed by his watch, it seemed like an hour, and all was still, Oh, so very still, like the grave... He switched off the torch and the darkness enclosed him again...

Julie was still banging on the trapdoor, but then she guessed that with the noise of the rain and the wind no one was going to hear her, and there would be no one in the garden anyway. She came down from the ladder tearful and afraid. She stamped on the panel, and shouted, and then listened, but there was no reply, *would Alan have enough air down there, and what would she do if anything happened to him?* She realized that crying was not going to help, she had to do something; she felt her way along the wall, to the passage, there was not a glimmer of light, and the total silence rushed in her ears. It was scary, she imagined all sort of things reaching out for her in the darkness, even though she knew she was there alone, *but, was Honeybeck there? Was he there, watching,* waiting... She shivered, trying to put that eerie thought out of her mind – what would she do if he materialized, she couldn't run screaming in the dark, but then what could he do? She then thought it better to go back to the sconce and give it another try, even though Alan was trapped she felt closer to him, and the darkness scared her more than she could say. She might feel her way along the passage, and miss the stairs to the library and *then both she and Alan would be lost forever.* But what a stupid thought, they had left the bookcase door open and there would be some light, *and Rick or Charles would come in to investigate... Wouldn't they? Should she wait? Should she?...*

Her thoughts kept going around and around, the dense darkness made her head spin she couldn't think straight, she had to get a grip of herself. Her right hand now clinging tightly to the wall, she turned to go back, her left hand now on the wall, if she left the wall she would be totally disorientated. She felt her way slowly and carefully, step by step, holding the wall like it was a lifeline in a dense black sea. Thoughts of Gavin struggling in the sea came bright into her thoughts, she mustn't think if that now, *this was the dense black sea and she was struggling for her life and Alan's...* Then, suddenly, the rough coral stone wall finished and her left hand pushed into space and she almost lost her balance. She quickly stepped back feeling the wall again, and taking a deep and thankful breath. She swallowed hard – *what was the space?* – she stood dead still, and then realized that it was the archway, but she was afraid to take her left hand off the wall. A few steps on, maybe four or six, she trod very carefully as if suspended in space, her arms flaying in front of her, and with great relief she found the wall again, hoping that it was the other side of the arch, feeling around the wall above her head, she couldn't find the sconce, and she began to panic – was she on the right wall, was this the other side of the arch? She stopped, on the brink of tears again, peering into the pitch blackness – should she feel her way back to the passage and find Rick? What should she do? Tears clouded her eyes, and then flaying her hands above her head her hand hit something – she thought it was the sconce, it was, *it was!* She felt relief, but it was locked solid, as she knew it would be, and also a bit high for her to really put any pressure on it. She tried and tried, standing on tiptoe, and suddenly it moved just a fraction. She anxiously tried again, and the rust squeaked, then as it moved she felt tiny bits of rust falling on her head and on her brow. She closed her eyes tight, it moved a bit more with a rusty grating sound, and the panel on the floor under the arch moved just an inch, the torch flashed, "ALAN!" she shouted, and to her relief he answered.

"You OK?" His voice came out of the ground as a glimmer of light got bigger.

"Yes, but I'm struggling with this sconce, it's completely rusted up," she hung on to it with all of her full weight, "I can't move it," and suddenly it jerked down an inch with a rusty grinding sound. She lifted her feet again and hung on with all her might, and it just moved very slowly and with a feeling of relief she saw light and heard the floor slowly opening and Alan's head came up in the dim torchlight, "ALAN!" her voice echoed hysterically, "Oh Alan, oh, Alan!" She was breathless and crying with relief. He pulled himself up, and she put her arms around his neck and clung to him, "Oh Alan, Alan, I'm so glad you're alright."

"So am I," he smiled and sighed with relief, and kissed her hungrily and lovingly for the very first time, and she melted into his arms, as they clung together, he whispered into her dark hair, "I love you."

"And I love you too, Alan," she looked up into his shadowed face, "I love you," and she hugged him with a tearful cry.

He kissed her again hugging her and smiling into her hair. Then he pulled away, "What happened? I thought I was going spend another three hundred years down there with the treasure," he chuckled.

She smiled happily with relief, "You knew I wouldn't leave you there, what would I do without you." She smiled, and then explained hastily about the ladder falling and the sconce locking and she had tried to get some help, but the trapdoor was closed, "...and I think there is something on top of it because there is no glimmer of light now from the broken floorboards, and then I tried the sconce again, it's very rusty, but it worked." She took a breath.

He hugged her tightly again they were both relieved, and knowing how scared she must have been here in the dark, he'd also been worried, but was confident that she would get him out, or somebody would, it was just a matter of time – and now, glancing at his watch it had been the whole afternoon. It was eerie.

"Did you see the treasure? Is it down there, can I see it?" she asked him anxiously.

He nodded in the dim torchlight, "Yeah!" He sounded a bit dazed and had a smirk on his face which she didn't see, "Yes, but not right now, I think we should have Rick down here, you can't go down there on your own – for one thing the steps are too steep, and we don't want to both get stuck down there, do we?"

She knew he was right, "Is it, lovely?" Her eyes lit up anxiously, "Is it just as you imagine pirates' treasure would be – a chest, like you see in children's fairy tale books?"

"Yeah, something like that," he grinned, "Yeah," he nodded, "Yeah, it's just like that. The torch, the battery is running out," he took her by the hand, "Come on, let's go and find Rick, before the battery really goes. And we'll need those lanterns, this torch has nearly had it." They made their way slowly along the passage, the light gradually dimming, and as they almost got to the bottom of the winding steps before the library, the torch just blacked out.

"The door must be shut or the light would be shining down," said Julie anxiously.

"Just a minute," Alan got his phone and switched on, the light was dim but enough for them to climb the steep steps, Julie on all fours. They reached the top, "I've got the key, but where's the keyhole? I didn't think – we should have checked that before we came in here." He ran the small light up and down the doorway, but it revealed nothing, "What we need is another sconce," Alan joked.

"There is one, up here somewhere, I remember seeing it when we came in," Julie was feeling around above her head in the darkness.

Alan helped, "Got it!" He twisted it, and like the others it moved with a rusty squeak and to their relief the door began to slowly open and Eddie started barking, and Rick was standing right there in front of them.

"Oh we are so glad to see you," Alan sounded exhausted, as he stepped out of the passageway.

Rick looked dumbfounded to see them, and the bookcase opening. For a minute he didn't know what to say, "Well

Eddie has been driving us mad barking all the afternoon, have you been down there all that time?"

"Yeah," Alan nodded with relief, "I've seen the treasure," he flicked up his eyebrows with a grin.

"WHAT! Really! You have! It's down there?" Rick was amazed, "REALLY! Is it gold?"

"Yeah, some of it," Alan grinned at the astonished look on his face, "Show you later, right now I need a drink." Alan closed the bookcase and turned the key, "Well go back down there after dinner. Come and have a drink with us and I'll fill you in."

The rain had stopped and the wind had dropped, and they went out onto the arched patio, it was too wet to go to the gazebo. Eddie made himself comfortable under Julie's chair, and Rick rang Charles for the drinks.

They waited until Charles had gone and they both started talking at once to Rick. "I haven't seen the treasure yet," said Julie, she told him about the ladder falling and Alan being shut in, "and I was fumbling around down there in the pitch darkness."

"Yes well that's why I want you there to stand guard," said Alan, "Julie can't go down there on her own, and should we get shut in again, no one would ever find us."

"Can't you prop the door open?"

"No," said Alan, "too heavy."

Rick was getting anxious to hear more as Charles served them dinner and he sat at the table with a drink listening while they talked.

Rick asked anxiously, after Charles had gone, "Well what is the treasure like?"

Alan shook his head, "You'll see," he grinned.

"I can't wait," Julie smiled.

Charles was standing in the shadows, away from the gazebo; he'd got snippets of the conversation as he attended the table, and stood now hoping to hear more. He raised his eyebrows, with surprise, as he went back to the kitchen.

After dinner, Julie was tired and although anxious to see the treasure, she thought it too late to go exploring through the passage again, the treasure had been there for over three hundred years, it wasn't going to disappear overnight. Alan was in full agreement, and Rick left to go home, his head full of wonder.

Julie went to bed, but although tired she couldn't sleep.

Alan went to his room, content that he had seen Honeybeck's treasure, but with a feeling of unrest. Honeybeck, although ghostly, was evil and threatening. He had never thought about ghosts before, but now he was in no doubt, after seeing ghostly images and hearing ghostly voices, and seeing the rocking chair moving unaided. There was something very mysterious attached to this house, and Julie's words kept ringing in her ears, it seems that anyone who has seen the treasure is DEAD! He found it very disturbing.

The sun streamed in through a gap in the drapes. Alan blinked, surprised to find himself still alive, then dismissed the thought as stupid. He showered, shaved, and dressed in green tee shirt and white shorts, and made his way to the gazebo. The early morning air was warm but fresh from last night's rain; it was peaceful and quiet, apart from the birds singing. He wandered down and stood in front of the silver lady, wondering if Honeybeck had a real purpose for standing her here, he knew now that it wasn't for the treasure – and what made her glow at night? He glanced up and saw Charles coming across the garden with a tray, and made his way back to the gazebo, "Morning Charles."

"Morning Mr Stone. Coffee, Sir?"

"Yes please." Charles put down the tray and poured him a black coffee, "bit better this morning," Alan looked up at the sky.

"Yes, Sir, but the weather is unsettled, they forecast more rain and thunderstorms and gale force winds."

"Well, I guess we can do nothing about the weather."

Charles inclined his head. "No, Sir." He finished laying the table, and then went back to the kitchen. Alan sat at the table quietly sipping his coffee, the humidity was still high and everything was damp, the table was sticky. The garden was bedraggled, the lawns covered in torn branches and soggy leaves, the trees still dripping from the heavy rain; it was brighter but the sky was still overcast, the birds didn't seem to mind, they still twittered happily, sitting on the backs of the chairs, their heads nervously twitching while waiting for the first crumb. Charles brought toast, butter, croissants, jam and marmalade; the birds were on the table in a second and Alan shooed them off, just as Julie joined him.

"Morning, Alan, at least the rain's stopped."

"Yes but we are going to get some more, so Charles said," Alan poured her coffee, and she buttered toast. They were almost finished when Rick came across the garden.

"Morning, Mrs Anderson," he smiled and nodded to Alan, "I'm just going over to have a look at the damage."

"Oh, we'll come with you," said Julie, folding her napkin and putting it on the table; Alan did the same, and they walked with Rick across the lawn still wet but drying in the humidity. When they got to where the barn stood, it was a mess – sawdust everywhere from the tree, wet and soggy like pulp, branches, leaves, wood from the half fallen barn, and wooden roof tiles.

"Oh, *what* a *mess*," Julie put a hand to her forehead.

"The tree people will be back here soon, I'll get them to clear it up," said Rick, "looks like a lot of water there in the barn too."

"That's probably why the barn was built over the cave," said Alan, "with rain storms like yesterday, over the months I guess the cave could have held the water – it would have been like a pond."

"Yeah," Rick agreed, "and would cause a lot of mosquitoes too. I'll get it cleared up." They made their way back to the house and Rick went back to the office.

Charles related snippets of conversation that he had heard last night, to Oliver and old Gibbons, as they sat enjoying a beer in the staff room, and that Denny Bell's ghostly experience was actually Mrs Anderson screaming to be let out of the cave. Old Gibbons had laughed and left to find Denny.

"Do you think they have found the treasure then?" said Oliver anxiously, now that old Gibbons had gone.

"Well it seems *they've* found *something!*" Charles inclined his head and arched his greying eyebrows.

"Wow!" Oliver's eyes popped, and he pursed his lips, "Fancy, I wonder if it *is* the treasure?"

Charles shrugged his shoulders and went about his business.

Old Gibbons grinned as he told Denny Bell later that his ghost had been Mrs Anderson screaming to get out of the cave.

"Cave!" He screwed his face up in a puzzled frown as he watched old Gibbons walking away. "Cave?" He now felt quite stupid.

The day was clearing up, and the sun was hot once again and Alan and Julie took books and went to sit by the pool. "I didn't sleep very well last night," said Julie.

Alan grimaced, "Neither did I, I kept thinking about what you said, everyone that found the treasure, *is dead!* I felt I nearly was, *and*, I don't think it's a good idea for you to see it either."

"Oh! But Alan!" She was most surprised, "I want to! What, after searching everywhere for that key, I *must* see it! I *must!*"

"Well I don't think it's wise! I think it's dangerous!"

"Well you'll be there. And you've already seen it. *Please*, Alan!"

"Yes, I've seen it and I want to stay alive, and I don't want you worrying about it. You said you loved me yesterday, or, was that because you were scared in the cave, or did you really mean it? I don't want to lose you, Julie." He sounded most anxious.

She smiled gently at him, "I meant it, Alan. I do love you." She said gently, "And I don't want to lose you either. You said you loved me too. Did you *really* mean it? Or was it just relief because I rescued you?"

He looked at her open-mouthed, a little bewildered, "I always say just what I mean." He pulled her to him and was kissing her when Charles came down the steps with ice cold lemonade, they both sat apart. Charles sort of grinned to himself, but just put the glasses on the table and left.

"Now where were we," Alan grinned, taking her hand, and pulling her to him again, "you know, I've loved you for some time, but I really thought it a bit too soon to air my feelings. But I do love you, Julie."

"Well it is a bit too soon, Alan, but we can't go on forever mourning can we... We both know how we feel," she sounded tearful. "And Alan, you have been such a great support to me, and I really can't thank you enough, and I think it's too soon but I do love you too." She put her arms around his neck and hugged him tightly, "What would we have done without each other?" and he kissed her again.

She sat back, "It'll be alright, you know, I do have to see the treasure Alan, if I don't see it, it will be between us forever."

"Do you really want to be with me, forever?" he said sincerely. She nodded urgently up at him with a smile, "Yes I do."

"Me too," he smiled. And kissed her.

Sitting quietly now with her own thoughts. Julie suddenly said, "I really am excited to see the treasure, Alan! Do you think before he died, that skeleton Joseph saw it? He must have got the silver coins from somewhere, mustn't he? There *is* silver down there isn't there? And that Jackson Verity said that he had a broken back and a broken leg, maybe *that's why*, perhaps he found the sconce, and grabbed a few silver coins from the chest before the slab closed, probably that was all he could carry, and then when he came up they beat him, maybe he was running with that jar of silver coins in his hand and they were whipping him and he just sat down exhausted and died."

Alan grimaced, "Maybe, you could be right."

"I'm dying to see it all, I can't wait, what time have you arranged with Rick?"

"I haven't," he arched his eyebrows and shook his head, then checked his watch, nine o'clock, "but we could go now if you like." He phoned Rick who was in the office, and asked him to bring the lanterns from the barn to the library, "And come in quietly, I don't want the rest of the staff knowing about the bookcase."

Rick went to the old barn or what was left of it, the lanterns were near the door where they had left them – one was completely smashed, and the old barn was very rickety, perhaps the tree men should take the whole thing down, no sense in trying to rebuild it. He made his way back to the library where Alan and Julie were there waiting. Knowing that Charles would not be coming into the library, until eleven o'clock with the coffee Alan suggested that they go right now, have a couple of hours and be back here by eleven, and no one would know that they had left the room. He took the key from his pocket.

Rick was amazed at the passageway, he'd only glimpsed it when he'd come in to see why Eddie was barking and they had come out. "Yer, know, I only thought his sort of thing happen in films," he grinned.

"Mmm, you wait 'til you see the treasure," Alan had a twisted grin.

By the way he said it, Rick wondered if it was anything worth seeing. They stepped into the passage and the bookcase door closed behind them, Alan thought it must be on a timer, at least now he knew how to open it. The bright lantern lit up every indentation in the cold coral stone walls and Rick felt a shiver go through his body, the silence clogged his ears it was like stepping into a tomb.

Alan held the lantern high and Rick followed behind Julie, as they made slow progress down the deep and winding uneven steps. The long passage was narrow, dry and dusty and a strong musty smell rose as they moved. Rick found it claustrophobic; a lizard ran up wall frightened by the light it then stopped, its big eyes watching them. Alan stopped as they came to the next set of stone steps, he warned Rick there were only five but they were steep and narrow; then he turned to take Julie's hand, then they were in the short narrow passage facing the blank wall. It surprised Rick when it opened up and then he was more surprised to find that they were in the cave near the ladder and close to the Amerindian drawings on the wall. "How ever did you find your way down here?" Rick asked.

"Through Edward Turner's manuscript," Julie turned to him in the shadows, "and with Eddie's help," she chuckled. "He found the key."

He was about to ask how, but Alan moved to the archway and they followed. He explained to Rick about the sconce and as he twisted it there was the squeaking and scraping of dry rusted iron, and in the lantern light he saw the floor panel opening. "We can't all go together," Alan explained, "so I want you to stay here, and make sure that the sconce does not slip back and close the panel," Rick nodded. "Sorry, but we'll have to leave you in the semi dark, being as we've only got the one lantern."

"That's OK." Ricked smiled, "I'll keep my hand on the sconce and make sure it stays in place, but I'd like to have a look at the treasure while I'm down here."

'Sure, sure, you can afterwards," Alan nodded to Rick, "but I can't let Julie go down on her own, the steps are a bit dodgy anyway." He took her by the hand and Rick waited, watching them disappear into the ground and was left in total darkness.

At the bottom of the steps Alan held the lantern high.

Julie nearly fainted at the sight before her – it took her breath away, her hand covered her mouth. The cave was vast and there were chests everywhere brimming over with golden plates and vases, goblets, jewels and even more jewels that sparkled and glittered in the light, brimming with pearls and precious stones, diamond tiaras, bracelets and necklaces. Between the chests stood golden statuettes with glittering emerald eyes, and large vases, painted portraits in golden frames – there seemed to be gold everywhere, she had never seen such a sight, it was stunningly out of this world, "It's so unbelievable is it *real?*"

"I guess so," said Alan. She went to one chest brimming over with golden coins, "Oh!" Her hand went to her mouth "there's a skeleton on the floor."

Alan came to her side and looked, then said, "Look there's another one," he held the lantern high, and saw yet another one, there were four in all, "these are the guys that brought the treasure from the ship," Alan said, "it said in the manuscript that the bearers died, Honeybeck killed them so that they wouldn't talk."

For a moment it gave Julie the creeps, but then she moved on to another chest brimming with silver pieces of eight, and yet another chest full with precious stones, it was so unbelievable her head was spinning, "What's this sand?" She took a handful lifted it and it ran through her fingers, "Gold dust," said Alan. It was just like Aladdin's cave, everything sparkled and shone in the lantern light, she expected it to disappear it couldn't be true. "It must have taken years to collect all this. It's unbelievable," she turned to Alan, "it must be worth millions, I never imagined *anything like this.*" She picked up a large emerald, almost the size of her palm it sparkled, "This *surely* can't be *real*. Can it?" Her eyes shone in absolute amazement, "where's it all come from! What are we going to do with it?"

Alan shook his head, arched his eyebrows and splayed his hands palms up, "I haven't got the foggiest idea, it's mind-blowing." There was a low chuckle, they both looked up, as a mist rose in front of them and Honeybeck materialized, all white as they had never seen him before, a pirate, tallish and robust, wearing a three-corned hat with an ostrich feather, a sword at his side and knives and a pistol in his belt. It was all so clear, his face features fuzzy and not really discernible, but there seemed a leering smile on his lips, or did they imagine it? It stunned them both. There was no doubt that it *was*, Honeybeck, he was *very* impressive. He appeared to float about a foot off the ground and as he came closer Julie gasped and stepped back, frozen to the spot as the white image towered over her, and his right arm lifted slowly and she felt a freezing shiver and cringed her shoulders reaching her ears, as the emerald was taken from her open palm. She held her breath and her eyes were wide in fright and disbelief as the emerald floated slowly on the air held by icy white fingers and was put gently back into the chest. She felt she could hold her breath no longer, too afraid to even blink, then she felt Alan put a protective arm around and the figure of Honeybeck faded leaving them both mesmerized and staring into space.

An anxious shout from Rick brought them both back to reality, and Alan went quickly to the steep steps, crawling up on all fours, as quickly as he could in case the slab closed and then poked his head out of the open panel to be faced with a double barrelled shotgun. The face of the man holding it was in darkness...

Alan was really taken by great surprise to see a shotgun pointing so close to his face that he didn't argue when the voice behind it said "GET BACK!" He turned his head to the right and saw the soles of a pair of trainers, he guessed it was Rick, obviously lying down and knocked unconscious.

The voice behind the gun said again in a low and menacing tone, "GET BACK!" and the gun was pushed close into his cheek. Alan didn't argue, he slowly backed down the steep steps on his hands and knees. The gunman followed awkwardly and unsteady after him, with unsure footage, each step jagged and almost calf-high, and needed careful negotiation in the shadowed light from the lantern. Julie in the shadows saw the shotgun waver, and recognized Denny Bell, she held her breath.

Denny Bell gasped seeing gold and jewels glittering before him, and he momentarily lost his guard. In that split second Alan, now at the bottom of the steps, stood up quickly pushing the barrel of the gun up, and it fired into the roof showering them with splinters of coral stone as he grabbed Denny Bell's ankle and he came tumbling down the stairs with a shout of shock and pain as his back hit the hard sharp coral stone steps. But being young he recovered very quickly and he and Alan were rolling on the floor and fighting for the gun. Julie, scared, moved around them and Alan shouted "GET OUT!" She got to the steps, scrambling up on all fours in the half shadows and scraping her knees on the way, and as she came to the top Rick had now recovered and hearing the skirmish was about to go down. He grabbed her roughly by the arm and pulled her out, pushing her to the left of the open panel and into the second cave saying sharply, "Stay in the dark," he went down the steps slowly and with difficulty seeing Alan and Denny Bell in the shadowed light and as he was halfway down the steps Denny grabbed the gun again and was about scramble up, and without a word he stopped and waved the shotgun, motioning Rick to come down and then as he was almost down he put the gun behind him and pushed him the rest of the way. Rick came tumbling down the last two steps, head first, with a shout and landed flat on his stomach, pushing Alan who was scrambling to get to his feet back down flat on his back, and knocking the lantern over and the light went out, as Denny scrambled back up the steps in the darkness and was gone through the panel. Before they could sort themselves out and reach the steps, the panel was closing over them.

Julie, in the darkness of the second cave, was scared; she had heard the noise of the fight and heard Rick ushered down into the cave at gun point. She could now hear Denny Bell fumbling about but could not see him, and then she heard the scraping sound of the panel closing.

Both stunned, Alan and Rick sat in pitch darkness at the bottom of the steps, then Alan switched on the low light on his phone. Rick was rubbing his shoulder and held his head and he groaned. "Are you alright?" asked Alan. Rick nodded, "Yeah," although his head hurt, and he felt blood running down his cheek where the butt of the gun had hit him and knocked him out.

He told Alan, "I was standing by the sconce in the darkness, and heard a sound by the ladder. I turned and he hit me – where he came from I don't know, I suppose I blacked out," he winced, holding his head. Then caught his breath, "Well this is enough to take the pain away," he grinned and winced again, squinting into the low light, astonished at the vast cave, he picked up the lantern and shook it. The bright light lit up the cave, he stood up then, holding it high and walking around, "My GOD! This is some treasure, it's unbelievable, and it must be worth millions, what the hell are you going to do with it all?"

"Dunno," Alan shook his head, "where's Julie?"

"In the second cave, I hope, I told her to stay in the dark. Hey there's a couple of skeletons here."

"Yeah I know, there's four of them, I guess they're the guys who brought all this stuff in here, and Honeybeck killed them." Alan then shook his head looking around the cave, as Rick moved around and the light picked out the shining gold, and the sparkling jewels, "I would suggest just shutting this all up and forgetting about it. If we tell anyone, we'll have the police here, and then the press. Wouldn't do to let them know about this, the house would be overrun with fortune hunters, and there'd be break-in's, and tourists, and I just don't know what! And it could never be lived in, there would be no peace or safety here again. Better to shut it up and say nothing."

"Hmm, guess you're right," Rick agreed, "and not only that, there's all the antiques in the house to be considered as well."

"And… Honeybeck was here just now," said Alan.

"Was he? *Honeybeck* was here?" Rick sounded most surprised, but he wasn't really.

"Yeah, there was a thick white mist and then he was very clear, Julie and I could see every detail; and *do you know*, he actually took this emerald right out of Julie's hand and replaced it there in the chest. I'm not going to touch it, it really was *uncanny*, I must say bloody *scary*! I don't like it! And I think this lot is better left alone."

"Out of her *hand?*" Rick's eyes opened wide, "He took it out of her *hand?*" He screwed up his face, wanting to pick up the emerald, but heeded Alan's warning, of "Don't touch it!"

The day was grey with stormy rain clouds, but the humidity was high. The men were sweating as they piled the last of the sawn-up logs on to a trolley, and three of them wheeled them out to the front drive via the back of the house past the old stables, now unused after hundreds of years, and they were transported on to a truck. It had taken four of them almost a week to saw up the mahogany tree. Tommy Baker was in charge, and when Pete, Trev, and Gordon came back all four of them were to try and tackle the roof of the rickety barn as Rick had suggested; they couldn't leave it in the precarious position, there were still branches and soggy leaves hanging on it, and it was unsafe, and as they attempted to move it the wooden roof tiles slipped off one by one. Then one of the stays holding up part of what had once been a hay loft and was now heavy with straw that had been there for years and now wet from the storm it suddenly gave way, and the gutter full with rain water and leaves that had accumulated over many years just poured out. There was a loud rumbling behind the heavy grey clouds and a terrific clap of thunder followed, and the fork lightning lit up the sky and seemed to shake the whole of the island and then a few spots of rain. Tommy Baker urged them to hurry and lift part of the roof that they were still holding or they would all get a good soaking. Then there was another clap of thunder and then the rain came down in torrents.

Julie strained her eyes into the darkness, standing quietly in the darkness of the second cave; there was just a glimmer of grey light, where Alan had moved some of the greenery from above. She could hear Denny Bell moving about on the other side of the archway, she could hear him grumbling to himself and fumbling about in the darkness to reload the gun then he must have dropped a shell, as she heard him swear, and then more fumbling – he was probably on his knees feeling for it, and then a click as he closed the barrel of the shotgun, and then in the pitch darkness she heard him feeling along the wall, she thought hopefully towards the ladder, obviously that was the way he'd got in through the trapdoor. Then suddenly and without warning there was a deafening crashing sound of heavy timber falling as the old barn collapsed through its own floor and down into the cave, and Denny cried out before he was crushed to the coral stone floor of the cave. Julie saw a flash and as the gun fired the shot echoed through the cave, lost in the sound of falling timber and rubble. Scared in the darkness, she bent low, leaning close to the sharp coral wall, covering her ears, her eyes closed tight, shaking with fright thinking that the whole cave was caving in on her. Then all seemed quiet, and surprised to find she was still crouching low and unhurt, she tasted the choking dust that rushed through on the draught, and billowed in the darkness filling the whole of the stone cavity and covering her as she went right down onto his knees, her hand over her mouth and her nose. Unable to breathe, she felt as if she was suffocating, and then coughing and choking as she took a deep breath in, feeling dust clogging her throat. It took a few minutes for the dust to settle, and then there was complete silence again. She took her hands from her face, feeling the gritty dust in her mouth, and her sinuses were clogged. She got to her feet very slowly. And then she heard distant voices – it was the tree men, still in the garden they had obviously not heard the gunshot. And of course what she didn't know, was, that at the moment of the gunshot there had been a loud clap of thunder, and just as the roof of the barn had slipped from their grip it had caught their ladders knocking all the tree men down sprawling flat out on their backs on the wet lawn, and of course they were shocked at the impact and not knowing about the cave or that anyone was down there.

Julie moved very quietly, feeling her way in the darkness crossing the panel, not knowing if Denny Bell was still there, and knowing that both Alan and Rick were down below and hoping that Denny had not shot one of them. As she emerged from the archway into the first cave, there was dim light coming from above; she looked up into the open cloudy sky hearing a rumble of thunder and then a flash of lightning, and felt the rain and a wisp of the fresh air, and she breathed deeply. The light was dull and the rubble heavy underfoot, with jagged pieces of wood and large sharp nails and metal rubble of the old barn and tree branches. Above, the roof of the barn hung half intact, and part of the wall hung precariously, with wet straw just hanging, swinging in the wind and could fall any minute; the rest filled the floor of the cave amongst the wood and rubble. She then saw one trainer sticking out from under it, and she knew it must be Denny Bell, and surely he must be dead! She stood very still just looking for any sign of movement. She came nearer, creeping carefully and cautiously in case Denny Bell should suddenly get up. Her feet slipped over broken and wet timber, and felt wet straw poking through the toes of her sandals, but her only thought now was to get to the sconce, it seemed untouched by the mess and she sighed with relief reaching up to find that it still worked, and the panel moved with the rusty scraping sound and Alan and Rick came out – Alan anxious to know if she was alright and she so relieved to find them both alright; they were both amazed at the devastation, she very quickly filling them in on what had happened. Alan then twisted the sconce and the panel closed over the treasure, supposedly for the very last time. Julie indicated the trainer, and they guessed that Denny Bell was dead. The ladder was gone, and they could hear voices of the workmen, but Alan suggested that they not call up, the least people that knew about the cave the better, and when they came to remove the rubble, they would find Denny Bell.

The three of them made their way back with the light from the phone as the lantern had gone out again. It was very creepy in the short narrow passage, as Alan turned the sconce and the wall closed on the cave leaving them in deadly silence. They mounted the five stone steps into the long narrow passage and they just stepped into the library as the French clock was chiming eleven, and they were sitting casually getting their breath back when Charles came in few minutes later with the coffee. He put the tray down, noticing the gash on Rick's head, and the dust on Mrs Anderson's hair and clothes, but of course did not remark on it, thinking that they maybe had gone out of the French doors in the storm and over to the tree men. He asked should he pour, but Julie said no she would do it, and asked him to bring another cup for Rick, "Thank you, Charles." He then left the room quietly and went back to the kitchen, and remarked his thoughts to Oliver who was busy making pastry – he just lifted his eyes, not very interested.

Julie was pouring coffee, and they talked excitedly about the treasure, and then sadly about Denny Bell. Charles came back with another cup and saucer, when he'd gone, "He would have left us to die," said Rick.

"Well, what *was* he doing there anyway?" Julie shrugged.

"Do you think he knew about the treasure?" Alan frowned.

Julie shook her head. "How could he?"

About an hour had gone by, when Charles tapped on the door and came in with the sad news that the tree men had found Denny Bell. Julie caught her breath.

"Mr Baker is in the drawing room, Madam."

"Thank you, Charles." The three of them exchanged glances and made their way to the drawing room, where Tommy Baker looked so worried and upset, and almost in tears, "It just collapsed, Mr Holland, Sir," he turned to Rick, "we couldn't stop it. I'm so sorry, Mistress," he turned to Julie, "I think the lightning struck it, I'm not sure, we were holding it and it just suddenly went, and we were knocked off the ladders – it just slipped away from us – I'm so sorry," he wrung his hands and shook his head gently, looking down at his mudded boots, "and of course we didn't know anyone was down there..." He was looking pleadingly at them all, "And did you know there is a cave down there? Under the barn?" He looked at Rick wide-eyed with surprise, they were all a little taken aback at this question, and Rick really didn't know what to say.

Alan with a surprised look said, "Oh! Yes! We have heard that there was a cave somewhere, haven't we, Rick?" Rick nodded.

"What about Denny Bell?" Julie said anxiously, changing the subject and trying to sound a little sad, but in her mind, thinking *he had been prepared to let them all die down there.*

"Well Mam…"

"It's not your fault, Mr Baker," Rick cut in.

"No, we are sure it was not your fault," Julie, sympathized. "Whatever Denny Bell was doing, he shouldn't have been in the barn anyway." *Well,* she thought, *that bit was true anyway.*

"Where is he?" asked Rick."

"Well we've laid him under a tree, Mr Holland, it's terrible," he was in tears shaking his head, "I'm so sorry," he was rubbing her hands nervously.

"I'll come," said Rick, he went out with Johnny, and while he was there he phoned for an ambulance, and of course the police came too. Johnny and his men were worried and scared, as the four of them with Rick and Alan stood in the pouring rain under the tree with the police sergeant while the ambulance men did their job.

Julie was watching from the patio with Charles and Oliver and old Gibbons.

"I can't think why on earth he was down there," said Julie.

"I told him it wasn't a ghost," said old Gibbons.

"*Ghost?*" Julie frowned.

"Yes, Mistress, he come in saying 'eeh 'eard ghostly screamin' in the barn."

"Yes," Charles nodded, "I gave him coffee and rum to calm him down."

Julie frowned again, "Well, what was he doing in the barn?"

"Well, Mr Rick sent him to fix the roof 'cause it was dangerous swing' in the wind, and he said he heard ghosts," said Gibbons, "but I didn't think 'ee'd have gone back in there." Gibbons shook his head. He didn't say that he knew it was her screaming to get out.

Back in the drawing room, Alan and Julie watched from the window while waited, for Rick, "Another dead body after

230

finding the treasure," said Alan. Julie looked at him and took a deep and faulting breath.

"Yes, it's sad, he was so young, but thank goodness it wasn't you," Julie reached for his hand affectionately, "But, he was prepared to let us all die, and I don't want to lose you."

Alan smiled, "And I don't want to lose you either," he put a comforting arm around her, and was kissing her gently when Rick came back in, "Oops, sorry."

"It's OK, come in," Alan smiled.

"What about Denny Bell?" Julie was anxious to know.

"The ambulance has gone," Rick pulled a face, "crushed every bone in his body so they said." He took a deep breath. "Sad," there was a long pause… "Sad," he said again, shaking his head gently, "he seemed such a nice young guy, but thank God you were there, Mrs Anderson, when Denny Bell died, or we would have done… nobody knew we were down there." There was another pause…

"Well, whatever made him come down there with a shotgun?" said Alan. "Did he know about the treasure?"

"He was looking for a ghost so old Gibbons said," said Julie.

"No," Rick half chuckled, "he was after the treasure. You don't chase a ghost with a shotgun."

"Well how did he know?" said Alan.

"He must have heard us talking. Why does the talk of money or treasure make people do these things," Julie shook her head in despair. Then she took a deep breath, "But what now! What about *the treasure*? What are you going to with it?"

"Nothing," Alan flicked his eyebrows and shook his head taking his hand out of his shorts' pockets, "I don't think we should do anything! I think, it's best left where it is! It seems, well, according to that manuscript that anyone that has ever found it, or *touched* anything has died… It's best left alone, Denny Bell could be Honeybeck's last victim."

"But it wasn't Honeybeck," said Rick, "it was the storm."

"How do you know?" asked Alan.

"Well it's obvious," Rick splayed his hands.

"Hmm, well I'm not so sure," Alan raised his eyebrows, "look what happened when we moved the gold cup, that was just a warning – we could be dead. Even though it sounds a bit ridiculous."

"Well, we've all seen the treasure now, actually been locked in with it, and we're still here," Rick raised his eyebrows, a bit surprised and relieved.

"That's as maybe," said Alan, "there's still time and, we *don't* want to steal it…"

"Do you think Honeybeck knows that?" Rick nodded thoughtfully… then looked up, "What about the key to the bookcase?"

"I put it back," Alan grinned.

"Where?" Rick now looked curiously wide-eyed.

Alan grinned, "Right where young Benjamin left it!" Alan gave him a comical smile, his eyebrows still arched.

Rick frowned at him, a sort of 'where?' in unsaid words, but knew that Alan wasn't going to say, so he never asked.

The rocking chair started to rock, had Honeybeck been there all the time and could he have heard their conversation? Alan thought he heard a contented sigh, it could have been imagination but he never said anything. "Let's go outside on to the patio," he took Julie by the arm, and Rick followed them. The rain had eased and so they made it to the gazebo. "I think Honeybeck listens to all we say," Alan raised his eyebrows.

"No, *no!*" Rick inclined his head with a smile, "Although, you could be right. He knows we've seen the treasure."

"Then he knows that we won't touch it," Alan smiled, "he went wild when we moved the gold cup, just think what he would do, if we touched the treasure, I think we should just forget about it from now on, he hasn't troubled the house now for some months, perhaps he won't come back, now he knows his treasure is safe."

"Well he was in the drawing room just now wasn't he?"

"Well we don't mind, as long as he just stays there rocking. Did you hear that, Honeybeck?" Alan grinned at all around him. Julie felt an icy chill.

CHAPTER TWENTY-ONE

The weeks had gone on and the weather was still a little unsettled, the humidity was high, and the mornings sunny and bright. Julie sat by the pool but not for long, by lunchtime the sky was overcast with intermittent heavy showers, so she went to the library taking her book, or still glancing through Edward Turner's manuscript.

Alan was at the office and some days she had met him for lunch, that broke the day up for her, and in the evenings they had dined out or at the Silver Lady, sometimes inviting Zena and Perry, or Loretta and Dan, who could just walk from their house and always followed by Eddie who would not be left behind. But Julie was pleased to see him, especially in the day time, he was company to have around. There was one day when he decided to bury a bone that Oliver had given him, and he dug a deep hole in front of the silver lady. Old Gibbons then got young Jim Westerly, who had replaced Denny Bell, to fill in the hole. Jim had very black skin, he was tall and thin, very athletic – played most sports and worked out in the gym every morning, and had hard muscles. He slammed the spade down and the lady fell over, Jim was then apologizing and saying he was sorry – "the wood was rotten at the bottom and she just fell over."

The now forlorn lady was lying on her back with her bright eyes staring up at the sky. Old Gibbons explained that the lady had stood there untouched for 300 years. Jim, worried and still apologizing, as old Gibbons went to fetch Rick, who came to look and suggested that Jim dig out the rotten wood and put some cement into the ground and stand her up again. Jim set to work; the rotten wood went deep into the ground that was hard, even though they had had a lot of rain, and the deeper he went the drier it became; the spade struck something, and looking into the hole he saw a coffin. He quickly called old Gibbons, who again called Rick, who was with Alan and Julie, and they all came anxiously to see.

"Honeybeck, do you think?" Alan looked at Rick.

"Who's Honeybeck?" asked young Jim. No one answered and he stood there with wide and scared brown eyes wondering what he had done.

"Do you think we should take a look?" said Alan.

Rick, wide-eyed, held his breath and bit his bottom lip then said to Jim, "Yeah, clear off the rest of this earth."

Jim's eyes were wide with alarm, he shovelled away the rest of the earth and stood back, hoping they wouldn't ask him to open the coffin; the expression on his black face was aghast, he even looked pale. "Whaa! You gonna *open it up?*" His eyes showing white with fear were ready to pop, and his voice a high-pitched squeak.

Julie felt a sickness in her stomach, it would obviously be a skeleton, but to open up a *coffin*, she held her breath. "No, don't!"

Rick took the spade from Jim, the wood was rotten, and creaked and broke away at the corner as Rick levered it up.

Julie, wanting to see, peered into the hole, but then turned away in horror, although she'd seen absolutely nothing.

"Well! What'll you know?" Rick stood back, chuckled and looked at Alan who grinned, and they chuckled together. Julie and Jim looked at each other and came closer and old Gibbons joined them.

"Lovely meal," said Dan, sipping at his white wine.

"Yes, the snapper was lovely," Loretta smiled at Julie, "it's my favourite fish, and your chef is very good, I'll have to have the recipe. We've had Bella now for five years, and she's a good cook," she wrinkled her nose, "but she's not a chef."

"What, do *you* do now?" Alan asked Dan.

"Well, I'm retired, but I keep busy, got some financial stuff on the move – stocks and shares. Phone and email – you know."

"And the dogs keep me busy," Loretta smiled at Julie, "I hope that Eddie doesn't bother you too much, we can't keep him in, and I'm so sorry he dug up your garden, Alf Gibbons told us." She sounded sad and ashamed. Charles came to clear the plates and replenish their glasses.

'Must have been awful digging up a grave," said Dan, "Jimmy Westerly told us it was gruesome – all those bones and stuff, and just the hat left."

Alan glanced sharply at Julie, a smile touched the corners of his mouth and his eyes twinkled, they both burst out laughing. Dan and Loretta glanced at each other.

"Well wasn't it bad then?" asked Dan.

"Well," Alan raised his eyebrows wrinkling his forehead with a chuckle, "it certainly was a surprise, and it was a nice hat, a bit dusty of course, but I'd hardly call a three-cornered hat with a faded red feather, gruesome."

"Is that all that was in there?" Loretta looked at them both, "Jimmy said it was terrible a gruesome sight."

Julie laughed, "Yes that's all there was, a three-cornered hat and under it one silver coin, or piece of eight, as I suppose it would have been called in that day and age."

"That Jimmy was having us on," Dan glanced at his wife and they smiled. "I see you've stood her up again, cemented her in this time then, so Jimmy said?"

"Yes," Alan smiled, he thought – *they knew more about it than he did!*

"See she's not glowing tonight," said Dan.

"No, we disconnected the electricity."

Dan looked amazed, "Electricity?"

At last, thought Alan, *something they didn't know.* "Yeah, she was connected to the security lighting, someone has had that coffin up before, it's very old, we wondered if it had been full of silver, obviously we were expecting to see a skeleton. But all there was, was the hat, and one silver coin."

"I would think the hat is Honeybeck's," said Julie, "it looks the same as the one in the portrait in the library, so I put it on a shelf nearby, I'm sure he will be pleased to have it back."

"So where's the body then?" Loretta looked puzzled.

"Dunno," Alan grimaced, "I would think Honeybeck was buried there once with treasure, probably someone took the treasure and just turned out the body or the bones, maybe that is why Honeybeck haunts the house, he's not at rest. And maybe they left the hat and the silver coin by mistake, *or*, it could have been left for people like us who would eventually dig up the coffin thinking it was the treasure, and then it would be a joke. But whoever it was fixed the lady up to the electricity and a very low small bulb, so I don't know how long there has been security lighting here, how long has she been glowing – do you know?"

Ben shook his head, "I haven't been up here that much, it just is more so now that Eddie keeps coming here. I think the last people that were here with the bank had kids."

"Hmm, well someone has messed about with it. But it puzzles me why anyone would want to do that to a grave, no matter how long it's been there."

"Yes," Loretta wrinkled her nose, "what a horrible thing to do. Might have been youngsters, who knows what they get up to these days."

"Yeah! Dunno! Maybe somebody thought it was funny."

"Well, it could have been the Turners, I would think that there has been security lighting here for some years," Alan put his elbows on the table and rubbed his hands together, "I looked it up, on the computer, apparently electricity was discovered by the ancient Greeks."

"Well I'm sure they didn't live here," laughed Dan, they all laughed.

Alan grinned, "It was in 1600, that a William Gilbert, who was English, called it 'electric', so I suppose, it could have been years ago, depends how long the electricity has been here on the island or put in the house, before that, it would have been candlelight. And, I should think *that* coffin's been opened more than once over the years. I bet the Turners must have been curious about Honeybeck's treasure, especially as he haunts the house, and where else would you expect him to be buried, it seems obvious that it would be under the silver lady.

But my guess is that while the house has been empty for so many years, it was vandals."

"Are you still looking for the treasure?" Dan chuckled, thinking the treasure was all a big joke, "I hear you lost your barn in the storm and it was over a cave wasn't it? I bet that was a surprise, old Gibbons told us," Dan went on, "Shame about poor Denny Bell, nice young lad he was, he used to do a bit of gardening for us until I caught him pinching the new plants and selling 'em. Down there looking for ghosts, so Alf Gibbons said. I thought, in a storm," he wrinkled his nose, "no, he must have been sheltering, when the whole barn collapsed on him."

Julie took a breath, "Well yes, I think that *is* what must have happened."

"But the barn has been locked for years, hasn't it?" said Dan.

Alan frowned, "Yes, we've never found a key. I just pulled the door one day and the lock broke."

"Well, he shouldn't have been in there anyway so Gibbons said, he'd been warned that the floor was not safe. You fell through the floorboards too, didn't you?" Dan went on, "so you knew about the cave then…"

Alan nodded, "Yes the floor *was* a bit unsafe," thinking, *was there anything that these people didn't know?*

"Did you get any storm damage?" asked Julie, changing the subject.

"Just a couple of trees down," said Loretta, "but they were just small ones. They said that there is more to come, gale force winds and floods next week, doesn't sound too good, but I suppose we are still in the hurricane season, it won't get any better until the end of October, will it?"

It was about 10.30 when Dan and Loretta left, and Alan and Julie went to the garden gate with them, saying goodnight as they walked arm-in-arm, down the long drive, followed by Eddie.

Alan and Julie went back to the gazebo, "Good God," Alan flopped back down into an easy chair and picked up his glass again, "is there anything that they don't know?"

"Yes," Julie whispered with a smile, "They don't know that we found the treasure…" there was a pause as Charles came to clear away the rest of the glasses; he said goodnight, and left them to finish their drinks.

"I wonder what happened to that shotgun?" Julie suddenly asked.

Alan pulled a face, "Dunno, probably still down there under the rubble."

"What will happen when they clear the rest of the rubble and they find it?"

"Oh they'll think Denny Bell was out shooting birds or something."

"WHAT! In a raging storm?"

Alan smiled, "Well, if they find it we'll just say don't know."

The week went by. The funeral of Denny Bell was sad – Julie thought it her duty to attend as he was an employee, Rick, Charles, Oliver, and old Gibbons went with her and the church was full. Denny Bell was obviously a very popular young man. She had never found out why he was down there in the cave anyway, but old Gibbons had made her laugh about Denny hearing her screaming and thought that it was a ghost so she suspected that he had come down there to investigate just as the floor panel to the treasure was opening, but why he was carrying a shotgun in a raging storm was a mystery.

The weather had not been good; there had been some sunshine but heavy intermittent rain showers and thunderstorms. It was a Saturday morning a week later when the rain storms seemed to have cleared, and the workmen came back to finish clearing the rubble left from the old tree that was now wet, and soggy sawdust, and now after more inspections after finding Denny Bell in the cave they had brought a large grab to reach down through the top of the first half of the cave to remove the collapsed mess of the old barn. They had been there a few hours.

Julie was sitting on the patio with coffee, and Charles had cleared the breakfast things. It was noisy with the continual heaving and droning of the heavy engine, and the crashing and banging as the timber was removed and piled into a tip, that they had driven away several times to empty on to a truck. Above the noise, men's voices rose as they shouted directions to the driver and to each other. And now it was dull and drizzling with rain again, but the humidity was still high. And so she removed herself into the library once again; it was quieter in here and cooler with the fan running and she made herself comfortable in one of the deep winged-back chairs, but the book wasn't very interesting anyway, and she resorted back to Edward Turner's manuscript – there was still a lot that she hadn't read.

Now sitting at the desk, she turned the papers; there was a mention of Honeybeck – he had materialized, in the drawing room and the candles had moved across the room, and terrified one Marie Lou, age 17, daughter of Gilbert and Alice Turner, it seemed that she had a weak heart and she had died of fright in the drawing room. He had also appeared in the drawing room to Edgar and Jessica, while entertaining their friends, who it is said would never enter the house again. Honeybeck had laughed loudly, scaring the servants, and of course word spread about the ghost and they left and Edgar could not get any staff for months and so he took slaves from his cane fields and then had to buy more slaves down on the beach at Carlyle Bay that had become not only a busy port, but a trading post for slaves. And then it seemed that Honeybeck had disappeared, and not been seen for many months, at least Edward Turner had not mentioned a word about him in the following chapters.

She read that up until 1665 the majority of people living in Holetown were white English males under the age of 55, and this applied to most of Barbados anyway. The early males were mostly Irish indentured servants, this guaranteed them freedom after a seven-year period. There had been an outbreak of cholera somewhere around 1835 – the date had been scribbled on the bottom of the page and was smudged out, and there was a mention of a hurricane in 1955.

Suddenly there were loud shouts to almost hysteria, and she ran out of the library. Oliver, Charles, and young Robbie the kitchen boy came out of the hall door that led from the kitchen and were running across the lawn, so she followed. There was a lot of confusion, the men were rushing round and then she could see that the huge grab had toppled on its right side and was half fallen into the cave, the driver still inside. The whirring of the heavy engine was deafening, the left-hand track still rotating in the air and three men were trying to get the driver out, but as they put their weight on the cab to open the door so the grab fell a little further. They said the driver was struggling, but thought it better now to stay still, each movement inched it further down; then there was a tremendous noise as the right track deep down was crunching against the coral stone. Then the driver must have turned off the engine for it all suddenly went quiet. Julie overheard one of the workmen telling Charles that the coral stone had been a thin layer of rock on the top and under the weight of the digger it had just collapsed into the open space.

The men could do nothing but wait. It was an hour before another larger grab came to haul out the fallen one, and the driver was then free and virtually unhurt, but for a pain in his arm and his ribs where he had lain so long in an awkward position, but the doctor had come and said that all was well. But had also sent him to the clinic in Holetown for an X-ray.

The foreman told Rick that they would clear the rock from the cave, but Rick told them to leave it as it was almost filling the cavity. He told Julie, quietly, the rock fall had sealed the treasure forever.

Julie's days were mostly the same; sitting by the pool she had sent and received her emails, and she sat daydreaming looking out through the trees on to the vast ocean, and her thoughts were of Gavin, *he was out there somewhere*. And then looking at the reflections of the trees in the pool, while sparrows and yellow birds, flitted from branch to branch, and then she was fascinated to see a humming bird, hovering before the white orchids that grew on a high bow of a mahogany tree, then a small green-grey kingfisher swooped to take insects off the surface of the pool, disturbing the water, and the reflections of the trees moved with the slow rippling motion. The humidity was tiring and she lay down under the green umbrella with her eyes closed behind dark glasses, listening to the whistling and calling of the birds. Her mind went to Honeybeck's treasure, *it was sad that it was now lost forever under a ton of rock, but it was a relief, she would have feared break-ins, but she thought now it would have been nice to have saved just a little something, a piece of jewellery, but it was too late now, and what she had never had she would never miss, and no one knew about it anyway which was just as well. As Alan had said, it would have been a nightmare if the press had got hold of it. The cave no longer existed, it was now just a large pile of coral, and the old barn had been an eyesore anyway, but it was a shame about the Arawak drawings, but Michael would have photos in his Antiques magazine and Alan had said that it was all better forgotten anyway, and she agreed. Maybe Honeybeck would never come back now that his treasure was safe.*

Alan, had stayed for the whole weekend again, and on Saturday they had driven around the island to the east coast, where the scenery was very rural. The quiet coast road separated the rolling green hills to the right from the high bearded fig trees to the left that edged the long golden deserted beach; beyond this, the rough Atlantic Ocean forever rolled in over the a rocky reef. They stopped the car and sat looking out to sea; it was quiet, not a soul about anywhere, and so peaceful with just the rushing sound of the sea. They stayed in the car, not wanting to walk on the beach – the sea held sad memories for them both. "Barbados takes its name, from the bearded fig trees," Julie suddenly said, "did you know that? A Portuguese captain named the island, Barbados, it means bearded fig."

"Really, does it," Alan turned to her in surprise. "I didn't know that, I didn't even know that they were bearded fig trees either."

She smiled, "I read it in Edward Turner's manuscript." They sat with their own thoughts, hearing the rush and thunder of the waves crashing on the shore.

"We're lucky to have found each other, you know!" Alan smiled turning to her. But his eyes were saddened.

She nodded, sadly, "Yes, but maybe Gavin and Suzie were also lucky to find each other, in heaven. I wonder if they think of us like we think of them." They smiled sadly and thoughtfully at each other.

"Come on," he touched her hand with a smile, "we're getting morbid, let's go for lunch." They drove along the coast road passing a few small chattel houses but saw no one, and then up a steep and winding hill, past dense jungle greenery and a banana plantation, and then a sharp turn to the left and the road went down very steeply. They stopped at the 'Round House', a restaurant that looked like the turret of a coral stone castle. They had a table on what might have been the battlements. A strong cool breeze blew off the sea far below rocking the large umbrella that shaded them from the blazing afternoon sun. They returned later to the Silver Lady for cocktails and dinner.

CHAPTER TWENTY-TWO

Julie was suntan creaming her legs by the pool the next morning while waiting for Alan who was making a phone call, when her mobile phone rang – it was Michael Prescott, saying that he was back on the island, he got in on the late flight last night, and Julie asked him to come for lunch knowing that he would probably have no food in the house.

"Oh. Are you here on your own?" Julie looked up in surprise as Charles showed Michael up on to the gazebo, where she and Alan were now enjoying a glass of light white wine. She nodded with a smile to Charles to pour Mr Prescott a glass.

"Where's Mellissa. Working again?" asked Alan.

"No!" Michael shook his head, "It's all off! Here," he turned to Julie, "I brought you copy of the antiques magazine, there are picture of the cave drawings."

"Off?" Alan, dipped his head and arched his eyebrows.

"Oh, I'm sorry," said Julie. Although she was not really surprised, "when did this happen?"

"A few weeks ago. Well, we were never really together," said Michael, "the modelling was taking all of her time, we haven't seen each other now for some months, she's been down in Mexico again, and then London," he shook his head, "and she's never liked it here anyway, and so we agreed to call it a day."

"So how long are you staying?" Alan raised his eyebrows.

He shook his head, "Dunno yet, cheers," he lifted his glass, "maybe a few weeks or so, I've got nothing on in America at the moment. But I have got a girlfriend Dianne, we've known each other for a few years, she's a make-up artist, and we've been together now for a couple of months."

"Oh, so you were seeing her while Mellissa was away?" said Julie

"Yeah…"

There was a bit of an awkward moment… "Anyway," Alan cleared his throat, and lifted his glass, "Cheers, again." Michael seemed to relax a bit, he smiled nodded and sipped at the wine.

Julie thumbed though the magazine, "These are good, and you've got the drawings on the front cover too," she smiled and showed Alan.

"These are very good," Alan flicked his eyes at Michael, "so clear, considering the light down there. But, *now*, we've lost the cave."

"No! Really! You found *that treasure* yet?" Michael said eagerly, chuckling.

"No!" Both Julie and Alan said together, glancing at each other.

Michael flicked his eyes; *he wasn't sure what that really meant.* Alan then explained about the storm. "We lost the barn and now cave is full of rubble."

"Oh what a shame," Michael frowned.

Alan nodded, "But still we've got your photos in the magazine."

"Had any more trouble with that ghostly pirate?" Michael grinned. "I'd still like to get a good shot of him."

"Yeah! We'd like to get shot of him too," Alan chuckled.

"No," Julie smiled, just as Charles was serving the lunch, "We haven't seen much of him lately, we had the Paranormal Group here, it seems to be a bit better, but I don't think he will ever leave the house."

"Oh, so I might stand a chance yet." Michael smiled.

It was on Wednesday evening that Michael took them both out for dinner. He said he was settling down and he had engaged Emma, she was a maid and a cook, and that he was still sorting though his parents' things. "I heard you'd dug up a grave by the silver lady?" He looked at Alan, "But there was no body, was there?"

Alan half chuckled, "How did you know that?"

"I met old Alf Gibbons in the coffee shop early this morning." He grinned, shrugged his shoulders, "had nothing in the house, so, went down for a bun and cappuccino. I think I'll be OK. Now I've got this maid, I'll get her to do the shopping."

"Did you know all we found was a three-cornered hat?" Said Julie.

Michael's eyes opened wide, "Yeah?" He was greatly surprised, "Did yer? Coo, I didn't hear that bit, I'd liked to have photographed that."

"Well you can do," said Julie, "I put it in the library, near old Honeybeck's portrait, I thought he might like to have it back, I put it near the gold cup."

"But we won't touch *that* again," Alan grinned.

"Why?"

"Well! We looked at the gold cup and left it on the desk, didn't put it back again in the alcove and he ransacked the whole of the library. It was the night that we had dinner with you and Mellissa, when we got back the staff were all out in the garden scared stiff, we're surprised that they stayed on."

"Really," Michael chuckled it was all a big joke to him, "I'd love to get a shot of old Honeybeck but I think he's camera shy, all I get is mist." He laughed, as the waiter poured more wine.

They said goodnight to Michael, it had been a pleasant evening. Alan drove Julie home, they were sitting in the car in the driveway of the Silver Lady Cottage. The drink had mellowed them both, he kissed her and she responded warmly, he kissed her again, and then whispered, "You said you loved me, in the cave."

She leaned away looking dreamily into his keen brown eyes in the semi-darkness, "Yes," she whispered, "yes I meant it. How could I not love you, Alan. You have been such help to me, I couldn't live without you now. I really do love you."

"And I love you, Julie, I have done for a long time, you have also been a great comfort to me too, I couldn't have gone on alone especially out here in Barbados, I think I would have chucked the job in and gone back to the UK. But now, I feel that I can't live without you. But I didn't say anything before, because I didn't know how you felt, and I thought that it might be too soon… But we do have to live on don't we?"

She nodded up at him feeling a little tearful, thoughts of Gavin came into her mind, but Alan was *right here*. She had to let Gavin go. He pulled her closer and kissed her passionately for the very first time since they had known each other. She clung to him, feeling content and safe, in the strength in his arms, "Oh Alan, I do love you…"

"Will you marry me?"

"Yes," she nodded, "yes." They kissed again and that night, for the very first time, in almost two years, they shared a bed.

Two weeks went by, and Alan had arranged a dinner party on the Saturday night in their favourite restaurant. Julie had informed Michael on the phone of their engagement, and asked him for dinner, he had said that Dianne was arriving and could he bring her too.

Loretta and Dan, and Zena and Perry, and also Rick and Chrystal were all there for the celebration, and the girls admired the diamond solitaire that Alan had given her.

Dianne Forester had arrived from New York. She was a make-up artist for the models that Michael photographed. She was beautiful, with long dark hair and dusky skin, big brown eyes and long curling black ashes – needless to say that her make-up was perfect. She was American, but of some African or Indian descent. Julie found her to be of a quiet nature, polite and graceful, easy to talk to, and very down to earth – a complete contrast to the fancy and finicky blonde Mellissa – and she thought that his mother Mary, if looking down, would approve of this one. All the girls got on well, while the men as usual seemed to be talking business. Dianne said that it was her first time in Barbados, she only arrived last night but had had a lovely day and was sure that she was going to love it, although only here for a week. She had known Michael a long time, and he was planning to come and live here, and he had asked her to live here too and she was thinking about it. They did not live together in New York, but saw each other nearly every day during the photographic sessions, and they had been seriously together for six months. The evening went well and Michael, a little intoxicated, went down on one knee in the busy restaurant, asking Dianne to marry him, and she accepted, and they all had more champagne. The people on the tables nearby clapped and congratulated them and then, after the restaurant, the celebrations went on, as they went from bar to bar.

Two nights afterwards, they were at a barbecue, at Michael's house, and Dianne was flashing a beautiful sapphire ring.

As the merriment went on, Julie suddenly had sombre thoughts of Gavin. The last time she was in this house he was here, she had that feeling of nearness, she stared hard at the garden chair where he had been sitting the night before the terrible disaster... It brought tears to her eyes but she mustn't let go, and was startled as Michael was at her elbow, saying "More champagne, Julie?" She quickly brightened.

CHAPTER TWENTY-THREE

Some months had gone by, and Honeybeck was still around. Julie felt his presence, she looked behind her many times especially when going up the stairs, but of course there was nothing there, but there was the occasional grunt, or sigh – it made her feel a bit on edge, but at least she was used to it now.

Looking now at the portrait in the library, she thought the eyes flickered, but then brushed it off as her imagination, *well it had to be didn't it?* She felt somehow that Honeybeck was mocking her; *it was all in her imagination wasn't it?* Even though she could feel a presence, "Why are you still here?" she asked the portrait quietly, "if it's your treasure you're worried about, it's sealed for ever in the cave, and I'm not going to touch it. I retrieved your hat, did you like that?" She picked up the hat and put on her head, suddenly loud harsh laughter filled the room which startled her and she spun around to find Honeybeck standing there in the centre of the library. She stepped back, her eyes wide, her heart beating fast, she blinked.

"I'm still here…" he chuckled. The voice was rough and husky, but it was a clear drawn-out hushed whisper.

She was stunned, it took her breath away, her heart thumping loudly in her ears. He stood, six feet tall, robust, broad-shouldered, fully dressed as in the portrait, in red damask. He swept the hat from his head and bowed. Julie's hands went to her head, the hat was gone, this certainly was not her imagination! She was speechless, she spun around looking at the portrait – he was still there in the portrait. She turned back, he was still here in the centre of the room, and he was so real. She took a deep breath, "Captain Honeybeck?" She was bewildered, *he would vanish any minute.* But he didn't…

248

"At your service, Madam!" He smiled, his teeth were white and even – he was quite handsome in a rugged sort of way – his skin bronzed from being open to the element for too long and his brown eyes had a roguish twinkle. There was a devilish, boyish, air about him, she imagined that at a minute's notice he could have drawn the sword and gone into action with jubilant pleasure at killing his opponent. She held her breath, *was she dreaming?*

"I thank you for my hat," he put it back on his head and faded away.

Julie was spellbound she let out her breath slowly feeling her breast heavily deflating, and clenching her hands tightly together it seemed to be holding her body together, she was shaking, it couldn't have happened – could it? She had imagined it hadn't she? "No!" She shook her head. It had happened, hadn't it? She turned back to the portrait, did the eyes flicker? *"No, no!"* she whispered, it was all imagination. The hat was back in the alcove where it always was, she'd had it on her head – how did it get there? Perhaps she had absentmindedly put it back. She felt numb and sat down in a chair, her hands clasped in tight fists, her toes clenched tight in her sandals, she was scared, a bit excited, a bit fascinated, the quick thumping of her heart seemed to shake her body. She said very quietly and warily to the portrait, "Captain Honeybeck, are you here?"

"Mmm?" There was a low chuckle.

She caught her breath feeling a tightness clasp her whole body, "Can you move that hat?" It lifted up and then down. She held her breath again, her eyes scanned the room, she jumped up and raced to the door, then glanced back before closing it, hearing a low chuckle that sent a shiver down her spine. She closed the door again and stood frozen to the spot.

Alan came home from the office and they were on the gazebo, with drinks before dinner, she couldn't wait to tell him, "Alan…" she started slowly, "you'll never believe what happened in the library," and then she told him…

"Really!" He had a slight frown, and looked sceptically at her, finding it hard to believe, knowing that she had a brilliant imagination, but surely she wouldn't have made it all up? Charles came up onto the gazebo, with a tray, saying that the dinner was served. They took their seats at the table.

"Well, you don't believe me do you? It happened Alan, I know it's hard to believe but it happened, I didn't imagine it. *He was there! He was real!*" Charles turned, hearing her high pitch as he was half way across the garden.

Alan nodded, "Yeah, OK."

"You don't believe me do you?"

"Yeah, of course I do. Yeah!"

"You don't!" she said with annoyance, feeling heat rising through her body, "it happened, Alan, he was there, fully dressed in *red,* just like the portrait…" She was so annoyed to thank that he didn't believe her! And they ate in silence.

The next morning, at breakfast Alan was down first; he was drinking coffee when she arrived, he half smiled and got a glare. "Mmm, is this our first fight?" He frowned, a little comically.

"It did happen!"

"Friends?" He inclined his head with arched eyebrows and a smile.

She nodded, with a smile, "Yes… But it did happen!"

"Yes, I remember Oliver saying that he had rushed through the kitchen in red."

"Oh Alan, you *do* believe me?" He nodded

Charles came to the table, "Good morning, Madam," he gave her the post. "Coffee, Mam?" he began to pour.

"Oh, look at this," she turned to Alan showing him the wedding invitation from Michael and Dianne.

CHAPTER TWENTY-FOUR

The flight had been good. It was the first time that Julie had been to Miami, and after Barbados the shopping was marvellous; they could walk from the Ritz Carlton Hotel into the town, which was alive and busy both by day and by night, with restaurants and bars packed and there was an all round holiday spirit. By day they marvelled as skate boarders swerved in and out of busy fast moving traffic, and some hanging on the backs of cars and trucks, and roller blades swished in and out of people on the sidewalk along by the beach. The beach was long, straight and wide, and white, and people crowdedd there from 6.30 in the morning until 7.00 at night when it got dark – it was all very exciting.

Dianne looked beautiful in white silk and veiling. They were married under an arbour of white roses in the hotel garden, and witnessed by fifty guests and then there was dancing under a starlit sky to a large band until the early hours of the morning, Julie and Alan stayed on in Miami for the rest of the week while Michael and Dianne, honeymooned in Barbados.

Now back home Alan was once again in the office. Julie was this morning lying by the pool with her eyes closed, thinking back on the wonderful week they'd had with the excitement of the wedding, that was now two weeks ago, and the shopping had been great. Alan had been so patient while she had tried on dresses and dozens of pairs of shoes, she thought he was an exceptional man, as most men do not like shopping. But for all that, it was nice to be back, quiet and peaceful once again.

The day was cloudy, and there were intermittent rain showers, and so she curled up under the umbrella, until it got worse and then she had to go back to the house where she spent most of her time in the library and luckily there had been no trouble with Honeybeck. In the afternoon the wind had got stronger. In the evening, the dinner had been laid in the gazebo as usual, but it was very windy and Charles had a problem balancing the tray coming across the garden and apologized as a glass got blown away and broken. There had been warnings of a storm, and the rain was heavy and the wind got even stronger, and Charles brought them umbrellas to go across the garden but it was hard to hold on to them and they ran.

Julie lay awake through the night, as the rain lashed at the window panes, and the wind howled in ghostly tones and rattled the louvered doors on the bedroom balcony and around the house. Then there was a rumble of thunder and a flash of lightning, then a rumble and another loud clap of thunder and fork lightning flashed like daylight through the drapes. There came a loud bang as branches and twigs had flown through the air and rolled down the roof and the thunder roared and the lightning flashed as the rain lashed at the window pane when the storm was at its peak right overhead. There was no way that they could sleep. "Are you awake?" Alan's voice came out the darkened shadows.

"Yes, it's terrible isn't it?"

Alan got up and opened the drapes and cringed back quickly as lightning flashed directly in his face, and there was a tremendous clap of thunder that made him duck his head, seeing the trees blowing in a frenzy and the palms almost bending in half. Debris flew through the air as the storm raged on, lightning crackled snapped and sizzled as it zigzagged into the ground and the windows rattled. Alan saw a tree fall, "Come on, get up I don't think it's safe here."

"Why, where can we go?" It was then that Julie started to get a little anxious.

"Down into the passage. Come on, put a dressing gown on." She did as she was told and slipped into her flat sandals. Then there was a most explosive bang that shattered the whole house and as the ceiling fan slowed the electricity suddenly went. As Alan opened the bedroom door, there was a light coming from below, and Charles' voice came out of the shadows.

"Are you alright, Sir?" He shone the torch upwards for them to come down the stairs. "I think a tree has crashed on the roof."

"Is that what it was? What a night," said Alan.

"Yes Sir, I've taken Lucy and Rosalie down to the basement, will you and Mrs Anderson come down?"

"Thanks Charles, but we'll be OK. You go ahead, man."

Charles hesitated thinking where will they go. "But, Sir?"

"Go man, go," Alan urged, and Charles nodded and went down the stairs following the maids. Oliver was to give them his apartment and he was to move in with Charles for the rest of the night. They heard Charles telling Oliver that Mrs Anderson wouldn't come down.

Then Alan took Julie's hand, "Come on." They made their way down the long panelled hallway with flashes of lightning coming through the skylight showing them the way. They reached the library door, and as Alan opened it there was an explosion of lightning that made them both stop short; he rushed across the room and drew the curtains on both windows and took the key from the louvered doors, then put the key into the safe and turned it. The door began to open very slowly, and he pushed Julie inside just as a branch came crashing down on to the patio hitting the window and splattering glass across the room, and tearing the long curtain down from the pelmet. A piece of branch landing halfway across the desk, he dived into the passageway after Julie, and then looking back thinking if it had come minutes before it could have killed him. There was an enormous crash of thunder, and lightning streaked across the room, just as the door to the passage closed leaving them in darkness, and all was deadly quiet.

"We haven't got a torch," said Julie.

"Wait a minute, the lantern is here somewhere, I left it in here," he was feeling around the floor near the door, and suddenly the light lit up making eerie shadows around the cold coral stone walls. They sat on the steps, the faint sounds of the thunder sounded miles away. It was almost five o'clock in the morning when Alan looked at his watch; he opened the passage door, the storm had cleared but it was still raining.

Julie came out of the passage, her sandals crunching on glass, "Oh, my God what a mess!" the library was a mess, a large bough from a mahogany tree lay across the patio and a branch lay across the desk, Edward Turner's manuscript was half on the floor, and everything was wet and soggy.

"Well never mind, it will soon dry out," said Alan, "come on let's see what else is damaged." As Alan opened the door into the hall he could hear raised excited voices although muffled; he knew it to be Charles and Oliver, and the maids all babbling at once. He and Julie hurried along the panelled hallway. On opening the door into the main circular hall there was chaos – a huge mahogany tree had fallen through the roof, it looked forlorn now, its soggy leaves and branches were blocking the stairs and most of the hall and part of the roof was hanging. The round table lay on its side, the large antique vase was broken, and everything was soaked from the rain. The staff all turned quickly as they entered, "Come quick Sir, come quick," Charles was beckoning, Julie and Alan joined the staff. To their astonishment the tree had crashed down and broken the banister rail. They stared in absolute amazement to see the snarling jaws of the serpent still spewing out silver pieces of eight...

CHAPTER TWENTY-FIVE

It had taken almost three weeks to get the house back in order again. Although the roof had been hanging, Tommy Baker said it was not too bad and his men had soon put it right, and his carpenters had mended the serpent handrail but no one had mentioned that it had contained silver coins.

Julie wondered where else Honeybeck had hidden treasure. Alan had called Jackson Verity, who had come and collected the silver coins; Travis Braithwaite had come with him. While there, Alan had shown them around the house, they had whistled in amazement at the antiques in the rooms, and then a week later Jackson had phoned back to say that he had had the silver valued at twenty-two million dollars, plus the silver and the jar from the cave, which Jackson had told them previously, the jar was worth a fortune, and the total was now a hundred and fifty-five million dollars. Both Julie and Alan were amazed, and obviously excited, but they didn't mention that they had found the real treasure – no one should ever know, they both thought that it was best forgotten.

The weather had brightened up to the normal sunshine, and the temperature was back in the mid-eighties. Within the next month they decided to marry, and arrangements were made for the wedding in St James' church in Holetown. Rick had picked up Julie's parents from the airport and they were to stay for ten days; Michael and Dianne came from Miami; Zena and Perry were delighted with the invitation and of course Rick and Chrystal – Alan had asked Rick to be best man – and Dan and Loretta Carding, and for once Eddie had to stay at home.

At three thirty on the Saturday afternoon, the small party came out of the church, Julie looked stunning in a short white silk dress, with a wreath of white flowers in her dark hair, and carrying a posy of pink orchids. Of course Michael had his camera flashing, before they all drove back to the Silver Lady where the staff were all waiting with confetti and Charles with a tray of champagne, and then a celebration dinner provided by Oliver that went on well into the night.

On Monday afternoon Julie's parents left, Rick drove them to the airport for the overnight flight back to Gatwick. Julie was sad to see them go and there were tearful hugs and kisses, but during their stay she and her mother had had long talks. Her mother had liked Alan, and of course wished them every happiness. And then Julie and Alan were off on honeymoon the next morning for the very early flight to Miami. Rick drove to the airport again, wishing them a safe flight, and telling them to have a wonderful time.

CHAPTER TWENTY-SIX

From Miami, after three days of shopping, a car took them to Fort Lauderdale where they had decided to put the past behind them – they couldn't keep running away from the sea, and so they had booked for one week on a cruise ship.

The cabin was reasonably spacious, and on their first evening they met some nice people sitting around the bar. The food in the restaurant was delicious, and they were to call at a different ports during the week. The weather was perfect and they sunbathed around the pool on the deck, and the week went far too quickly; and now with super tans, and feeling happy and relaxed, they were back in Miami Airport, where there were hundreds of people – some rushing to catch a flight, some shopping, some just wandering and waiting for a flight. It was a long walk to the departure gate, they had over an hour to wait and there were not many seats left. They then found two, just near where it said RESERVED FOR WHEELCHAIRS ONLY. They took the two seats. Alan read the paper, while Julie liked to people watch. Soon after, a black middle-aged nurse came with a wheelchair, she took the appropriate seat just to the side of them. Her patient was a hooded lifeless man. Julie gave the nurse a sympathetic glance and the nurse smiled back, then she bent to attend to him, and Julie caught a quick glimpse of his face – he had a wide red scar across his head and down his cheek and his right eye drooped badly and he had a vacant stare. The nurse touched his shoulder there seemed no reaction.

Julie smiled sadly at the nurse, "Car accident?" she asked.

"No," the nurse shook her head, with a slight smile, "he was found by fishermen swimming in the middle of the ocean – his head was almost severed; he has no speech and is completely paralyzed, and is blind, we don't even know who he is. He's wearing a wedding ring, we think his wife must have drowned. We've just been to see the specialist in Miami, they are hoping that his sight might come back," she wrinkled her nose and shook her head gently, "but there is really nothing they can do."

"Oh," Julie put her head on one side sadly, her thoughts were on Gavin. "Shark attack?" she asked.

"Oh they are calling our flight," the nurse looked up quickly as the girl on the desk called and beckoned her to come to the gate first. She stood up and took the brake off the wheelchair, and started to push her patient away, then she turned back to answer Julie's question, "No, not a shark!" She shook her head, "We think it was a catamaran accident, we think he must have got caught in the propeller."

Julie heard the loud pang in her head, the words hit her like a rock, she was stunned!

Alan, half hearing the conversation, slammed down the paper and saw the nurse as she was walking away, and before either of them could recover the nurse had gone through the barrier. They looked at each other wide-eyed and open-mouthed, there were unsaid words between them, *could it have been...?*